Encrypted Emotions

B. Lynn Hedge

To my wonderful husband, thank you for encouraging me to "just write the damn book".

Love you lots,

-Your wife

Thank you so much to anyone who takes the time to read this, it's only taken me 8 years to finally finish a story... but here we are!

"If you are always trying to be normal, you will never know how amazing you can be."

- Maya Angelou

Contents

Foreword

Foreword

Before jumping into this story it's important to note that there may be some triggers along the way.

Lottie is a very special character that I decided to write about. She has Asperger's, or ASD as Asperger's is an outdated and non-accurate diagnosis, and while this is nothing to be looked down on, she does face some challenges within the book, and her coping mechanisms are not the best.

This is the first book of the series, it is also a slow burn - like a very slow burn. So, I apologize in advance, if you were looking for something with a lot of spice then this is not the one for you. This book will focus on Lottie developing relationships with each of the guys, but it will not go much further than that, for now....

Please be aware that the book will contain some forms of self-harm, both intentional and unintentional. There is also a lot of talk about anxiety and panic attacks throughout.

Not to be forgotten, the book also contains mentions of parental neglect, sex trafficking, kidnapping, abusive behaviors, violence, mental health and bullying.

Your mental health is important, so please keep that in mind before reading.

If you are okay with all of the above, then please continue and enjoy Charlotte's journey, with her overbearing and protective men at her side.

-Charlotte-

The human brain is fascinating. What one finds joy and comfort in can bring another equal discomfort and disgust. Some love casual conversations and socializing, while others would rather bathe in bleach before having to even speak to the cashier at the grocery store.

No two minds are completely alike. Our behaviors reflect our preferences and personalities. Fundamentally, we are all the same, but these details add layers that make us all appear different.

I find solace in computers; simple machines programmed to respond to commands and achieve what the user tells them with the stroke of a few keys. Computers are all logic and information; there's no room for emotions.

When I left home 4 years ago, one state away from where I grew up, to attend Oceancoast University, my parents probably hoped I'd venture out, make friends, and experience new things. They would be disappointed to learn that I've spent all my time much like I did today: wake up, go for a run, attend classes, grin and bear all the people around me until I can retreat back to my dorm and fall back into my virtual reality.

Firing up my monitors, I instantly feel more at ease; all the discomforts from the day fade away. Following my normal routine, I spend about an hour completing any assignments given today before jumping into a new certification project. I've been coding for years, ever since I got my first computer at twelve. I quickly fell in love with writing code, manipulating the machine before me to follow *my* commands. Back then, I learned basic scripts from children's coding websites, learning how to create a webpage or a nutrition label. Now, I have over 30 different certifications and am always searching for new things to learn.

In six months, I'll complete my degree in computer science, but the classes I've taken here can never compare to the experience I've gained working on real projects and building my own programs from scratch. In years of seeking out new information, I'd ventured into the dark web a time or two, learning much more complex skills that could be questionable ethically, the main one being hacking. I'd gotten ridiculously good at it over the last couple of years.

About three hours into practicing, my stomach protests loudly, and my bladder insists I take a break. I move about my room, taking care of business before using the small kitchenette to heat up a bowl of ramen. Oceancoast is a ridiculously expensive school for the social elite, and while the whole show-and-dance seemed a bit excessive, at least it meant the dorms were more like small apartments. Perfect for a hermit like myself; I hardly ever had to leave. I myself was not part of the social elite by any means, but my parents were well known and respected by many elite members of the community. I just happened to reap the benefits.

As I clean up, I grab one of my energy drinks from the fridge along with a bottle of water to wash down one of the little white pills that taunt me from the orange bottle on the counter.

Somewhere around high school, my parents became frustrated with my lack of desire to socialize with my peers and my "odd" behaviors, as they so kindly put it.

They insisted that I see a therapist, who quickly diagnosed me with Asperger's syndrome along with a heaping side of anxiety. Thus, the medication began. It's not actually necessary to medicate for Asperger's, but my parents believed in quick and easy solutions, so they'd put me on the pills. Imagine their disappointment when the pills weren't some magical cure-alls, and I didn't become "normal" by taking them. Nonetheless, they believed that I was somewhat more functional on them, so they had conceded to not hassle me constantly about my life and social behaviors as long as I continued taking the medication.

Easy decision if you ask me.

As I wash down the pill, a notification pings from my computer. Settling back at my desk, I see it's a message request from 'CobraKai69'.

CobraKai69: Dragonlight? I need to let off some steam.

CharlotteGirl: Of course!

When I started at Oceancoast, I spent a lot of time gaming online those first few weeks. It was a break from coding, and it allowed me to stay lost in virtual reality in a different way. I quickly found a companion in Kai, also known as CobraKai69. Like me, he was one of the only players in the area skilled enough to reach a level 30 dragon tamer. So, in a mystical world of dragons, warlocks, and knights, we were something of experts, and we'd bonded quickly over our love for the game.

Before the game is fully queued up, an incoming call rings through my headset.

"Lottie girl! How's my favorite dragon lady?" Kai's cheerful greeting comes through, instantly bringing a smile to my face.

"Hi, Kai. I'm fine, how are you?" I wish I didn't always sound so formal when I spoke to him, but if he thought it was weird, he never said so.

"Just fine? Now that just won't do. Who do I need to beat up? Who made your day less than amazing?"

"No one," I laugh at his dramatics, "Just a long day. I had 5 lectures today, so I was out for a while before I could get back home."

"Ah, too much people-ing and not enough computer time for one day?" Understanding rings through his tone.

"Pretty much".

"Well then, let's get lost in the land of dragons, shall we?"

We game for a couple of hours, not really talking as we do. Well, Kai talks. He always fills the silence, telling me anything and everything about him, his day, or his brothers. Whatever comes to mind, he tends to speak freely.

At 9 o'clock, my phone alarm starts blaring, scaring me from my mid-game trance. I reach over to quickly silence it.

"Do you need a minute to take your meds?" Kai asks gently.

Kai is one of the only people I've ever told about my meds. We had been playing together for months, with my phone alarm going off every night. One night, after a particularly rough day, he asked what the alarm was for, and I told him, not thinking much of it. Six months later, he asked what the meds were for, and I'd shut him down completely.

"No, I took them with dinner before you called."

5

"Wait, let me guess." I can hear the smile in his voice, "Another packet of those crappy, overpriced noodles that you love so much?"

"Maybe..." I won't confirm or deny; we both know that I eat them practically every day.

A laugh spills from him at my refusal to answer. "I swear you need to buy stock in them. For how much you eat that crap, that is not food."

I fake a gasp of outrage. "How dare you! That 'crap', as you call it, is one of the best things ever invented. It makes me happy."

"Apologies, Lottie," He chuckles. "If it makes you happy, then by all means, help yourself. Hell, I'd buy you a lifetime supply if you'd let me."

"Thank you. I will accept your apology and await my lifetime supply of crappy noodles." My cheeks are starting to hurt from smiling so hard, and I feel the blush covering my face.

"Yeah, I'll get right on that. Though that would mean I'd need to know where you live and hide away all day so I could get them to you." He tiptoes around the topic.

"Kai..." I say warningly.

"I know, I know. Virtual friendship only. I can't help it, Lottie-girl." He lets out a heavy sigh, "We started gaming together years ago by a location match, so I know at least then we were somewhere near each other. Now, I can't help but wonder if we still are, and it drives me crazy. I

6

could've been behind you at the grocery store last weekend and wouldn't even know it." He adds matter-of-factly.

"Well, I hardly go to the grocery store, so I highly doubt it was me," I tell him derisively.

"You know what I mean, Lottie." He groans, frustrated with my aloofness.

I do know what he means. I've often wondered if I'd seen him around campus. I had been curious enough to periodically use the software on my computer to see his true location, past the barriers set up by his VPN, and I knew that, as far as locations go, we were practically on top of each other. Same city, same college, and yet I had no clue what he looked like.

But I made the rule early on that our friendship could only be surface level, only through the safety of the computer. No details, no faces, and absolutely no suggesting or agreeing to ever meet in person. I'm not even sure if he knows that Charlotte is my real name, or if he just assumes that I lived there and thought it was a clever username.

I won't lie and say I've never considered breaking my own rules, but I haven't been able to bring myself to even try.

Our friendship works because of the safety and comfort being behind the screen grants me. Here, I feel safe and comfortable. In person, I would be a disappointment, a frazzled ball of anxiety and awkward conversation. Our friendship would be over as soon as it starts in the real world. I can admit that I'm lonely enough not to want to lose the one friend I have, even if he is just a virtual companion.

"I know, I'm sorry," I tell him gently.

"Don't be sorry, Lottie-girl. I respect your choices. But..." He hesitates, "Can you tell me why you stick to that rule? It's been like four years; would it really be so awful for us to get to know each other a little? Even just a little bit?"

I contemplate what to say. I don't want to share everything about myself with him, but I can't keep shutting him out. As he said, it's been 4 years of his comforting presence, and he's never questioned me or pushed me to share anything with him.

"Not getting personal keeps it safe." I try to explain to him, "Learning more about each other or even meeting you in person is terrifying."

"Because you think I'd be awful in person?" He asks, hurt seeping into his voice.

"No!" I quickly try to reassure him, "Even without knowing you, I can tell you're a great person, and I don't doubt that I'd feel exactly the same way if I met you."

"So, then what is it that's so terrifying?" Thankfully, he sounds less hurt and more curious.

"I just think that if you met me, you'd be very disappointed in what you'd find."

"Lottie, I can promise you that I'd never be disappointed in who you are," He tells me fiercely. "I may not know everything about you, but I know enough to have figured out that you are a wonderful, intelligent, and unique human being. And I'd be proud to get to know you one day. Whenever you're ready, I'll be here."

Emotion clogs my throat. No one has ever said they were proud of me, or that who I am is enough. Even my own parents call me a disappointment, yet Kai is quick to say I'm enough without having even met me.

"Thank you." My voice can hardly be heard, but he catches it anyway.

"I'll tell you that every day if you need to hear it, Lottie," he promises. "And I'm an open book if you decide to break your rules and want to get to know me. Baby steps."

"Baby steps. I just might take you up on that." I won't promise him anything, but I make a promise to myself that I'll try to consider the possibility of letting him into my carefully constructed reality.

"I'll be right here when you're ready."

Soon after, Kai signs off for the night, mentioning that his brothers needed some help with work. From what he's told me before, they run some kind of company together. I continue messing around on the computer for a while before deciding to turn in for the night.

I make quick work of shutting everything down and cleaning my space of any trash or clutter before settling under my weighted blanket with my e-reader, determined to get lost in the new dark romance I'd downloaded.

As I try to read, my mind drifts to Kai and what it'd be like to meet him. Would he be as wonderful in the real world? Could he actually meet me and think I was anything more than just a disappointment?

I drift off, imagining the real-world version of the man behind the screen that I'd grown so familiar with.

2

-Kai-

Logging off with Lottie, I shut everything down quickly before heading into the living room, where Maverick summoned us. I wished I could stay online and chat with her for a little longer, especially after the bomb she just dropped about feeling like a disappointment. That was hard to hear.

Lottie has been one of my best friends for years now. Anytime we game together, it's an outlet for me to vent, a chance to talk about anything and everything. Even though I know almost nothing about her, I'm drawn to her. I want nothing more than to get to know the girl behind the screen. I just need to find a way to convince her that it'd be worth it. That *I* could be worth it.

Maverick and Cooper are already seated on the armchairs situated on either side of the living room, leaving the couch open for Eli and me. I settle into the corner of the couch moments before Eli stumbles into the living room, clutching his laptop and looking like he just rolled out of bed.

"What's up, big bro? It's a little late for an impromptu family meeting." I ask Maverick, his face set in his typical stony mask.

"We have a new case to work on," he says, pointing to the file folder laid out on the coffee table. "You guys have been working on smaller gigs up until this point. Since you want to hit the ground running after you graduate Coop and I figured this was a good way to get your feet wet, learn what you'll be dealing with and try a case that's not as cut and dry as you're used to."

I lock eyes with Eli, who looks unimpressed. "So, is this an intro or a test?" he asks dryly, clearly sensing Mav's hidden implication

"Think of it as a skills assessment, and a test if you must." Cooper chimes in. Confirming that this is indeed a test.

I pick up the folder and read over the contents. Notes cover the whole page, detailing a 19-year-old girl and her last-seen whereabouts, as well as information about her life and family.

"Our skills assessment is a missing person's case? We've worked on like ten of these with you guys by now. What makes this one so special?" I ask, passing the folder to Eli to read.

Maverick shifts in his seat, crossing his arms and staring us down. "This one is special because it's not *just* a missing person's case. The missing person file has been combed through by countless detectives who couldn't find anything, so the girl's family hired us because they refuse to give up. A quick preliminary look at the file led us to evidence showing the girl was taken intentionally. Our job is to find out by whom and for what reason, in addition to locating her," He explains bluntly.

"There aren't enough leads for the police to spend all of their resources looking into it, so that's where we come in," Cooper adds.

Eli tosses the folder back onto the table. "And you think that we have enough resources to solve a case that the police won't even touch?"

"That's the plan. You both wanted in, now you got it." Maverick raises a brow, waiting for us to argue. Neither of us does. Eli and I have wanted to join Maverick and Cooper at Golden Locke Security since they started the company years ago. From the ground up, they'd built GLS with our dad's help and worked on confidential contracts with all types of people. If the police couldn't or wouldn't touch it, then they called us. Until now, Maverick and Cooper would only let us help out with the lowest priority cases just to get our feet wet, nothing in the big leagues. Missing people who were clearly runaways, with all the evidence laid out, or easily spotted drug deals gone wrong. Everything we'd touched up until this point required no thought, no problem-solving skills;

13

all of the information had been easily identified and didn't involve much effort.

They were finally giving us a shot. A shot in the dark, but I knew that both of us would do whatever we could to not waste it.

"Now, in the spirit of jumping right into the deep end, we decided that you both will start by speaking to the family. Go over all the details that they provided when the police interviewed them originally." Cooper looks way too happy to be giving us our grunt-work assignment of gathering information.

Eli stands with his laptop. "Alright, fine, we'll head out in the morning and get on it."

Maverick stands as well, stopping Eli from retreating to his room. "You'll head out tonight. The family is in Atlanta. The faster you get there, the faster you get the information you need confirmed to start digging for any leads." He hands him the file folder before heading into his office, shutting the door behind him.

"Awesome, I was really looking forward to getting no sleep tonight," I say caustically.

Cooper laughs at our expense, standing to pat me on the shoulder. "Y'all want the job, you've got to start somewhere."

He gives Eli a pat as he walks past. "Call if you get into any trouble." He calls over his shoulder, leaving us alone.

Eli stands motionless in the middle of the room, looking lost in thought.

"Well, brother, let's get on the road, I guess. I'll drive if you want to fire up your laptop and see what information you can dig up." Breaking out of his trance, he just nods before leaving to gather his stuff.

As much as I'd love to call it a night and crash, this assignment stirs up a new energy in me. Anticipation bubbles within me – I'm ready to get my hands dirty.

***

Six hours later, we've made it to Atlanta and checked into some crappy motel off the interstate about 15 minutes away from where our missing girl's family lives. Eli taps away at his computer as I devour my way through a takeout bag of fast food we picked up.

"Did you find anything we can use about the girl?" I ask through a mouthful of fries.

Eli's tapping stops briefly as he shoots me a disgusted look over his computer. Raising my brows at him, I wait, adding in a hearty belch for good measure. He rolls his eyes before turning his attention back to the screen.

"Not much. Ivy Gilbert, 19 years old, was last seen leaving a bar called the Tilted Kilt on the night of November 14th, 2022. So, she's been missing for just shy of a year now. Friends of hers at the bar said that she arrived with them but texted that she was leaving with a guy she met after going to the bathroom and not

15

returning; that was around 1 am." He reads the facts with no emotion, spewing facts and dates that he pulled on the drive up here. "No sightings of her since that night. Her family called the authorities the next day when no one could get a hold of her. None of her belongings were ever recovered, and she seems to have fallen off the face of the Earth."

"So, we have nothing. Seems like a great start." I let the sarcasm seep into my words as I tear into one of the burgers from the bag, tossing him one to eat.

"Basically." He chews the burger for a few moments thoughtfully. "I do want to try and see if there's any way I can get access to the bar's security feed, if they even have one in place. Typically, security feeds are written to a hard drive and retained for a set period of time. So if they have a system that stores all their footage, I may have a way to see the feeds from that night. If we can find the guy that she left with, then we might have a decent starting point."

"Do you really think you can do that?" Eli has always been good with computers, obsessed even, but that's impressive even for him. Not to mention, it'd be a huge lead we could jump on, since meeting with the family isn't likely to give us anything new.

"I'm not sure, but I'll see what I can do." He finishes his food and goes back to his computer. "You should get some sleep before we go see the family," he suggests.

Finishing off the food, I agree with him, rolling over to get a couple of hours of rest before a reasonable time to visit the family and get our questioning done. Listening to Eli tap away, I start to drift off before my phone buzzes with a notification. Taking a look, I see its Lottie.

CharlotteGirl: I'm going to be online for a while if you want to join :)

She's up early today, which isn't very odd given how random her sleep schedule has been over the years.

Normally, on Saturdays, I game with Lottie for most of the day. In the rush to leave last night, I'd forgotten to send her a message that I'd be offline for a bit. Locking the phone, I make a mental note to message her when I wake up to let her know that I'll be away for a couple of days, before I fall into unconsciousness.

I'm woken up by Eli cursing at his computer. Rolling over, the clock reads just around 10 am, meaning I got about six hours of sleep. I sit up to stretch, cracking my neck and taking in Eli's disheveled hair, which looks like he's been tugging at it for the last six hours, hunched over the computer.

"Everything alright, there?"

Eli startles a bit, lost in his own world and not expecting my voice. "Yeah, fine. You ready to head out to talk to Ivy's family?"

"Just give me ten to shower, and I'll be ready," I tell him while I gather up a clean change of clothes. "Did you find anything in the security footage?"

He takes off his glasses, dropping them onto the desk to rub his eyes, frustration evident on his face. "Nothing yet, but I have a few other things I can try."

Leaving him to gather his thoughts, I rush through showering and changing into fresh clothes before we make our way to Ivy's family's home. We pull up to a typical suburban home with a welcoming front porch and neutral siding, all complemented by neatly trimmed shrubs and colorful flowers in a well-kept front flower bed.

Such a normal-looking home. From the outside, no one would know that the family within has suffered such a tremendous loss.

Eli follows me out of my truck and to the front door. Ringing the bell, we wait. A middle-aged woman answers the door, wearing a floral print apron and a kind smile; she takes us both in, confusion flooding her features.

"Can I help you?" she asks hesitantly.

Smiling at her, I show her my GLS ID. "Hi, Carol? We're with Golden Locke Security. We recently took over your daughter's case. Just wondering if you had some time to sit down and answer a few questions for us?"

Her eyes fill with sorrow upon hearing our reason for being there and the reminder of her daughter.

"Oh, of course, please come in." She ushers us into the house, leads us to a sitting room off the front door, and motions for us to take a seat. "Let me just go get Patrick, my husband, he's the one who hired you all."

The house is nice, everything in it looks high-end, but that shouldn't surprise me, considering I know just how expensive it is to hire us for a case like this.

Eli sets up his laptop to take notes while we wait. Minutes later, Carol returns with a grim-looking Patrick in tow. He, like Carol, is also middle-aged. Thinning grey hair and wrinkles around his eyes show his age, possibly more than normal, with the stress of his daughter's disappearance. We stand to shake his hand and make our introductions before we all settle into our seats.

"Thank you for your time today. I'm Kai, and this is Eli." I break the ice. "As I told Carol, since we're taking over your daughter's case, we just need to go over some of the information that you would have relayed to the police back when the incident occurred."

"Ivy, her name is Ivy." Patrick grits out, trying to tame some of his irritation before continuing, "And yes, of course. We'll give you whatever information you need to find out what happened to her and who took her."

We go over the basic information from the police report made the day after Ivy was taken, no surprise, everything matches up with the original.

"Ivy's friends weren't originally questioned by the police." Eli suddenly speaks up. "Do either of you know why they didn't provide any details at the time of the event?"

Patrick rolls his eyes while muttering a curse, and Carol stiffens next to him, speaking before Patrick gets a chance to reply.

"All of them refused to answer any questions from the police when they started asking about that night. Since there was no suspicion of foul play from them, the police weren't very motivated to push them," she explains.

Eli and I share disbelieving looks. What detective refuses to question anyone who was close to the victim in an abduction case?

"So, none of her friends who were with her last gave any information to the police?" Eli clarifies.

"Only one, Liv Roberts." Patrick spits out, disgust coating his words. "Fat lot of good that did. Mousey little girl was always a follower, and she had nothing of use to tell the police."

Eli taps away, taking notes of everything Patrick and Carol can tell us, as we finish our questioning.

"Look, Maverick was very convincing over the phone that he would do what he could to find Ivy and bring her home. Do you all really think you can do something that the police weren't able to do?" Patrick asks as Eli packs away his computer.

I struggle to find the words to reassure him. The few cases we'd worked with Maverick and Cooper were easy and successful with a quick turnaround, but none of those were as intense as this one I already proving to be.

"We have a lot of resources, and we are going to do everything we can to get to the bottom of Ivy's disappearance." Eli jumps in to reassure them.

"Please. Whatever you can do, please just do it," Carol tells both of us, tears filling her eyes. "We just want our daughter back. We'd give anything to have her back."

We both give them our reassurances before heading back to the truck. Driving for a few minutes down the road before I break the silence between us.

"So, our grunt work assignment seems to be a dead end. Where do you think we should start when we get back home?"

Eli stays silent, fidgeting with one of his snake bite piercings as he tends to do when he's lost in thought. I let the silence build between us before it makes me uncomfortable.

"Okay, so we'll talk about it with Mav and Coop when we get home, I suppose," I say, resigned to his silence. He won't speak up until he wants to.

"We can't go home yet." He finally speaks.

"What? Why?"

"Ivy's parents said that none of her friends were questioned except for Liv."

"Okay, and?" I try to keep the impatience out of my voice, but I'm failing to follow along with his train of thought at the moment.

"So, it's a bit odd that none of Ivy's closest friends would tell the police anything they could to help find her." He explains, "I think it stands to reason that we need to try to question Liv for anything she may know, and maybe even get the names of Ivy's other friends so we can try to track them down."

Determination flows freely from Eli. Like any of the other cases we've worked on, once he gets an idea or an inkling of one that can lead him towards new information, he sticks with it. It's one of the things I've always admired about him. He follows any trail he can find until he's absolutely sure it either yields results or leads to a dead end. We haven't had to resort to finding our own leads very often on other cases, though, and doubt still lingers in my mind.

"Do you really think a couple of college girls are going to have some groundbreaking information from their friend's disappearance over a year ago?"

"I don't know, but it's worth looking into." It's clear that Eli is sticking with this idea. "What kind of friends wouldn't be devastated at the fact that she was taken so suddenly like that, without any trace?"

As I contemplate his words, we arrive back at the motel. We settle into the room, Eli sets up his laptop again, while I'm lost in thought.

"Fine." I concede. "We'll question Liv and the others if we can find them. I'll call Mav and Coop, and then you can tell me how I can help."

A quick phone call to Mav, and then Eli and I both sit down to get to work. Possibly working a dead end, but if Eli is this eager to follow through on checking it out, then I'll do whatever I can to support him. He never chases leads he doesn't think will get us anywhere, and we both want to do whatever we can to convince the guys that we deserve a full-time spot with the company after we graduate.

Cracking open some energy drinks for us both, I settle in, ready to take notes as his hands fly over the keys. It's going to be a long night for sure.

3

-Charlotte-

Returning from classes on Wednesday afternoon, I go about my normal routine of working on my assignments. As I try to work, my mind wanders to Kai. I haven't heard from him since Friday night.

I get that he has his own life and isn't obligated to get online with me every day, but something feels off. In all the time I've known him, he's always given me a heads-up if he's going to be offline for any length of time. He even messaged me when he'd gotten appendicitis to tell me he'd be away for a couple of days while he got surgery and recovered. This sudden silence from him is odd.

Not hearing from him in days is making me feel uneasy.

We'd left off on a good note the other night, and I'd been left feeling almost giddy at the thought that he wanted to get to know me.

Now, I can only sit and wonder if it was all wishful thinking. Maybe he took the time to think about what I said and realized that I would only be a disappointment to him, and decided to cut his losses and ghost me.

As much as I put up a wall between the two of us, I was just starting to accept the idea of letting him in, and I can't deny the hurt that swells deep in the pit of my stomach at the idea of not having him around anymore.

A notification pings through my computer, pulling me from my self-pity party. I feel hopeful as I jump up to check it, but quickly deflate when I realize it's not him.

A message from '**Eli2X**' pops up from an online chatroom I had used a few times previously, whenever I'd gotten stuck while writing code. I hardly ever use it, and I'm a bit surprised to see someone messaging me.

Curiosity wins out, and I open the chat.

Eli2X : Hey, Charlie. Sorry to bother you, but I'm working on a project, and I'm stuck. Was wondering if you had some time to help out?

Now there's someone I haven't heard from in a while. 'Eli2X', or Eli and I, have chatted on and off for years. Anytime either of us has gotten stuck on a coding or programming problem, we have looked to the other for help. We'd even shared some mundane conversations here and there, mostly centered on our computer preferences, but also a few good-natured, heated debates about which programs and scripts were best.

As with Kai, the conversation flowed behind a screen; it was easy to talk to him, and we seemed to get along well.

Eli was extremely smart, and I enjoyed conversations with him. It'd been months since I last heard from him, but that was normal for us.

Following my curiosity, I message back.

CharlieCipher: Hi Eli. It's no bother at all. What are we working with?

Eli2X: Just testing out some new skills. I need two things, if you're able to help. I'm working to see if I can access security feeds to see at least a year of backlog footage. It's a friend of my family's bar, and he gave his blessing to pick around since he's looking for a girl he met there one night while he was working. If we're able to get access to the footage, I also need to figure out good software to run for facial recognition to try to get a basic ID on the girl.

CharlieCipher: Wow...that's quite a hefty load there.

Eli2X: I know. I get it if you can't or don't want to help; I know it's a shot in the dark. But you're one of the smartest programmers I've talked to on here, so I figured it'd be worth it to ask.

Of all the things Eli could have asked for help with, I would have never guessed anything to this degree. We'd never tossed around ideas of doing anything this extreme.

Accessing a security system for a business? It was doable, but not exactly ethical. And facial recognition software was typically reserved for law enforcement and similar uses. It wasn't illegal to use it on your own, although I'm sure it was frowned upon.

Eli had never asked me for much, and as my only friend outside of Kai, I wanted to help him. Or at least try to.

CharlieCipher: It will take me some time to work through it, but that sounds doable. Send me over the details, and I'll let you know what I can find.

Eli2X: Thanks, Charlie! I've been racking my brain for days now and can't quite get through. I'm dropping the file to you now. Let me know if you need any more info.

As I finish reading the message, an .ipynd project file follows. Taking a quick glance, I see pages and pages of information to be sorted through.

Eli had already sorted all the information he had, showing the security system the bar ran and all the location details. He was thorough and organized, one of the many reasons I always enjoyed working with him.

CharlieCipher: Just got it. I'll let you know when I have something.

With something to keep my mind occupied, I jump right in, seeing what I can make of this perfectly packaged mess that Eli just unleashed on me.

***

Days go by, filled with nothing but working on Eli's project and attending classes, where my mind stays occupied with how to solve it.

Now, Monday morning, my brain is officially fried. After barely sleeping for days while working away at the endless lines of code, I finally think I've got it. I even skipped my lectures today because I thought I was close.

Taking a deep breath, I cross my fingers and hit the key to run the program, and wait. After a few moments of nothing happening, suddenly something shifts, and the bar's security feed pops up on my screen.

Holy Shit.

I wasn't sure I'd actually get it. Quickly jumping back into the program for the feeds, I look through the lines of code, searching for anything that can lead me to the backlog of footage that's kept.

It takes a few minutes of trial and error before I finally find what I'm looking for. Opening a new window with the backlog, I start plugging in dates to see how far back I can access. A few runs show me that I can go back as far as two years.

I almost want to jump up and celebrate for figuring this out. After days of trying, it actually worked. Before I jump the gun and tell Eli, I try the facial recognition software that I had downloaded. Picking a random date, I pull the security footage from that day. Finding a random customer from the bar that I can get a clear shot of, I plug them into the software. It takes a few minutes to run, but then suddenly, yet another window pops up with a full profile of the customer I selected. All three of my monitors are now filled with windows of information and codes to sort through.

A full window of information shows me the person's full background. From copies of a driver's license to lines of credit in their name, addresses, phone numbers, anything I can think of sits before me.

Accomplishment floods through me, overshadowing the exhaustion I felt from before. Eager to share the news, I pull up the chat with Eli.

CharlieCipher: I got it! The bar's backlogs date back at least two years, and that can be paired with the facial recognition. It pulls from different sources, so you'll have access to background information on anyone whose face you can get a clear shot of in the feeds.

Eli is usually quick to respond, so I wait a few minutes to hear back from him. When I don't get a reply, the same feeling of disappointment I have towards Kai's silence washes over me, but I quickly try to smother it. He's probably just busy. It's a weekday; he could be working or at school. I forget sometimes that other people have social lives and don't wait by their computers every minute of the day.

I tinker with the program for another hour before stepping away for a bit. Cleaning up my space, I decide to shower and eat some food, since it's been days since I remember doing either.

I barely manage to finish off my noodles before I fall into my bed, shutting off the rest of the world and falling into a blissful nothingness.

My alarm rings through the room, startling me awake the next morning. It takes me a minute to drag myself out of bed and freshen up.

Even having slept for a solid eight hours, my body feels weighed down and sluggish. I want nothing more than to crawl back into bed and forget the world around me. But I need to see if Eli responded to my message.

Booting up the computer, I wait, sipping away at a fresh cup of coffee.

Checking the chat, I'm sad to find that he still hasn't replied. Now, I'm not only being ignored by Kai but Eli as well, it seems. I'd be lying if I said that didn't royally suck.

I spent most of the morning organizing the code I worked on into folders and then compiling them into a zip file to make it easier for Eli to navigate. Sending it over, I do my best not to let it upset me when that message goes unanswered, too.

I try to distract myself with other projects and catching up on my assignments, but my mind keeps coming back to Kai and Eli. What could be happening for the only two people I speak to not to be responding? Eli's message had sounded urgent, as if he were actively working on this project. But now he wasn't even reading my messages? And Kai had gone radio silent with no warning days ago, and that wasn't like him at all.

Against my better judgment, I find myself digging into Kai's VPN again, something I haven't done since shortly after we started chatting online. Finally pushing past to see his true location, I can't find anything for the current time. The only thing I can find is a last known location showing somewhere in Georgia.

I always thought we were closer in proximity than that. Granted, Jacksonville is close enough to Georgia that he could have been there this whole time, but something about that didn't feel right. My gut is telling me that something is off.

Digging further, I do the same thing through Eli's profile in the chat room. He is even more protected and harder to work through, not giving me much except where he bases his VPN. This location is a lot closer, in the same city as me.

Looking up the address, I find a business's webpage.

Golden Locke Security.

I guess that answers the question of where Eli works. I make a quick decision and copy down the address, getting up to throw on some clothes before I can talk myself out of it.

I print out some of the information I was able to pull from the security feed and shove that along with my personal laptop into my bag before leaving the dorm.

Since Eli hadn't responded, I was going to seek him out and give him the information I had found. He would get what he needed, and I would get confirmation that he didn't disappear into oblivion.

I would try to dig more into what happened to Kai later, once I sorted this out.

Pushing back the anxiety that was threatening to overtake me at the thought of seeking out a virtual stranger, I navigate my way through the streets near campus, making my way towards Riverside, where the business is.

It takes me about 30 minutes to get to the street where Golden Locke Security is located. A sheen of sweat covers me, and my hair is sticking uncomfortably to my face. My stomach threatens to revolt the second I turn the corner and see the sleek and modern office before me. With a glass front and 'G.L.S' written in blinding, but elegant, gold script.

The website noted that GLS was a private security firm, but it didn't suggest it was a larger company. The office screams professional and high-end, making me question why I thought this was a good idea. Everything inside me begs to turn around and go back to the dorm. But I've made it all the way here, and I have all the information for Eli to help him with his project. Seeing where he works, something tells me that it goes beyond just some fun little project or helping his family friend find a girl.

My anxiety wars with my concern for Eli in my mind, making me lightheaded with the tug of war to see which will prevail.

My hands start to shake, and a weight settles on my chest, constricting each breath I try to take in. I can feel my heart beginning to pound, each beat resonating in my ears, loud and insistent.

I swallow hard, my mouth dry. I close my eyes and try to focus on lines of code I'd written for Eli to ground me. Giving myself a few minutes, I feel marginally better.

Finally, feeling like I can breathe again, I open my eyes and jump at the sight of someone standing in the entryway to GLS, watching me.

He watches me with a furrowed brow and a deep-rooted scowl on his face. His hulking frame takes up the entire doorway, large muscles on display through his fitted polo shirt that stretches across his chest, where his arms are folded, his khaki slacks fitting every contour of his tree-trunk thighs.

He looks like he could break me in half, and he's watching me with nothing but disdain washed over all his features.

We stay in a standoff, staring each other down. Neither of us says a word. The longer we stand, the more the nervous anticipation builds within me. I shift my weight and start twisting my fingers to try to alleviate some of the nervous energy before he finally speaks.

"Can I help you with something?" His voice comes out with a measured calm, a deep baritone rich enough to wrap around me.

"Uh. I'm, uh.." words stick in my throat, unable to escape in his dominating presence.

He lifts a brow at me without breaking his stoic mask.

"Look, if you need something, come inside. Otherwise, you need to get moving. You've been standing out here for half an hour. Someone's going to get concerned if you don't move."

A half hour? No wonder my hair was practically glued to the back of my neck. The heat, paired with the mini anxiety attack I'd face, would do that. I tended to lose time every time I fell into an episode. Sometimes it'd take minutes to pull myself out, and on the really rough days, it could be hours before I surfaced again.

Realizing it would be more awkward for me to turn and run now, I have no other choice but to follow him into the crisp and lavish interior of the office. A wide front desk sits just inside the glass windows, gunmetal grey with sleek black tops, a stark contrast to the warm wood flooring, but somehow they complement each other. A waiting room of sorts is set up off to the right of the desk, whereas a hallway leading to what I'm guessing are offices is off to the left.

The guy from outside rounds the desk and rests his folded arms on it, looking at me expectantly.

"I'm Maverick, one of the owners. Is there something I can help you with?"

"E-Eli. I need t-to talk to Eli." It takes everything in my power to get the words to come out. I mentally curse my stutter. It always intensifies when I'm nervous or stressed, or when I try to lie. It's difficult to get people to take you seriously when you choke on your own words.

He just stares at me, that damn eyebrow raised again. "Eli, who?"

"I don't know. E-Eli, I think he works here."

"So, you think you know he works here, but you don't know his last name?" His words drip with condescension.

"Right. He asked for help with something, but then he hasn't responded to any of my messages." Now that I'm talking, the word vomit starts spilling out, and I can't stop it. "I was worried since I hadn't heard from him, so I looked up his location, and this is where it is set up. So, I came to give him the information I helped find. It sounded urgent, and I want to make sure he has it." I do my best to explain.

Now, both of his eyebrows are up high on his face, and he stands to his full height so he can look down on me, literally. He looks pissed.

"You tracked his location? Can I ask how you went about that?" He asks, "And what 'information' do you have for him?"

Okay. So, he not only looks pissed, but now he sounds pissed, too.

"I can't tell you," I tell him simply.

"You can't tell me?" exasperation rings through his words, "You just told me that you were tracking one of my employees, but you won't give me any information as to how you did that, or what it is you need to give to him?"

"Yes." It seems pretty straightforward to me. I'm not sure why he's getting so upset over this. Whatever Eli trusted me with is between him and me. I'm not going to just dump it all out for this guy, whom I don't know.

His demeanor suddenly shifts, giving me whiplash as a mask of indifference cloaks his features.

"Alright then." He motions to the hallways leading to the offices. "Please, join me in my office for a moment, and we'll see if we can get a hold of Eli for you."

I hesitate, unsure of his sudden change of heart, but I decide to follow, knowing I have nothing else to work with here.

He leads me down the hall, closed doors lining each side, before stopping in front of one that looks just like the rest. Turning a key in the lock, he opens the door, gesturing for me to go first. As I step over the threshold, Maverick suddenly snatches my bag off my shoulder, taking me by surprise. The door slams shut as I turn around to face him, leaving me inside the room while he's left in the hall.

I hear the click of the lock being turned, and my pulse spikes with it. Knowing it's no use, I grab the handle and pull, but the door doesn't budge. I turn to take in the room and find what looks like an interrogation room, as you'd see on T.V., complete with a stainless-steel table and chairs in the center and a mirror along the back wall.

Dread washes over me, starting at the back of my neck and spreading down. My skin prickles with a cold sweat as my lungs constrict, making it impossible to breathe properly. My chest constricts as my breathing quickens, making me feel lightheaded.

I lean against the wall for support while I try to work out what the fuck just happened. My thoughts spiral, jumping from wondering why I'm being locked away, to what's going to happen to me, and who the hell this guy thinks he is doing this. All of these thoughts bounce around in my brain, making my head pound.

I slide down the wall as my legs suddenly can't support me. Sitting on the cold cement floor, I draw my legs close, as if closing in on myself will protect me. I blink rapidly, feeling tears sting my eyes as my vision blurs at the edges, tunneling slightly.

I fight to gasp for breath, struggling to draw in a full breath of air.

I lose the battle and continue to gasp for every morsel of air into my lungs. My hands start to tingle, numbness beginning at my fingertips. I clench and unclench my hands into fists to get it to go away, but the sensation only grows with each passing second.

The darkness in my vision only continues to grow as my fight for air proves to be futile. I feel myself slipping into unconsciousness, and I'm powerless to fight it.

With no other choice, I welcome the darkness with only the hope that when I come to, this will all have been some fucked-up nightmare.

4

-Kai-

What should have been a quick overnight trip to Atlanta to interview the family turned into days of chasing down Ivy's group of friends and trying to get them to give us something to work with. The closest we got was Liv, the friend who had previously spoken to the police; she could recall only vague details about the guy she'd seen Ivy leave with.

Days of a crappy motel room and running all over Georgia, and we still have no leads to start pursuing. I'm ready to go home, shower in a shower with hot water and decent water pressure, then face-plant into my bed. But of course, the universe hates me. That has to be the reason that Cooper called us, saying that Maverick was pissed and demanded we head straight to the office. Because after a 6-hour drive, a pissed-off Maverick is just the thing I want to deal with.

Not.

Eli has been silent for most of the drive home. Not getting any leads from Ivy's friends, on top of making no progress hacking into the bar's security system, has really put a damper on his mood.

He hasn't even touched his laptop the entire drive back; it's weird to see, considering it's practically an extension of him at this point.

"We'll find something to look into for the case once we get home and settled," I try to reassure him. "Maybe that's why Mav called us straight to the office; he could have something for us to look into."

"Doubtful, he's probably just calling us in for wasting four days to come home with nothing." He retorts, sounding like he's dreading this meeting as much as I am.

He has a point there, not that I'll admit it.

Pulling up to GLS, we get out and make our way inside, both bracing ourselves for Maverick's temper and Cooper's smug satisfaction of sending us on a wild goose hunt. Approaching Maverick's office, I can hear him and Cooper in the middle of an argument, both their voices raised and tense.

"Are you out of your freaking mind? What the hell is wrong with you? This is insane!" Cooper sounds livid, his voice booming through the entire office.

"It's not insane. I'm looking out for all of us with this. We don't know who she is; she could be psychotic!" Maverick fires back.

Eli and I both stop just outside his office, listening to their exchange.

"Exactly! You don't know her, and rather than trying to sort through it like a normal person, *you* became the psycho by doing this! Nothing about this is ethical, I'm not even sure it's legal."

"Right, and since when have we cared about doing something illegal?" Mav questions. A silence falls over the room. I can picture Cooper pacing the room while Maverick watches with his stony mask in place.

"We bend the rules when it comes to solving a case that we've been hired to work on, not when it involves some random chick off the street!" Cooper seems to be escalating again.

I step into the room, Eli right on my heels, and look between the two of them. Maverick is hunched over his desk, a messenger bag sitting next to a rose-gold laptop I've never seen on top of his usual pile of case files covering the surface. Cooper stands in front of the desk, his white-knuckle grip locked onto one of the chairs facing the desk, threatening to puncture a hole in the fabric.

"What is going on? We could hear you guys from the lobby." I look between both of them, not knowing who will answer.

Cooper shoots us a look that could cut glass. "Maverick has lost his fucking mind. That's what happened," He growls.

"I haven't, but it's come to my attention that Eli has." Maverick counters.

And the plot thickens.

Raising my brows, I spin to face Eli, who stands in the doorway, shock and confusion evident on his face.

"How so? I haven't even been here in days." Eli looks past me to ask.

Maverick pushes to stand up, supporting his weight on his hands on the desk. "You haven't been here, but it seems that didn't stop you from reaching out to a stranger to have them help you on a classified case." He is pissed. The vein in his forehead bulges as he waits for a response.

Eli folds his arms over his chest, staring defiantly at Maverick. "I didn't ask anyone for help on a case." His voice is pitched low; I have to strain to hear it.

Spinning the laptop to face us, Maverick points at the screen. "So, you're not 'Eli2X' and you didn't ask for help with accessing security footage from the bar where Ivy went missing over a year ago?"

Eli doesn't respond. If looks could kill, then Maverick would be a cold corpse on the floor by now.

"That's what I thought." Maverick retorts, sounding every bit like the smug asshole that he's coming across as right now. "What the hell were you thinking, Eli? You know better than to share information about our cases or our clients. That shit is confidential!"

Eli storms forward, matching Maverick's stance, the desk the only thing standing between them.

"I didn't share anything confidential; I asked a trusted friend for help running a program. That's it." Eli glances down at the foreign laptop. "How do you even know about that anyway?"

"Yes, Maverick, how do you know about that? Why don't you enlighten us?" Cooper chimes in, his voice full of implication.

It feels like I'm watching a tennis match, the way my head is snapping back and forth between them. I shouldn't be enjoying this, but I'm thrilled that it's not me in the hot seat for once.

Maverick doesn't say anything; he just sits back in his chair, arms crossed, staring defiantly at all three of us.

"Okay, I'll share." Cooper snarks, "Maverick here knows because a girl showed up here today asking for Eli, when she then told him that she had information for him but wouldn't inform dear old Maverick of what it was, he proceeded to take her bag and lock her in the interrogation room so he could go through her laptop himself." Cooper's voice rises the longer he speaks, and by the time he finishes, he's practically yelling yet again.

It takes a moment for the information about what Cooper just told us to sink in.

"What the fuck, Maverick?"

"You went through her shit?"

Eli and I speak in unison, both equally furious at our brother's impulsive decision. He's clearly lost his mind because, under no normal circumstances, would we ever take someone's belongings and lock them in a room unless we had an explicit reason to question them.

"Yes, what Cooper failed to mention is that I did this only after the girl shared with me that she *stalked* Eli by tracking his computer location to find out that he worked here. That was the reason she showed up out of the blue." Maverick informs us, clearly thinking that his actions are justified. "So, in the interest of the safety of all of us, I felt it important to find out what she knew and why she would be tracking anyone's location, let alone one of my employees."

"Wait, what?" I ask, dumbfounded. Mav is known for being a bit overprotective, but this is insane even by his standards.

Eli processes the information for a moment, looking lost in thought, "Wait, you said some girl showed up?"

Cooper rubs the bridge of his nose, looking annoyed with Eli veering off the topic of Maverick imprisoning someone.

44

"Yes, Eli. A girl. Tiny little thing, looks like she can't be older than 19. Currently passed out on the floor in the room across the hall where Maverick left her," He tells us drily.

"I never talked to a girl. The only person I've ever talked to is some guy named Charlie, he's a genius with all things programming, better than me at most things, and he can hack into almost anything."

Maverick just raises a brow, "Well, I don't know what to tell you, Eli, but whoever you've been talking to is most certainly not a guy. I found the chats with you two on her computer."

A nagging feeling tugs in the back of my mind, but I ignore it while I watch Eli spin the computer around to start opening tabs and folders, combing through whatever's on the laptop. We're all silent for a few minutes while he taps away.

"Fuck." Eli lets out a breath as he falls to sit in the chair behind him.

"Yeah, Eli. *Fuck.*" Maverick growls.

Cooper narrows his eyes at Maverick, ready to tear him a new one again. Before he can, Eli speaks up.

"It's not that big of a deal, Maverick. So she's a girl. I've still been talking to her about coding and programming for years. She knows her shit. And I didn't tell her anything about the case. As far as she knows, I was helping a family friend find a girl he met." Eli clicks a few buttons on the laptop and turns it to show Maverick, "She figured out how to get access to the bar's footage all the way back to when Ivy was there, and she found a newer facial recognition program that runs directly to the footage to use to ID the guy Ivy left with. This is *good*." He tries to stress to Maverick.

"It's good, except now we have a girl locked in our interrogation room. Oh, and we've just rummaged through her personal belongings, all because Maverick doesn't know how to function like a normal human being." Cooper interjects, still livid.

A growl spills from deep in Maverick's chest. "She admitted to stalking Eli, then wouldn't tell me anything else. What was I supposed to do?"

"Literally anything but what you did, bro," I tell him. I feel as though that should be obvious by now. But Maverick won't admit that what he did was wrong. In his mind, he was protecting all of us, and that's something that he'll never apologize for. His narrowed gaze snaps to me, silently telling me to keep my mouth shut.

"It's not a big deal, Maverick. Anyone can track a location; it's my fault for setting it here." Eli tries to placate him. "She wouldn't have been able to see anything past GLS. I'll talk to her and sort it out, but I'm fairly certain she's harmless."

"Well, I'll know for sure once I question her."

Cooper pushes off the wall, taking a step towards Maverick's desk. "Whoa, Mav. No, I'm sorry, but you're not going anywhere near this girl after you forced her into a room against her will."

"I can, and I will. If she's harmless, then she should have no issues answering some questions."

Cooper is already shaking his head before he finishes.

"No, if she's harmless, then the only thing that you're talking to her is going to get us is a big fat lawsuit." Maverick's jaw tenses at Cooper's words. I can hear his molars grinding together from here.

Eli closes the laptop and starts throwing all of the belongings back into the messenger bag. "I'll go talk to her, try to smooth over all this bullshit." Venom seeps into his tone, clearly directed at Maverick as he shoots a glare his way.

As Eli leaves the room, the three of us follow closely, entering the room next to the interrogation room where we can watch the interaction through the two-way mirror. Cooper and Maverick both stand near the glass, tense as they observe. I stand just behind them and get a glance at the girl that Maverick imprisoned.

If she was passed out earlier, she's since woken up. She's a tiny little thing, sitting curled in on herself near the door. Her silky brown hair shields half her face as it falls in a curtain reaching her waist. Her small face is covered mostly by wide, gold-rimmed glasses. The hoodie she wears swallows her tiny frame, but her leggings hug every curve of her legs, all the way down to her well-worn Vans.

The click of the lock echoes through the room, startling the girl, who jumps to her feet, immediately retreating to the other side of the room as far from the door as she can get. Eli's head pokes into the room, searching for the girl before his soft gaze settles on her. He steps into the room slowly, clearly afraid to scare her anymore.

They stand at opposite ends of the room. Eli relaxed as he took her in. She holds herself stiffly, her trembling hands clenching and unclenching repeatedly at her sides.

Her eyes snap up to Eli's as he clears his throat to gain her attention.

"Hi, uh, Charlie, right?" She doesn't respond. "I'm Eli." She still doesn't respond. She doesn't acknowledge him as she continues to stare, her breathing picking up slightly.

"I heard you were asking for me. I just got back from a work trip, and I'm really sorry for how my brother handled everything with you today." Eli's tone remains patient and remorseful as she tries to put her at ease.

"I'd like to go h-home, please," she finally speaks, her voice coming out as a low, raspy whisper barely to be heard in the large room.

"Of course," Eli quickly reassures her, "I have your bag here. I just wanted to make sure you were okay. I know this is probably not what you expected when you came here today. I know you were just trying to help, and really, this is my fault for not seeing any of your messages. Again, I'm really sorry about all this."

She eyes him up for another few moments, looking distrustful at his immediate reassurance that she could leave. Not that I can blame her, she's spent the past few hours locked in a room after coming to help out a friend. I'm not sure I'd be too trusting in her position either.

"Do you guys' o-often lock up a-anyone who shows up unannounced?" she asks him bluntly, her slight stutter not taking away from the anger laced in her words.

Something about her voice is familiar to me, though I can't seem to place it. That nagging feeling is back and screaming at me from the back of my mind, but I can't seem to make out what it's telling me.

"No, Charlie. We don't. Maverick is- well, he just is a bit-" He searches for the right words, knowing that Maverick is just beyond the glass listening in.

"He's a dick?" She offers. Cooper chokes on a laugh at her question, and I try and fail to hold back a laugh of my own. Maverick, on the other hand, is red-faced and fuming, shooting daggers at her from behind the glass.

Eli chuckles in the other room, grinning at Charlie's assessment.

"I was going to say overprotective and impulsive, but yeah, that works too."

They fall silent for a few more moments, sizing each other up.

"I will say, it's cool to finally meet you, Charlie. I've gone years thinking you were a guy, so this is a surprise."

49

"Charlotte. My name is Charlotte," She murmurs, a light flush taking over her cheeks.

Wait a minute. My mind races for a few moments, thoughts racing as the name Charlotte bounces around my brain. I zero in on the sound of her voice, and after a few moments, the lightbulb goes off.

"Holy shit," I whisper, instantly drawing Maverick and Cooper's attention.

"What is it?" Cooper asks.

Ignoring him, I rush out of the room and to the door leading to Eli and Charlotte. Swinging the door open, Charlotte startles again while I take her in, from head to toe. I can barely contain my excitement, finally putting a face to the voice I've talked to just about every day for the last four years.

"Lottie?"

Her eyes shoot wide, and her lips part on a gasp. She studies me the way I do her, taking in every detail before her eyes quickly shift to Eli, flicking between us before settling on me again.

"Kai?" She pieces it together, still sounding confused.

Holy shit, it's her. My Lottie, here and in the flesh. She's even more beautiful than I could've ever imagined. Small, petite, and so cute. Finally, here in front of me, instead of hiding behind a screen.

I can't hold back the grin that stretches across my face as I take a small step closer, needing to be closer to her.

"Hey, Lottie-girl."

Standing closer, I can make out the dusting of light freckles that cover her cheeks, obstructed by her glasses, and catching the light, I can see the sliver of a tiny gold ring looped through her septum. Fuck, that shouldn't be as hot as it is, but the dainty little ring captures my attention, and it's all I can see.

"Lottie? You two know each other?" Eli's voice pulls me out of my head and captures Lottie's attention, too.

"Yeah, Lottie-girl and I go way back. We've been gaming together for years now, ever since we enrolled at Oceancoast." I tell him, shooting a wink Lottie's way, causing that blush to make an appearance on her cheeks once again.

Eli shakes his head, speechless at the new information.

"Y-you two are t-twins?" Lottie asks, looking between the two of us.

I chuckle. The answer to that question is pretty obvious, as she's looking at the two of us, practically a carbon copy of each other.

"Yeah, Charlie, we're twins," Eli tells her lightly. "Ironically, you've been chatting with both of us for years now. I'm surprised it never came up."

All the pieces fall into place now.

"So, your Charlie and my Lottie have been the same all these years?" I ask, no one in particular, recalling all the conversations we've had about our virtual friend and how awesome they were. Hell, the guys had all given me a hard time about gaming with a girl and had told me on multiple occasions that I needed to wife up the girl who could tolerate listening to me as much as Lottie did.

Eli nods, flicking his eyes to me before settling on Lottie again.

"Yeah, we met in one of the chat rooms for programmers a few years ago. We've helped each other out with different projects we were working on from time to time," he explains.

Another laugh spills out of me as I can't ignore the irony of the situation. I instantly regret it when I see embarrassment flood Lottie's face.

"I'm not laughing at you, Lottie-girl," I quickly try to reassure her. "I've just been dying to meet you for years without any success, and in the span of one afternoon, you've met two of my brothers and me. This is amazing."

Lottie tries to force a smile that looks more like a grimace just as the door opens again, Cooper stepping into the room.

"And behold, brother number four. Right on time." Eli mutters.

"While you were all having your revelations about knowing each other, I figured I may as well introduce myself." He flashes a grin Lottie's way. "Cooper Locke, it's nice to meet you, Charlotte."

Charlotte has gone speechless again, her eyes bouncing between the three of us, taking us all in. She seems nervous again, twisting her fingers one at a time before starting all over again.

Cooper continues, not one to let silence linger too long. "I just wanted to apologize again for how Maverick reacted earlier. He was just a little surprised to hear how you went about finding Eli. It's not every day that we have someone tracking down our locations, and we tend to be a bit uptight with security. I know it may not seem like it, but he would never harm you. He just acted without thinking."

Still twisting her fingers, she averts her gaze to the floor. "I just wanted to check on Eli. He never responded, and that's not like him. I-I was worried about Kai, too, but I couldn't find him, and Eli had asked for my help. I was just trying to follow through. I didn't mean to cause any trouble."

Eli approaches her slowly, as one would do with a wild animal. Giving her plenty of time to pull away, he reaches out to lightly take her hands, halting her from twisting her fingers.

He leans down to try to catch her eyes, but she keeps them firmly fixed on the floor.

"I appreciate your help, Charlie. I forgot to check my messages after I asked you. I'm sorry for making you worry."

She nods in acceptance of his apology but doesn't offer him much more. Gently prying her hands from his, she continues her nervous fidgeting with her fingers, thankfully gentler this time.

"I should go. It's getting late, and I have class tomorrow." I push down the sting of her dismissal of us, understanding that this has to have been a lot for her.

"Of course, I'll give you a ride." I offer, picking up her bag from where Eli left it by the door, and opening the door to let her through.

Her shoulders tense at the suggestion. "T-that's okay. I'm fine to walk."

Exchanging looks with Cooper and Eli, I see the silent agreement between all of us that we'd rather streak naked through a field of bees, covered in honey, before letting Lottie walk back home by herself. Especially assuming that she lives on campus, which is about a thirty-minute walk, and the sun's already gone down. Jacksonville may not be the worst city, but walking alone at night is never a good idea.

Luckily, Cooper interjects before I can demand that she let me take her home.

"Charlotte, I know it might not be your preference, but I really do insist that one of us take you home. It's dark out, and you've had a lot of stress this afternoon; plus a panic attack on top of that, it's not a good idea to be walking home," he keeps his tone light, not demanding anything from her, rather, strongly suggesting. "Whoever you feel most comfortable with is fine. We just want you to get back home safe."

I can see the defiance simmering just under the surface, but it's quickly washed out with exhaustion falling over taking over all her features. Her eyes find mine, and she gives me a nod of affirmation.

"Okay."

5

~ Charlotte ~

I think somewhere between passing out in this room and waking up to see I hadn't imagined any of this nightmare, I must have lost my mind.

What else could explain the fact that I'm starting at two identical-looking human beings who swear they are my only two friends?

I urge my brain to think logically and analyze all the information they're giving me. But it's a little preoccupied between reliving their apparent older brother imprisoning me and salivating over their undeniably attractive bodies standing right in front of me.

I had no idea who Eli was when he walked in here, interrupting me from falling into another meltdown with nothing else to keep my mind occupied in this prison.

Instantly, upon seeing him, I was locked in. He was tall, well, tall to me, which wasn't hard to do. He had to be at least 6 feet tall. His jet-black hair matched the black snake bite piercings snuggled against his bottom lip, as well as a small bar through his eyebrow. Both match the black frames of his glasses. Piercing blue eyes stared back at me through the lenses, and tattoos peeked out from his shirt sleeves where they had been pushed up. His muscles were obvious through his black jeans and long-sleeve tee, but not overwhelming like Maverick - the one who'd thrown me in here like a puppy that had misbehaved.

Before I could even fully comprehend what Eli had been telling me, Kai came barreling through the door as well. I'd recognize his voice anywhere; it was an instant feeling of comfort for me. But that was quickly replaced with shock as I took in his appearance and thought that I was seeing double. It made me worry that I had knocked my head when I'd passed out, but then I took in the subtle differences.

Kai had the same striking blue eyes, didn't have glasses or facial piercings. His hair was the same jet-black color, but slightly shorter, and it didn't hang onto his face like Eli's. And while Eli had some tattoos, he had nowhere near as many as Kai. His tanned skin was filled with ink, from his neck down to his hands, beautiful and bold dark swirls wrapped around his skin. Also, unlike Eli, Kai wore lighter jeans and a short-sleeve tee, giving me time to fully appreciate all of the decorated skin he had.

My brain was already overloaded, trying to sift through everything going on when Cooper, the final Locke brother, had come to introduce himself.

Cooper looked nothing like Kai and Eli but had a striking resemblance to Maverick. Although Cooper wasn't nearly as built, he had more of a swimmer's body. That, paired with his tan complexion and shaggy, dirty blonde hair, made him look like your typical surfer. Unlike any of the other three, he had no tattoos. And he wore a simple GLS polo, paired with khaki pants that were truly working in his favor.

I don't know what to think or what to say.

How do you handle meeting someone you swore you'd never meet in person *and* their twin brother, whom you've apparently been speaking to for years? And let's not forget to throw their two brothers into the mix, because this wasn't fucked up enough already.

I should have known that leaving my dorm was a bad idea.

At least three out of four of them weren't bad. Everyone but Maverick is being really nice. Now I just want to go home, but even that's a problem because the three men in front of me don't think I should be walking back to my dorm.

I can see the determined look in each of their eyes; it's evident that none of them is going to cave on me getting a ride home. It's sweet, but unnecessary.

The only thing that gets me to let go of my urge to argue is Cooper presenting it to me as a choice; *I* get to decide who takes me home. It's a drastic enough difference from how Maverick handled meeting me earlier that it puts me at ease enough to think for a moment.

I've known Kai for years, apparently Eli too, but I've spoken to Kai almost every day for as long as I've been in this city. I know so much about him, and my gut is telling me that he's a good person.

Just days ago, I was trying to convince myself to get used to the idea of meeting him in person and finally ditch the screen. The opportunity was now laid out, right at my feet. All I have to do is take the chance and hope that I'm not stupidly naive for trusting a guy that I met on the internet…

My recently sparked determination to step outside of my comfort zone wins out. That's the only reason I finally meet Kai's eyes, taking a breath to compose myself before nodding.

"Okay.

6

~Kai~

I gently lead Lottie out of GLS and to my truck. She's so short that it takes her a lot of effort to hoist herself up into the seat. I stand behind her, wanting to help her up but not wanting to startle her.

Once she's up in the seat, I notice her hands shaking again. Moving slowly, I set her bag on the floorboard by her feet before reaching up to pull the seatbelt over her, clicking it into place. She doesn't move, sitting stiffly as I move around her. Gently closing her door, I rush around the front of the truck to hop inside, instantly taking note of her twisting her fingers as she stares straight out the windshield.

I still can't believe that the girl I've been obsessing over meeting for years is right beside me. And I can't shake the awful feeling of guilt I have at what Mav did to her today.

I haven't gotten a chance to really get to know Lottie yet. Aside from her daily routine and gaming skills, the only thing I've learned about her over the years is that she takes medication for something. She would never tell me what it was for, but I had just come to assume it was for anxiety or something, and given her behaviors I've seen so far, I think that I'm correct in that assumption. If it is anxiety, then that makes me feel even worse about Mav locking her in a room just because she showed up to check on Eli and me.

I clear my throat to grab her attention before I start talking. "So, do you stay at the dorms at Oceancoast? Or do you have a place around here?"

"The dorms," She nods her head at me, "I'm in Buckner Hall."

Her voice doesn't come out as shaky as it did in the office earlier, but it's still pitched low enough that I have to strain to hear her.

"Cool, I know just where that is. Do you want any music on for the drive?" I'm hoping she says no so I can try to talk to her more, but I want to make sure she's comfortable.

"Whatever you want is fine."

Foregoing the music, I set out towards the campus, paying extra attention to not exceed the speed limit to maximize my time with my Lottie-girl.

She doesn't make any attempts to fill the silence that wraps around us; she hasn't even moved since getting buckled in.

"So, not how I imagined finally getting to meet you. Although I have to admit, I'm not upset about it."

"Really? I always imagined that I'd meet you, and your brother would lock me into a room against my will. All while I meet your other brother while finding out that you're a twin as well."

I'm stunned for a moment before a laugh escapes me at her summary.

"Really? Now I see why you were so against meeting me if that's what you were expecting." I joke.

Lottie ignores my teasing.

"I didn't know you were a twin."

"Yeah, for 22 years now. We never really got around to sharing any details about ourselves in all those times we talked."

I glance over and see Lottie avert her gaze to stare at her hands in her lap, looking ashamed.

"I meant what I told you the other day, Lottie-girl. Now that I've met you, I can definitely confirm that I'm not disappointed in the slightest."

She doesn't acknowledge me, so I continue.

"After meeting you today, I'm even more intrigued by you, and I absolutely want to get to know more about you. As for me, you learned today that I'm a twin, and it seems you already know Eli. You unfortunately met Maverick; he's the oldest. Then there's Cooper; he's a year younger than Mav. Maverick and Cooper are our adopted brothers, or I guess you could say that we're their adopted brothers. Their parents took us in when we were six. We've all always been really close, and they've always been very protective of Eli and me."

Lottie continues twisting her fingers, not as harshly as earlier, and her gaze shifts from her lap to the console between us as I speak,

"Maverick and Cooper both founded GLS about 6 years ago, and it's gotten pretty successful in that time. We all live in a house that our parents passed down to us, a little outside of campus towards Riverside. Eli and I work part-time with them. We both want to start full-time once we graduate in a few months, so we're working our way up as we can."

"It sounds nice," Lottie whispers once I finish speaking.

"What does?"

She hesitates for a moment, contemplating her words. "Being so close to your family."

"Are you and your family close?" I think I already know the answer, but I ask anyway.

Lottie doesn't answer, shifting her focus back out the windshield as we pull in the parking lot for Buckner Hall.

Putting the car in park, neither of us moves.

She seems uncomfortable now and I feel like I should apologize for asking about her family. She's never wanted to share personal details, and it seems that asking about them may have been too much too quickly.

"Lottie-"

"Thank you for the ride." She cuts me off.

She unclips the seatbelt before reaching for her bag. I reach out to lay a hand on her arm, stopping her before she can grab it.

"Let me walk you inside."

"No, it's fine. I don't need-"

It's my turn to cut her off. "Please, Lottie. I'm not ready to leave yet, and after today and everything that's happened, I just need to see that you get in and you're safe."

Taking a deep breath, Lottie looks everywhere else before finally meeting my gaze.

"Okay," She relents.

I jump out of the truck before she can change her mind, rounding the front to open her door as she grabs her bag and jumps down to the ground.

I walk silently beside her as we head into Buckner Hall. We stay on the first floor, moving through the halls to the back corner of the building to the last door. Room 175. Unlike all the other doors throughout the hallways, Lottie's door is lacking any decorations, just plain dark oak with a shiny golden knob.

Lottie pushes open the door and steps inside the dorm. Holding the door open behind her, she looks my way, fixating on my chest rather than looking me in the eyes.

"D-do you w-want to come in?" She stutters a bit, most likely due to nerves.

She's stepping out of her comfort zone, she's letting me in. Offering for me to come into her domain, her safe space to show me a part of her that she's kept locked away for so long. No way I'm passing up this opportunity she's laying out for me.

"Sure." I play it cool as I step in behind her, softly closing the door behind me.

I take in the space around me as she moves to put her things down. Eli and I had never stayed in the dorms since we lived so close to campus, but this was nice. There was a bedroom off to the side with a full-size bed before it opened into a small living space where Lottie had a small sectional and a coffee table facing a TV. The corner next to the living space was filled with a large computer desk with three curved monitors mounted to the back. The space then extends further into a small kitchenette, complete with a small breakfast bar. There were two doors on the bedroom side, which I guessed were the bathroom and closet.

All in all, it was a nice space, very spacious, but lacking any personal effects. Aside from the computer set-up in the corner, there was nothing in the space that indicated anyone lived here. Even the bed was immaculately made up with a plain forest green comforter. There were no pictures, no blankets left on the couch, no dishes on the counter.

It was cozy yet lonely all at once.

Glancing over the space once more, my eyes finally land back on Lottie, standing uncomfortably in the middle of the room. Her eyes follow me as I step slowly around the room, moving towards her desk.

"So, this is where you work your magic?" I shoot her a grin over my shoulder as she shifts her weight uncomfortably.

A blush rushes through her cheeks as her eyes meet mine, nodding her head.

Stepping towards her, she takes a step back for every step I take, backing up until her legs meet the couch. She sinks down on the cushions, tracking my movements as I sit on the opposite end of the couch from her.

"I like your space, Lottie-girl, it's nice."

"I-it's not m-much. But it's m-mine." She whispers.

I reach out to rest my hand on top of hers.

"Thank you for showing it to me."

Her hands tense under mine as she draws in a deep breath, looking right at me.

"You shared a lot with me... I want to share with you." Biting her lip, her brows furrow with worry.

"You don't have to, Lottie, whatever you feel comfortable with. You already let me into your space. That means so much to me." I give her hands a squeeze, emphasizing my words.

"A-a-asperger's," She stutters suddenly. "You asked what the m-medication I take is for." She clarifies quickly. "I have Asperger's. My parents put me on the medication years ago to help with some of my symptoms."

I let her admission sink in for a few moments. I rack my brain trying to think of anything that I know about Asperger's, which admittedly isn't much. From what I can remember, it would mean that Lottie is on the spectrum to some extent. It's a surprise to me, but nothing that I would ever judge her for. But looking at the worry etched across her face, it's clear that's where her thoughts are taking her right now.

Squeezing her hands once more, I lean down so that I'm eye level with her, so she has no choice but to meet my gaze. She tries to look off to the side, but I keep squeezing her hands to get her attention back on me until I know she's listening.

"Lottie-girl, I would never, ever, think down on you because of that. I've known you were special for years, and your telling me this doesn't change how I think of you or how awesome you are. I can see this is something you think will make me run away, scared, but it won't. I'm really just thrilled that you trusted me enough to share that with me, so thank you again." I don't look away, forcing every bit of sincerity that I feel into my words.

Her eyes bore into mine, looking for any signs of dishonesty that she won't find before a sigh of relief rushes out of her, her shoulders releasing some of the tension they'd been holding.

We both relax and just take each other in for a few minutes, studying each other while we sit in the comfortable silence for once. For the first time, we're both able to finally see each other, and not just in the physical sense. We both shared things about ourselves with each other after years of dancing around any details, but now it's like we each have a small window into each other's souls. And my Lottie-girl's is even brighter than I could have imagined.

I don't want to break the peaceful bubble we're in, but after what's probably longer than acceptable, I cave.

"I should probably get going. Are you sure that you're okay after everything today?"

A hint of disappointment washes over her face before a mask of indifference shutters over her features. Damn, she could give Maverick a run for his money as far as masking emotions go.

"I'm fine," She tells me simply.

I look over her for a moment, looking for any signs that she's not before standing from the couch and making my way across the room. Lottie follows just behind me as I turn once I reach the door.

I don't want to leave, but I know she's had enough thrown at her for one day. I'm stuck in place, feeling like a teenager with his first crush.

"Get some rest tonight. If it's okay with you, I'd like to come by tomorrow to check on you. We can hang out and talk or just play some games if you want?" I hold my breath, bracing myself for her refusal but metaphorically crossing my fingers that she won't push me away now that she's let me in.

She reverts to staring at my chest as she slowly nods her approval, and I just barely contain my urge to fist pump at her acceptance.

I tell Lottie goodnight and let myself out before I embarrass myself, finally making my way back home. Pulling into the garage, I notice that Cooper and Maverick's cars are gone, so at least I can get some rest without them breathing down my neck.

Downstairs is silent as I make my way up the stairs. Stopping just before my room, I crack open Eli's door to glance in. His room is in its typical state of disarray, a little bit of light is cast from his laptop on the bed. Eli is passed out on his stomach with his glasses hanging half off his face. It looks like he crashed in the middle of working on his next lead. I'm not surprised; I didn't see him sleep the entire time we were gone. It was bound to catch up at some point.

I tiptoe across the room, easing his glasses off his face and setting them on the nightstand before silently backing out of the room, gently shutting the door. Heading into my room, I make quick work of stripping out of my grimy day-old clothes before showering and promptly faceplanting onto my bed.

I instantly fall into a much-needed deep sleep.

My alarm blaring through the room pulls me out of a deep sleep way too early. Rolling over to turn it off, I stumble out of bed and drag myself through my morning routine, heading down to the gym downstairs to get a quick run in before lifting a bit. Once I finish up, I head back upstairs to shower and get dressed.

Coming back down the stairs, I beeline for the kitchen to get some coffee in my system before facing the day.

Eli is half slumped over the breakfast bar, looking disheveled and half-asleep as he nurses a cup of coffee. Cooper is cooking up an omelet at the stove, and Maverick is throwing a bunch of green shit into a blender to make his disgusting morning concoction. Maverick's German Shepard, Zeus, sits patiently on the floor between the two of them, hoping for some scraps to fall his way.

"Morning." Cooper greets me as I grab the coffee pot to fill up a mug. I offer a grunt in response as I down the first cup before going in for a refill.

"Everything go okay with Charlotte last night?" Cooper asks as he continues working over the stove. Maverick freezes at the mention of her name before continuing to dump ingredients into the blender.

"Yeah, everything's fine. I took her back to her dorm, and we talked for a while. She's okay." I tell him as I round the bar, taking the stool next to Eli, who seems to perk up some hearing Charlotte's name.

"Good." Cooper says, "She seemed really overwhelmed yesterday. I'm glad she's doing okay."

"She had a panic attack. I think you're all being just a little dramatic." Maverick grumbles before turning on the blender.

Eli straightens at his words while I shoot daggers at him across the counter. Even Cooper abandons his breakfast to turn and stare at the back of Maverick's as he keeps his focus lasered on his task.

The sound ricochets around the kitchen before we're plunged into a deafening silence once he flips the blender off. Maverick ignores all of our stares at him as he continues making his drink.

"Are you fucking for real right now?" Cooper growls.

Maverick takes a big swig of his drink, arching a brow at Cooper. "What? You all met this girl for twenty minutes, and suddenly you're all worried about her?" Putting the glass down, he crosses his arms, taking on his typical defiant stance. "I put her in a room while I looked into things myself after she insisted on withholding information and admitting to stalking my brother! Nothing traumatic happened. She isn't scared for life, and she wasn't hurt."

"That's bullshit!"

"You were so out of line."

"You don't know anything about her or what will affect her!"

Cooper, Eli, and I all talk over one another, bombarding Maverick, who looks surprised for a moment before it's gone, leaving him to just look pissed.

Maverick raises a hand to silence us. "What's done is done. It's over with. Kai took her home, and that's the end of it." His words hold a cryptic edge.

"What do you mean that's the end of it?" Eli questions, clearly catching on to his tone as well.

"I mean, that's the end of it. I don't want you two chatting or calling this girl anymore. No asking her for help on confidential cases, no bringing up what happened yesterday, nothing." Maverick says, zeroing in on the two of us.

I'm instantly fuming, "You can't just dictate who we can or can't talk to. And you definitely don't get to make that call after the way you steamrolled over her yesterday."

Maverick stands his ground, though. "I just did. I mean it, leave it alone. No more contact with the girl."

"Charlotte. Her name is Charlotte." Eli jumps in. "And you can't expect us to just cut her off because you had a bad moment yesterday. Kai and I have been talking to her for years; she's our friend."

"And yet, neither of you even knew who you were talking to until yesterday." Maverick fires back. "I mean it, no more contact. I don't need some random girl showing up and sticking her nose into our cases or anything else that concerns the business."

"Mav-" Cooper starts, but I quickly jump up to talk over him.

"No, you can't just determine who we can talk to," I tell him. "You want to play the boss card and demand that we not talk to her about anything work-related? Fine, we didn't do that anyway. But you have no right to forbid us anything else."

"Forgive me for considering that it's a bad idea to attach yourself to some girl who has a breakdown from being isolated in a room with the line of work we're in. If she can't handle something so simple, then I doubt a close friendship will last when you can't disclose anything about what you do." Maverick counters.

"Oh, fuck off! You don't know anything about her, and it's pretty shitty of you to judge her for having a panic attack. That's completely out of her control. You don't know what she's been through that would cause her to react that way." I can't believe how boneheaded he's acting about Lottie.

"And you do?" Maverick asks.

"No," I admit. "But I know a hell of a lot more than you. Regardless, I won't judge her or think poorly of her because she had a bad encounter with your overbearing ass."

A tense silence falls over the four of us as we all take a moment to collect ourselves.

Maverick rolls his eyes and drops his glass into the sink. "Keep talking to the chick if you're so adamant, but nothing about work and no seeking her out for help when you get stuck on a case." The last part is directed at Eli, who just glares back at Maverick. Having said his piece, Maverick storms out of the kitchen with Zeus close behind him. A moment passes before the door to his office slams shut.

"Well, that was fun." Cooper tries to break the tension, but it falls flat.

"What crawled up his ass that he's so intimidated by us having a friend?" Eli questions.

Turning back to the stove, Cooper sighs. "You know he's just protective of you guys. Plus, this case is a huge deal, so I'm sure the stress is just eating at him a bit." he tries to defend him.

"Sure, but that's no reason to take it out on all of us." I point out.

"He doesn't mean it," Cooper argues weakly.

"Whatever." I just want to get out of here at this point. "We've got class. Let's go, Eli."

Eli follows me out of the house to my truck. Driving to campus, I can still feel the anger simmering under the surface for both of us.

"What do you think his problem really is?" Eli finally asks, just before we get to the school.

"Honestly? I think Mav's inflated ego took a hit when Lottie told him no yesterday." I admit. "Plus, add in that we both realized that we were friends. The four of us have always stayed close to one another and haven't had many outside forces interfering with that. We both jumped to her defense immediately yesterday, and I think Maverick just took it personally."

"I guess." Eli agrees. "Whatever the case may be, he needs to get over it. I'm not going to let Maverick dictate my personal life. I get enough of that with him as my boss at GLS."

"You and me both, brother."

"So, just so we're on the same page. Are you still going to be talking to Charlie? Because I want nothing more than to get to know the girl who can work around a computer better than I can."

"Yeah, I'm actually going back to her dorm later on after classes today. She agreed to let me come check in and see how she's doing. We may even hang out and play some video games." I say as we both get out of the truck and head into campus.

Eli looks surprised. "She agreed to that? After everything that went down yesterday?"

"Yeah. We talked a little bit, and she opened up. I figured I'd shoot my shot while I had a chance, and she let me in."

"Wow." Eli sounds like he's soaking in the information.

"I can ask if she'd be comfortable with you coming to hang out with us." I offer.

Shaking his head, he hikes his bag further up onto his shoulder. "No, it's fine. I was going to reach out to her to talk at some point; you don't have to play wingman on this. No need to overwhelm her."

"Fair enough. Just don't wait too long to reach out to her. We didn't talk much last night, but from what little we did talk, I picked up that she's lonely. There's no way she's as okay being shut out from the rest of the world as she likes to front that she is."

"I'll try. We'll see what happens. I need to run; my class starts in five. I'll see you back at home later." He veers off to the left, heading to his first class of the day, and I stay on the path to make my way towards mine.

Heading towards my class, I'm feeling optimistic to get through the day to see Lottie. Last night, she let me in, let me see just a small sliver of her world, and I'm eager to dive in and get to know her on a more personal level. I've wanted nothing more than in the past four years than to

76

get to know her, and I finally have my shot. And I'll be dammed if I pass it up.

7

~Charlotte~

It took me a few days to process everything that happened during my visit to GLS. Finding the two people I'd been speaking to for years and meeting their brothers had been a lot. I had tried not to think too much about Maverick locking me in the room; doing so only made me panic each time. The more I thought about it, the more I could see his side of things. I don't agree with how he handled the situation, but I could understand his motivation. He was trying to protect his family, and in that moment, he considered me a threat to those he cares about most.

Kai and Eli had both apologized countless times for what happened that day and in the days leading up to it. I've grown so tired of hearing them apologize that I made them agree to start fresh so we could all just forget about it.

I was also still trying to wrap my head around the fact that Kai and Eli were twins. What are the odds that the only two friends I've made in four years are *twins*?

It's been about a month since I invited Kai to come to my dorm. Since then, it's become a regular occurrence; he comes over when he doesn't have work, and we game together, watch movies, or just eat food and talk. Slowly but surely, I've gotten comfortable being around him. I've learned a lot about him and his upbringing, and at the same time, I've shared a fair amount about myself.

For the first time in my life, I find myself getting close to someone. I know things like how he likes his coffee and how much he loves his brothers.

Having someone else in my space hasn't been as nerve-racking as I once thought it would be. Kai knowing about myself and how I'm a bit different from others helps with my anxiety a lot as well. He admitted that after our first night when he brought me home, he researched what he could about Asperger's, so he has a pretty good understanding of things that can easily bother me and hasn't made me feel weird about any of it. He's asked questions along the way to better understand and has been wonderful all around.

Eli reached out after our initial meeting through our usual chatroom, and we've begun talking more frequently as well. Kai even brought him along to hang out and watch movies a couple of times. Eli seemed almost as awkward as I, which oddly made me feel a bit better.

Eli has been trying to use the software I sent him to work on his project to help their friend, but has run into some trouble along the way. So, in between our casual chats and getting to know one another, I've also been helping him; in secret, of course, because according to the guys, Maverick would lose his shit if he knew I was helping.

Tonight is one of the few nights that I have my dorm to myself. Kai let me know that he and Eli had to handle a work assignment, so I might not be hearing from him.

I spent most of the afternoon following my regular schedule, working on new codes and making sure all of my assignments are caught up with our Thanksgiving break quickly approaching. Finishing off my noodles and an energy drink, I clean up quickly as my phone rings.

Eli's contact flashes on the screen, I answer curiously.

"Um, hi, Eli. Everything okay?"

"Hey, Charlie! Everything's fine. How was your day?" He asks cheerfully.

"Same as usual, no complaints for now."

"Great, that's great..." he seems hesitant, like he's struggling for what to say next, but I don't interrupt him. "So, I was hoping that you would come with me to Myth tonight to check it out. I know a nightclub probably isn't your thing, but I thought it could be fun. I technically have to go to work, but I thought you might like to hang out and spend some time together outside of your dorm? Kai will be there too." His words flow out so quickly that I have a hard time keeping up with what he's saying.

A nightclub definitely isn't my thing, not that I would know since I've never been to one... But the general idea of them didn't appeal to me. Loud music, flashing lights, and crowds of sweaty bodies didn't seem like anything I would enjoy.

But a small voice in the back of my head reminds me that I promised myself I would try to be more open with Kai and Eli as we've grown closer over the last month. I weirdly trusted them both and knew that they wouldn't let anything happen to me. Could I let myself be a little uncomfortable to make them happy by going and doing what they wanted to do? After all, it really wasn't fair of me to make them spend all their free time holed up in my dorm room.

Plus, Eli said he technically had to be there for work, and I have been helping him with their case, so maybe my being there tonight would help.

"Okay," I tell him before he can start rambling again.

"I understand, I knew it was a long- wait, did you just say yes?" surprise colors his tone.

A small laugh bubbles out of me, "Yes, I said yes." I confirm.

"Awesome!" He cheers, quickly clearing his throat, "I mean, yeah, that's cool. Um, I'll be by to pick you up in about half an hour, is that good?"

"Sounds good," I tell him before we quickly end the call.

All my false bravado washes away the instant the connection drops, anxiety settling in its place.

A fucking nightclub. What did I just agree to? What does someone wear when they go to a nightclub? My wardrobe mostly consisted of leggings, T-shirts, and hoodies, and I don't think any of those exactly meet the criteria for a club.

I could call my mom and ask...but she never seems thrilled to hear from me, and she'd ask too many questions about where I was going and who I was going with. Maybe I could ask one of the girls in my hall? No, that thought alone makes my palms sweat just thinking about it.

I settle on a quick Pinterest search for club outfits as I scan my closet. I remember that one of our neighbors growing up had an older daughter who left for college a couple of years before me. She had given me some clothes on one of her visits home before I went away to school. She had said they didn't fit her anymore and that I should take them with me to school 'just in case'. I never thought I'd encounter a just-in-case moment, but here we are.

Digging in the back of my closet, I find a few dresses in the mix of gifted clothes. Flipping through them, I find some that look like outfits from my search and quickly choose an all-black one over any of the sparkly ones.

A glance at the clock tells me I have only about ten minutes until Eli will be here, so I quickly strip and squeeze myself into the dress before heading into the bathroom to sort out my hair. Looking at myself in the mirror, I see a stranger. The black dress is fitted and very short, only coming to just above mid-thigh. There are cutouts in the dress over my rib cage that have been covered with a sheer black lace that matches the lace sleeves going down my arms.

I wouldn't say it looks bad, but it feels like a second skin and looks worlds away from anything that I normally wear.

Being short on time and just not knowing what to do, I run the straightener through my hair letting the silky, dark strands fall to my waist. I stick to wearing my Vans since I don't have any heels, nor would I attempt to wear any.

I'm just sliding my I.D. and debit card into my phone when I hear a knock at the door. Rushing over, I try to push down my nerves as I swing the door open. Eli stands just outside, looking sharp in a pair of dark wash jeans and a fitted black button-up, the buttons undone at the top and the sleeves rolled halfway up. His dark hair still looks messy as always, but it's shiny with some gel mixed in. His snake bite piercings are black today, standing out against his pale skin and matching his glasses. The few tattoos that he has peek out from his shirt sleeves, and his chest is bare except for a thin silver chain looped over it.

He stands gaping, looking me over from head to toe without saying anything, making my nerves act up again, and sweat starts to collect on my palms.

"I-is this okay?" I ask as I nervously twist my fingers.

"Fuck, Charlie. You look amazing." Eli's voice fills with awe as he continues to look me over, a smile tugging at his lips when his eyes find my vans paired with the dress.

I feel the heat rushing to my cheeks at his compliment. "Y-you look good too."

His stunned expression slowly morphs back into his carefree demeanor as he offers me his arm.

"Well, let's get going, shall we?"

I carefully place my arm in his, feeling awkward at the contact but not wanting to pull away as he leads me out of the dorms to his all-black charger waiting out front.

His car is the complete opposite of Kai's, which seems fitting for them, given how their personalities differ so much despite looking identical on the surface. He helps me lower into the front seat before he quickly rounds the car to settle in the driver's seat.

He keeps his hands on the wheel while I keep my hands firmly clasped in my lap; the silence hovers between us. The silence isn't uncomfortable as it normally is; it's more peaceful, and both of us are content to just be sharing the space.

"Have you ever been to Myth?" He asks as we cross the Hart bridge, the bright blue lights from the Acosta reflecting off his face and shining dimly through the car.

"No, I don't really go clubbing."

"Right." his answer is short, like he doesn't know what to say from here.

"You said something about needing to work while we're at the club?" I ask to fill in the silence.

He straightens up in his seat, seemingly relieved to have something he can talk about without walking on eggshells.

"Yeah, Kai and I thought we could observe the club crowd and look for anyone who could meet a description for a guy, for one of our running cases. He seems to stick to bars and clubs close to college campuses. It's a long shot, but we figured it wouldn't hurt to look around and see if we can find anything." His answer is specifically vague, not giving me enough information to break Maverick's rule about not sharing anything about their cases, but still keeping me in the loop about what he and Kai get up to.

I don't know why Maverick was such a stickler for the rule. I get that he doesn't like me, but I wouldn't share any of their confidential information with anyone. It's not like I had friends to gossip to.

It was a bit unfair how much Maverick seemed to dislike me from what the guys have told me about their conversations with him. I didn't lock him in a room against his will, and all things considered, I wasn't rude to him. It shouldn't bother me, but for some reason, it did, and I don't enjoy the feeling of knowing that someone that close to Eli and Kai is untrusting of me and wants me to stay away from the only friends I have.

We pull up out front of Myth quickly, and Eli rushes to open my door while handing off his keys to the valet waiting out front. My body instantly stiffens at the sight of all the people waiting out front. Eli notices and quickly takes my hand to gently pull me close to his side so that he's almost shielding me from others as we walk through the doors.

My eyes take a few moments to adjust to the low light of the club and the hazy fog of smoke that covers the room. Strobe lights flash through the space periodically, disorienting me as Eli tries to guide me through the crowd.

Bodies are packed wall to wall, blocking any bar that sits in the space, and I can hear a DJ yelling in between the tracks, but I couldn't point out where he is if someone paid me to.

My heart rate quickly increases, threatening to beat straight out of my chest as it feels like the people around us are closing in. I feel trapped, surrounded. I try to focus on Eli's hand on me, wrapped around my torso, but even that gets lost in all the sounds and people surrounding me. I try to curl in on myself and make myself smaller, hoping that it will keep people from brushing up against me. I feel the numb feeling starting to radiate in my fingertips and try to squeeze them to keep the sensation from spreading as I squeeze my eyes shut. If I can't see the people around me, maybe that will help.

Nope.

Instead, I feel even more disoriented than before.

I feel Eli ushering me from behind to where? I don't know. I'm too busy trying to hold on to my sanity to open my eyes to see.

I feel weightless for a moment as I'm counting my breaths, trying to get control, and suddenly the sound of the club is muted, and I feel a cool surface beneath me.

"Charlie, can you open your eyes for me?" Eli's voice comes out strained and tinted with worry. I want to look at him and take that worry away from him, but I still feel on the edge of losing myself, so I keep my eyes closed and focus on twisting my fingers in time with my deep breaths.

The numbness in my fingers starts to lessen, and my breath starts to slow. As the numbness fades, I can feel Eli holding both my hands and rubbing circles on my hands in time with my squeezing. I let the feeling soothe me as I continue to come down.

Now that I'm more alert, all I feel is embarrassment at myself for having a literal meltdown from just walking into the club, which keeps me from opening my eyes just yet. But another hand rubbing circles on my back makes me pause. If Eli has his hands on mine, then who the hell is rubbing my back?

My eyes fly open to immediately crash with Eli's deep sapphire eyes, his face just a few inches from mine. I quickly turn my gaze to the left and see an identical set of eyes twinkling with humor at my initial confusion.

"Hey Lottie, you look absolutely fucking stunning tonight."

I take a quick scan of his outfit. Much like Eli, he's wearing dark jeans with a worn pair of combat boots, but unlike Eli, he went with a short-sleeved navy button-up that's open down the front to reveal his tattoo-covered chest. Dark ink swirls over the expanse of his chest, emphasizing the hard muscles that sit just beneath.

Their contrasting styles match their personalities, and it makes me laugh at the thought that they look so similar, but Kai looks more like the devil on one of my shoulders, and Eli looks like the angel on the other.

Kai's eyes don't leave mine as he tilts his head, still rubbing my back. "What's so funny, Lottie?"

I flick my eyes to Eli's questioning stare before dropping my gaze to my lap, heat flooding my cheeks.

"N-nothing. You look good t-too."

I'm hoping they don't point out my embarrassment. I'm not sure I understand it myself, but looking at each of them gives me butterflies. I feel drawn to both of them, though I know it's wrong to like two people at once, yet I can't deny what I feel about each of them when their focus is on me.

Luckily, they take pity on me. Eli quickly jumps in to change the subject.

"Charlie, I'm sorry. If I knew that bringing you here would upset you, I wouldn't have suggested it. I feel like such a dick." His hand fists some of his hair, messing up the perfectly messy style it was sitting in just moments ago.

I reach for his hand, and he offers it willingly. I rub soothing circles on his as he was doing for me just minutes ago.

"It's not your fault. You didn't know how I'd react, it's not your fault that I'm too screwed up to do normal things that should be easy." I tell him honestly.

Eli's eyes flash up to mine, but now they're hard and narrowed on me.

I don't have time to question his look before I feel Kai's hand gently on my chin, turning my head to face him until our faces are just a few inches apart. He doesn't look much happier than Eli.

"Lottie-girl, what did you just say?" He asks in a deadly calm voice.

Confusion washes over me, and I try to look back at Eli, but Kai's hand gently but firmly keeps my eyes on him.

Nowhere to go, I answer him. "I just said that I'm too screwed up to do normal things. No one else down there freaked out from walking into the club like it was a haunted house."

"You are not *screwed up,* Lottie-girl. Just because you had a moment with a new situation doesn't make you weird, and it doesn't make you weak." He speaks with conviction, his eyes boring into mine. "I will speak for Eli and myself when I say that we don't like hearing anyone talk down on themselves, but we definitely don't want to hear you putting yourself down."

"But it's not normal to have a panic attack at that. I'm not talking down on myself, I'm just saying what's true."

"Who told you it's not normal to have panic attacks? Or when you're entitled to have them?" He asks, leaning back some to give me space as he tries to understand me.

I hesitate, something tells me that the answer 'my parents always called me a disappointment and told me to get over it' isn't what he wants to hear right now.

"Lottie, no one gets to tell you when it's appropriate to have a panic attack. If you get overstimulated or triggered into a panic attack, that's no one's business to comment on unless it's to help you get through it," he explains calmly.

"And don't talk down on yourself, ever. But especially about shit that's out of your control." Eli chimes in.

"Why?" I ask, looking between the two, not certain who will answer.

"Let's just call it a friendship rule." Kai offers, "We don't like how it makes us feel when people we care about talk badly about themselves. So, for the sake of all of our sanity, let's just eliminate the problem, please?"

"Okay." I agree, not wanting to upset either of them and ready to move on from this topic, I can overthink their words and what they mean more later.

"Great." Eli stands back to his full height, "So, do you want me to take you home, or do you want to stay longer? We can stay up here in the VIP, it's much less crowded and quieter too."

I glance around the space, seeing multiple private booths lining the room, with a full bar across from them. Over by the railing, it looks open, like it overlooks the club below. It's not nearly as overwhelming as the space downstairs. I feel determined to stay and not let my stupid anxiety ruin my first night out.

"Let's stay. If that's okay?"

Kai lets out an excited whoop as he fist pumps the air. "Yes! More than okay, Lottie! We're going to have a fun night."

Eli offers me a hand to pull me off the counter he had me sit on, "We can go sit over by the railing so you can see the club. If it gets too much, just let us know, and we can come sit in one of the quieter booths." He offers gently.

We find an empty table by the railing and settle in, Kai to my left and Eli to my right. We have a perfect view of the club below, and now, from higher up, I can finally spot the DJ I heard earlier on a small, raised stage towards the back of the club.

I can feel the guys touching me on either side. It's comforting but also makes my skin crawl a bit, like I'm hyperaware of every movement I make, knowing they may be able to feel any shift in me. I subtly shift my arms around my torso, so I'm not touching either of them, giving myself time to breathe, and lean forward to make it seem as though I'm just getting a better look at the crowd.

Kai and Eli both must notice as they slightly shift away, giving me space on either side, but neither of them mentions it.

"So, what do you think? Pretty cool, huh?" Eli asks.

"It's a lot," I counter, "What do you have to do for work while we're here?"

Kai answers, "Not much, it's more just surveillance. Seeing if we can spot anything out of the ordinary."

I nod in understanding, not really sure that I can help them with anything while I'm here, but determined to stay and keep them company.

"First time in a club, do you want to try the full experience? Maybe have a few drinks?" Kai is gesturing to the full bar that now sits behind us.

I've never had alcohol. I never had friends to sneak out and get drunk with like I'd heard so many kids at school brag about, and my parents always just seemed to become angry when they drank, so it didn't have much appeal to me. But I'd made it this far, coming into the club, and I was determined to make the best of the experience, so that meant experiencing it all.

"I'll try some, just not a-a lot."

A cute, boyish grin takes over Kai's face as he turns to flag down one of the waitresses walking around, and Eli speaks up from my other side.

"Are you sure, Charlie?" He doesn't sound condescending, only genuine as he checks with me. "You don't have to do anything you don't want to do. If you're not a drinker, then that's fine, we'll still have fun either way."

"I want to try it. It's something I've never done, and you guys will keep me safe, right?" I watch his expression light up at my question, pride beaming in his eyes. That's all the confirmation I need to know that they will absolutely stay by my side and keep me safe.

"Always. You don't even have to ask." He promises.

We sit and watch the club below, enjoying the music before drinks are delivered, two bottles of beer and a bright pink drink in a tall glass with a light shining from the base. There are also three small shot glasses set before us.

"Shots, Kai. Really?" Eli sounds disapproving of the drink choices, but that doesn't deter Kai as he sits with a Cheshire cat grin, holding out the shots to us both.

"Yes, really. We are going to have the full experience, and that means at least one shot."

We each take the shots from Kai as he grabs his own. I hold mine tentatively while Eli seems reluctant. Kai just holds his out between us, waiting for a cheers.

"To new experiences." He smiles widely at me.

I clink my glass to his and look at Eli expectantly. He waits a moment before rolling his eyes and tapping his glass with ours, and we quickly drink the shots.

It tastes disgusting and feels like fire rolling down my throat, a warm sensation quickly filling my chest. I'm sure the face I make isn't pleasant in the slightest, and it's only a compliment to the hacking cough that starts immediately after swallowing the liquid fire.

"Fuck, that shit is awful. Lottie, here, try this." Kai sputters while holding the pink drink in front of me.

I quickly grab it, desperate for anything to wash the taste of the shot away.

I take several gulps of the drink, an explosion of fruit dancing across my taste buds, and the cold liquid soothes my throat. The shot is quickly erased, and I'm left chugging the delicious drink, desperate for more of its fruity flavor.

"Slow down there, Charlie, you don't want to drink too fast." Eli chides me.

I take a break, gasping as I come up for air.

"It's so good, it's sweet and cold and way better than my energy drinks," I tell him, wanting to go back for more.

Kai chuckles, "Never thought I'd hear you claim something as better than your energy drinks. But Eli's right, you have to pace yourself. This definitely won't give you energy like your drinks will."

I settle for a small sip of the drink before placing it down and looking over the club once more. The music seems nice now, not as assaulting as earlier, and a lightness starts to take over me. I'm not worried about whether the guys brush against me; instead, just content to sway along with the feeling of the music.

My head is clear, no thoughts or worries to be found. I'm simply floating above the club alone. I know the guys are with me, but for now, I'm content to just float and enjoy the weightless sensation. No thoughts, no worries, just peace.

I wish I could stay like this forever.

8

~Kai~

Our Lottie girl is definitely a lightweight, not that I'm surprised, given her tiny size and lack of experience with drinking and partying. She's completely gone from just one shot and two drinks. But she looks so fucking happy that I can't even feel bad about the hangover she may feel tomorrow.

I am surprised at how drunk Eli is, though. He usually has a beer or two, but tonight it seems he's decided to throw caution to the wind and just enjoy the club with Lottie.

They're both by the railing, looking down on the club below and dancing to Uma Thurman by Fall Out Boy as it rattles through the speakers and shakes the floor.

Lottie is moving wherever the music takes her; there's no rhythm, and she's not anywhere close to being on beat, but even still, she's captivating, like a sexy little siren just calling out to me. It seems she calls Eli too, as we both can't keep our eyes off of her.

A slower song starts to play, so I peel myself off the couch, grabbing Lottie's hand gently in mine as she dances with her back plastered to Eli's chest. As I pull her chest to chest with me, Eli follows right behind her, sandwiching her between us.

A *Lottie sandwich.* I fucking love it.

Her five-foot height puts her right at our chests. I raise her arms up to loop around my neck, testing to see if she's okay with touch right now. She latches on tightly rather than tensing up like she usually does when either of us brushes against her, telling me that she's okay with it for now.

Eli and I have learned over the past few weeks that some days Lottie doesn't mind us touching her, holding her hand, or putting an arm over her shoulder. But then some days she looks ready to jump out of her skin at any contact. We've both tried to be very mindful of it and only touch her when she's relaxed. We both know to pull away instantly if she shows any signs of discomfort, so we don't draw attention to it.

Lottie's completely off beat, moving too quickly, so I slide my hands down to her hips, moving them in time with the music, showing her how to roll them and match the rhythm of the song. She adjusts quickly, and Eli wastes no time moving closer, rolling his hips with her and causing her to rub against my thigh with each pass.

We move together for some time, switching up our pace with each song. With every song, Lottie gets bolder, running her hands down my chest, sliding them under my shirt to explore my arms, even reaching back to run her hand through Eli's hair, even though she can barely reach.

The more Lottie explores, the deeper the blush gets, covering her face and seeping down to her chest.

Lottie's got a natural beauty that overshadows others without even trying, but her innocence takes it to a whole new level. I'm struggling to keep myself under control and not take it too far, especially while she's drunk. As much as I'm drawn to her, I'd never cross that line of breaking her trust by not having her consent.

That's why, when I see Eli starting to get handsy, I know I need to put a stop to it before anyone gets carried away.

"This has been fun, but I think it's time to head out," I tell both of them, getting matching frowns and protests.

Lottie's arm practically strangles me as she latches onto my neck.

"I'm having sooo much fun! Do we have to leave?" Lottie gives me the biggest puppy dog eyes that threaten to bring me to my knees in a heartbeat, willing and eager to do anything she says, but then Eli chimes in behind her.

"Yeah, it's fun. Don't be a buzzkill."

His drunken tone snaps me out of my haze instantly, and I cut him a look, silently telling him to shut the fuck up before I punch him in the throat. Clear-headed, I refocus on Lottie.

"I'm really glad you're having fun, and I promise we can come back sometime. But it's been a few hours, and you're very drunk, so we need to get you home before you crash or do something that you may regret." I feel silly having to explain this to her, but I remind myself that she's never partied, never been drunk, so this is all new for her.

"Like what?" she blinks at me innocently, her eyes glassy but wide.

I scramble for what to tell her without sounding like a hypocrite, listing all the things that I'd like to do with her, but Eli beats me to it.

"Touching, kissing, fucking." He shrugs, "Those are the usual regrets people throw out there after a night of partying."

"What if I want to try any of those things?" Her nose scrunches as her face flushes a shade of crimson. I'm curious which activity she's thinking of, causing that blush to deepen, but I decide to leave it for now.

"There's nothing wrong if you want to, we just won't be doing any of them tonight."

I try to loosen her hands from my neck so I can start leading her out of here, but she grabs on like a Koala, determined to continue the conversation.

"But what if I want to tonight? What if I want to try while the noise in my brain is all quiet? Don't I get to choose?" Her voice slurs as she shoots me those damn puppy dog eyes; it keeps me focused.

I scoop her up quickly, lifting her by the backs of her thighs, wrapping her legs around my waist, and resting her back against Eli's chest, putting our eyes at the same level. I grab her chin firmly enough that she has to keep her focus on me.

"Any other time, yes, you get to decide. But neither of us is going to do anything that you can't consent to." She starts to protest, but I quickly cut her off, "And believe me, Lottie girl, when I kiss you for the first time, I want you to be completely aware. I want you to hear all that noise in your brain, because then you'll see how well we can silence it for you in a different way. And for that, I want you to be able to remember it."

Her breath hitches as her eyes remain wide and glazed, lost in my words. Leaning in, I press a gentle kiss to her forehead before releasing her back down to her feet.

Peeking a glance at Eli, he still stands behind her, his hooded gaze telling me that he's imagining the different ways we can go about silencing the noise like I just explained. He doesn't even acknowledge me, just waiting for her to turn her gaze to him before muttering a simple, "Ditto".

Her blush deepens as she reverts to looking at the floor rather than directly at either of us.

We lead her out of the club with no issues, making sure to box her in between us so no one can accidentally touch her as we make our way out. I keep looking down to make sure she's okay, as we walk through the crowd, but she seems relaxed between the two of us.

Outside the club, I ask the valet to bring Eli's car around the front, figuring that I can just drive them both home in his car since he's too drunk and I rode my Kawasaki here tonight. We wait for a few minutes. Lottie looks ready to crash and is leaning heavily against my side, while Eli leans against the wall of the club, eyes closed, and face upturned to the night sky.

"Sir, I'm so sorry, but it appears that the car has two flat tires, and we aren't able to bring it around to the front." One of the valet employees tells me, standing before us, looking nervous, like he might puke at any moment.

I arch a brow at him, "Two flat tires?"

"Yes, sir, unfortunately."

Eli's attention is finally piqued, pulling himself off the wall, he steps up beside me, his arms folded across his chest.

"I drove it here tonight, and it was perfectly fine. How do I now have two flats?" His tone is annoyed, and I'm sure that if he were more sober and if Lottie weren't half passed out standing next to me, then he'd make much more of a scene.

"Well, I'm not certain, but it looks as though, I mean, it's possible - but again we don't know-"

"Spit it out," Eli growls as the man stumbles over his words.

His next words come out in a rush, his nervousness kicking up a notch, "It looks as though they may have been slashed."

Slashed? Who the fuck would slash Eli's tires? And what the fuck has the valet been doing all night that they didn't notice someone sneaking into the lot to fuck with any of the cars? Eli says nothing, but his glare towards the man is murderous as he stands there shaking, waiting for any type of reaction.

Eli and I have both come to Myth often, for both work and fun. Maverick and Cooper are both longtime friends of the owners, so all the staff at the club know us and give us their best service when we're here. GLS provides extensive security support, and Maverick even helped with their start-up years ago and serves as a silent partner.

"You need to go inform your boss of what happened and figure out who the fuck slashed my tires." Eli finally spits out at the man. "And be sure to tell him that someone from GLS will be calling tomorrow to discuss the club's failure to protect their customers' property," he adds as the man hurries off to anywhere but here.

Once he's gone, Eli is seething, running his hand through his hair and looking for something to punch, most likely.

"What the fuck?" he shouts, startling Lottie a bit, but she quickly slumps back against my chest, barely conscious.

"I don't know, man, but we can look into it tomorrow." I try to calm him down, "You and Lottie are both drunk, and we need to get both of you home. You're not going to figure anything out tonight."

He glances at Lottie before taking a deep breath, letting his head drop back as he does.

"Fine." He concedes as he straightens back up. "You took your bike tonight, didn't you?"

"Yeah, so we can either order an Uber, or we can call Cooper to come get us."

"Just call Cooper," He tells me, running his hand down his face. "I don't want to drag Charlie in the car with some stranger."

Agreeing with him, I pull my phone out of my pocket and dial Cooper, watching Lottie as I wait for it to connect.

"Kai, where are you? Is everything okay?" Maverick's voice comes through after a couple of rings.

Fuck. Well, this should be fun.

"Hey, Mav. Everything's fine, I'm at Myth with Eli and Charlotte, and we need a ride. Where's Cooper?"

"He's in the bathroom, but he left his phone on the couch. Why are you at Myth, and why do you need a ride? Didn't you drive there?" He doesn't sound annoyed yet, so that's positive, but I'm too tired to play twenty questions with him. And no way am I going to tell him that Eli and I were checking the club-goers to see if we could find anyone who could match the descriptions for a drug-deal case we were working on. It was already a long shot, but we figured that targeting bars near colleges might be a trend of theirs. Also, we brought Lottie, and that definitely violated Maverik's stupid rules about blending Lottie and work. So, I opt for lying.

"Just a fun night out. And we did drive, but I took my bike, and now Eli's tires were slashed, so now we need a ride."

Maverick's silence fills the line for so long that I have to check to see it's still connected before he finally speaks.

"I'll be there in ten." The line quickly goes dead.

"Great," I say to no one in particular as I pocket my phone.

Eli's back against the wall, much calmer now than before. "What?"

"Maverick answered Cooper's phone. He'll be here in ten." I tell him as I try to adjust Lottie so she's not about to slump over onto the sidewalk.

Eli's eyes close as he drops his head back to the wall. "Well, this will be a fun car ride. He does know that Charlie is with us, right?"

"I mentioned it, but he didn't say anything," I tell him, stroking her hair lightly, reveling in her closeness as she stays blissfully unaware of everything around her.

It doesn't take long for Maverick's SUV to pull up, and I carefully get Lottie situated in the middle of the back seat as Eli stumbles around to get in on the other side. Lottie's much more coherent now, but still quiet. Once she's settled and buckled in, I take the seat next to her, shutting the door behind me.

Maverick watches in the rearview mirror, his jaw clenched with his usual frustration. Cooper is in the passenger seat and turns around to look at Lottie, grinning like a maniac.

"Good night?" He asks.

A smile tugs at her lips, her eyes meeting Coop's before seeing Maverick's stare in the mirror and quickly dropping to her lap again.

"Y-yes."

"We're going to be talking about this in the morning." Maverick suddenly speaks up, his tone firm, not amused in the slightest.

"Talk about what?" Lottie questions and surprise flickers in Maverick's stare at hearing her speak to him. Though

I'm not sure she realizes she's talking to him; otherwise, she probably wouldn't have said anything.

Cooper shoots Maverick a look before flashing a smile at Lottie, "Nothing. Maverick is just grumpy. You remember he tends to have mood swings?"

"Oh, yeah." She nods, "He locked me in a room last time he was grumpy." Lottie is so matter-of-fact that Eli and I both can't contain the laughter that breaks free, even Cooper is about to lose it as Maverick seethes in the front seat, strangling the steering wheel.

He finally pulls away from the curb and starts heading back towards Oceancoast, silence filling the car as we go.

"You want any music, Charlotte?" Cooper asks, handing her his phone through the seat.

"NO," Maverick barks, but Cooper just rolls his eyes,

"We're not sitting here in silence, Mav, it's just some music."

Maverick's jaw grinds so hard I'm worried that he'll crack a tooth. "Fine. Just no freaking Taylor Swift," He finally relents.

I don't know what he has against Taylor Swift, but I just know that it's been forbidden in his car for as long as I can remember. I'm not sure why he assumes her first choice would be Taylor Swift, but I look over and see Lottie pouting slightly, clearly wanting to have put on one of her songs. Now she stares at the phone, indecision written all over her face. In an instant, though, it's gone, and in its place is a defiant look as she searches for a song. I expect to hear Taylor Swift start playing over the speakers, but instead, "Primadonna" by Marina starts blasting, and once again, Eli, Cooper, and I are fighting to hold back our laughter as Lottie seems satisfied to have found an alternative.

Lottie sits next to me, beaming with pride, while we watch the vein in Maverick's forehead pulse.

The car ride continues this way, Lottie picking songs to poke at Maverick. Sorry Not Sorry by Demi Lovato, 10 Things I Hate About You by Leah Kate, and a couple of other songs by female artists, that she dedicates to Maverick, subtly telling him to go fuck himself. My personal favorite, though, has to be Femininomenon by Chappell Roan, as Lottie and Eli both are very into it, drunkenly singing along, and even Cooper jumps into the parts he knows.

By the time we pull into the dorm parking lot, everyone has settled down. Maverick looks ready to burst, and Lottie is slumped over on me, completely tired out from her musical 'fuck you' campaign. Opening the door, I help Lottie out after me, and Eli stays passed out against the other door.

"Be quick," Maverick orders over his shoulder.

"You can just head back to the house; I'm going to stay with Lottie to make sure she's okay," I tell him, catching Lottie as she slips stepping down from the car. That makes Maverick's head spin to glare at me, "You will drop her off, then come home. I didn't bring you over here to drop you off so you can get your dick wet."

I make sure Lottie is steady before shooting daggers at him, "Not that it's any of your business, but I'm not going to *fuck* her. This is her first time being drunk. I need to make sure she's okay."

"Kai-"

"Maverick. He's fine. If he says he's not going to do anything, then just leave it at that. Just let him look after her." Cooper cuts him off, coming to my defense. Not waiting to hear what else he has to say, I slam the car door and walk Lottie towards her dorm. She stumbles a couple of times before I finally scoop her up into my arms to make the walk faster.

She doesn't have a care in the world as she lets her head hang back, giggling the whole way down the hall. Once I get to her door, I ask her where her key is.

"I don't have it. I just leave it unlocked," She says simply, like it's no big deal.

"Lottie, you can't just leave your door unlocked. What if someone wanted to break in?"

She shrugs, "No one has the last four years, so I think I'm safe."

Right. We'll be discussing that tomorrow, right after I find her key and make myself a copy.

"Alright, do you want to jump in the shower and change before bed?" I ask her, sitting her on the edge of her bed, kneeling down to untie her Vans and slip them off.

"Bed," Lottie says above me, glancing up. I see her eyes already half closed, and she's starting to slump forward. There's that crash I warned her about earlier.

"Okay, let me grab you some clothes so you can change," I tell her over my shoulder as I head into the closet, looking through the shelves, I find rows of clothes immaculately hung and organized by color. Leggings sit beneath the t-shirts and hoodies on the shelf above. The floor is lined with Vans in every color you could think of, all perfectly aligned and spaced evenly apart, the laces tucked into each shoe.

It seems Lottie might be a little bit of a neat freak. Not a surprise considering every time Eli or I have been over, she obsessively cleans up any trash or wrappers before she sits down, and I've never seen a speck of dust anywhere in her dorm room. Even her desk, where she works, is perfectly organized: the monitors spaced evenly across the surface, the mouse pad always aligned with the edge of the desk, and everything in its place. I've sat and watched her adjust her keyboard for a solid five minutes to make sure it's perfectly centered on the desk.

I'm thrilled that Lottie has let Eli and me in so much over the last month. Everything we get to learn about her is like a little treasure, and we both lock every bit of information away, cherishing knowing that she feels safe enough to show us things about her. I waited for years to get to know the girl behind the game that I talked to daily, and she's better than I ever imagined.

Not knowing what she usually sleeps in, I just grab a hoodie from the top of the pile and quickly find some loose lounge shorts. Stepping back into the room, I find Lottie sprawled out on the bed, completely passed out and lightly snoring.

I drop the clothes off on the bed and head over to the kitchenette, knowing that she needs to drink something and take some aspirin to lessen her hangover in the morning. Looking in her fridge, I find a single bottle of water among the variety of energy drinks. Looking through the cabinets, I find one with some medicine in it and grab two painkillers with the water. As I turn to leave the kitchen area, I spot an orange pill bottle on the counter, and I remember her nightly alarm for her meds. I scan the bottle for her dosage and grab one of the small pills as well.

"Lottie." I try to keep my voice low to not startle her, but it doesn't work as she shoots up in the bed, confused and disoriented. I move quickly to reassure her, "Hey, it's fine, Lottie. It's just me."

She calms down instantly at seeing me, her eyes already drooping to drag her back into sleep.

"Lottie, you can sleep in a minute; you need to take these and change, then you can sleep." I try to coax her to take the pills quickly, but she just tries to roll away from me towards the other side of the bed. "Lottie girl, really quick, just take these. I'll help."

I keep her upright with one arm as I bring my hand to her mouth with the pills, waiting for her to take them. Once she does, I hold the water to her lips, making her take a few sips until she's finished at least half of it. Sitting on the floor, I keep one arm around her as she tries to roll away again.

"Come on, comfy clothes, and then you can sleep. Almost done." She grumbles something back at me, but all I can hear is 'bed,' so I lift her up off the bed and set her on her feet, steadying her as she sways. Once she's steady enough, I grab the shorts and help her step into them, pulling them up under her dress. I grab the hoodie and ready it for her to slip on. "Can you slip the dress off so we can get this on?" I ask her.

Lottie doesn't even open her eyes as she grabs the bottom of the dress and begins to pull it over her head, her arms only getting stuck in the sleeves for a moment. I look at the ceiling as she pulls it off, not wanting to invite myself to look when she doesn't realize. Blindly, I help her slip into the hoodie, only looking once I know it's one.

Lottie's eyes are still closed, trying to slip back into sleep, so I grab the comforter and pull it back, noticing that it's heavy, like a weighted blanket. Gently, I guide her under the covers and pull them up, so she's covered. Any irritation at being woken is wiped from her face in an instant, calm taking over as she settles under the heavy weight of the blanket. She's out in seconds.

As I go to move away, ready to find some blankets and a pillow to make a bed on the couch for the night, I feel her hand shoot out to grab my wrist.

"Stay." She slurs.

"I'm not leaving, I'm just going to sleep on the couch," I whisper.

Her hand pulls on my wrist again, "Stay," She says, more clearly this time.

Lottie is never the one to initiate contact; it's always Eli or me who makes the first move. I'm not sure if it's the alcohol or if she even realizes that she's doing it, but something in me can't deny her. I reach over to turn off the lamp, cloaking the room in darkness before lying on top of the blankets next to her.

I lay in the dark, just listening to her snores for a while before she shifts, putting her head on my chest as she settles again.

I'm not sure what I did to get someone as special as Lottie in my life, but lying here with her, feeling her touch me, listening to her breathing as she sleeps, I feel a warmth in my chest that I've never felt before. I know that for as long as possible I'll stay with her, as long as she'll have me. In the dark, I make a silent promise to myself and to her. She won't have to ask me to stay ever again.

9

~Eli~

My head pounds in time with my heartbeat as the sun seeps through the window, dragging me out of sleep. Memories of last night filter in, bringing a smile to my face as I'm pulled to consciousness. Getting to spend time with Kai outside of work-related events was always something I cherished. Though we went to the club intending to look for people of interest in another case, we quickly abandoned that task and just enjoyed the night with Charlie. We had been close our entire lives, but more often than not, it felt like all of our time was devoted to work and proving ourselves. Getting to let loose was rare, but I'm glad we did.

Charlie looked absolutely stunning last night. Seeing her let loose and have a good time brought me so much joy; all I could think about last night was how to bring that smile back to her face and how to keep it there forever.

I'm not stupid; she's definitely attracted to me. She's also attracted to Kai, maybe even Cooper, too, if her blush in the car as he was giving her his attention is anything to go by. But we know how to share, we've done it before. As long as I can call Charlie mine, I don't care if she wants my brothers, too.

Pulling myself out of bed, the clock on the nightstand tells me it's a little after 8 in the morning. I vaguely remember that Kai decided to stay with Charlie last night, given how drunk she was. Deciding that I want to take them breakfast and check on her, I quickly shower and throw on clothes before heading down the stairs to find the keys to Kai's truck.

I find his keys quickly and almost make it to the garage door before I hear Maverick's voice calling me from his office. Sighing, I turn back to his door, knowing that he'll just cause a scene if I ignore him.

Inside, I see him sitting behind his desk, typing away. Zeus perks up at my entrance from his bed next to the desk but settles quickly, realizing I'm not a threat. Dropping into one of the chairs in front of the desk, I wait for Maverick to finish up whatever he's working on. He must've been in here for a while, still in his pajamas, and his coffee mug sits empty on the desk.

Once he's done, he looks up, staring at me over the desk. Neither of us says anything. I'm not sure what he called me here for, but I don't want to give him the upper hand in asking.

Maverick is an awesome brother; someone I've always been glad to have on my side, but he tends to forget that life is meant to be fun and not so serious all the time. I think part of him feels like he needs to be a parental figure ever since our parents died a few years ago. Being the oldest, he seems to carry around that burden with him. We've tried to tell him that he doesn't always have to be the protector and the father we lost, but he can't seem to let go of the control it gives him.

He continues to stare, but I just sit and wait, lifting a brow in question at him. He finally caves, taking a deep breath, gearing himself up before speaking.

"Eli, I thought I made it clear when we last had this discussion that your little *girlfriend* was not to know anything about the work that you and Kai do for GLS." He waits patiently for my response.

I know I have to be careful with my answer. If I apologize, then I'm immediately admitting that Kai and I went against his stupid rules. But if I play dumb too much, then he'll just get angrier than if I admit it.

"I'd say you were pretty clear," I tell him simply.

Leaning back, he looks pleased with my answer, meaning that he knows something and he's about to drop into his condescending asshole role.

"So, tell me why she was with you two last night at Myth if you were there for surveillance? Because I think that would be considered very close to your work, wouldn't you?"

I scratch my head, seeming lost in thought, "I guess that depends on what one would consider close to work. I mean, if she didn't know why we were there, I wouldn't consider it close; she would just see it as a fun night out with friends, which it basically was, since we didn't see anything. One could probably consider her 'close to work' by attending Oceancoast with us down the street, you know, given the radius and the miles between the office and school. It's all really up to one's perception, I suppose." I'm being a smartass, but I can't help it; he gets under my skin when he tries to act like his word is law, always followed and never questioned.

His eyes narrow at the sarcasm in my voice. "I might've agreed with you for argument's sake *if* I didn't know that you two were still letting her help with the case. Having her help with the software she gave you for the security cameras and searches you've been running on people linked to it." His calm demeanor is starting to slip, his usual irritation creeping into his tone.

I go with avoidance, trying to steer the conversation away from the obvious.

"'*Her* has a name, Charlotte. What do you have against her anyway? You were the one who was a dick the first time you met. Aside from that, she's done nothing to you; she's hardly even spoken to you."

"It's not an issue with her, Eli." I glare at him for avoiding her name after I just called him on it. He drags a hand down his face, sighing. "*Charlotte* isn't the problem here; you and Kai disregarding my orders and sharing confidential information with someone not in our line of work is the problem. We have contracts and rules in place to protect the people we're hired by; going around and sharing that with your girlfriend isn't exactly the best practice."

I'm surprised at his ability to keep his temper in check; usually, he'd be yelling by now. Maybe he assumes that pretending to be calm and concerned about client confidentiality will lull me into a submissive state. He'd be wrong, though, because the calmer he is, the more my anger starts to bubble up inside.

"Do you hear yourself when you talk sometimes? Your 'orders'? We're your brothers, Maverick; not everything you say to us should be an order. I get you're our boss, but we're also family, and I'm sorry, but you haven't felt like our older brother since mom and dad died." Emotions flash across his face at the mention of our parents, but I'm not stopping. "I get that you're running a business and you're concerned with protecting our clients, we are too. We're doing what we can to find the fuckers that took Ivy, and we've hit nothing but dead ends. Charlie brings something to the table that finds leads where others see dead ends. Shit that I can't even find she picks up on in an instant, Kai and I have had trails to follow because of what she's been able to do so far. So as much as you want to spew shit about us just telling all our business to our friend, that's not it. She's an asset to us, and you're deluded if you think that we're going to ignore the help she can offer and risk having this case go cold just because you're afraid to let someone help."

I sit back, breathing heavier now after saying my piece. Maverick is silent, mulling over my words, looking torn.

"Eli, I'm sorry if you think that I haven't been acting like your brother, but it's hard to navigate being your older brother and your boss." I'm stunned to hear an apology coming from him. I can count on one hand the number of times he's apologized to me for anything. Of course, he has to ruin it by continuing, "But the fact of the matter is that regardless of how helpful Charlotte has been thus far, she's not a part of GLS and therefore has no right to be anywhere near the work that we do."

"So, hire her," I say, my mouth moves faster than my brain. Honestly, though, I'm not sure why Kai and I didn't think of it sooner. Charlie's skills are next level. I wasn't lying when I said that she's an asset. She can work for GLS, help us with the case, and do something she enjoys. And we can continue to get to know her. It's a win for everyone, well, except for Maverick.

"You want me to hire your girlfriend to work for us?" Maverick asks, crossing his arms, staring at me like I've grown a second head.

"Our *friend*. But yes, that sounds like a perfect solution to this whole argument." I explain, "You won't have to worry about what Kai and I are doing when Charlie's around. We get some help that we seriously need on this case. Not to mention you'll have a fantastic hacker on your staff, which will be a big help to other cases we get."

"How do I know she's even qualified? She's a college student, with no job experience, and, don't take this the wrong way, but I think your judgment may be a little biased."

"She has experience," I quickly tell him. "I've been talking to Charlie for years. She's worked a few freelance jobs, and I'm sure she has references from those. As far as qualifications, I'd say that her program that you found on her laptop for the backlogged security feeds and facial recognition speaks for itself." I remind him.

He's silent again, the gears turning in his brain, probably trying to find another excuse to say this is a bad idea. The longer he sits, the more evident it is that he can't come up with anything else.

"I'll consider it." I start to feel excited, but he quickly tries to squash it, "But she has to interview. I have to actually have a conversation with her more in-depth than her drunkenly playing music, telling me to go fuck myself." His brow arches as I try to smother my laugh, "When could you get her to GLS to meet?"

"Today, I'm sure. I was about to take her and Kai breakfast; I can talk to her when I get there and have her at the office around noon?" I may be getting ahead of myself, making plans before I even run it by Charlie, but I know this is a good thing. It's good for us, and it will be something good for Charlie as well.

"Okay." I'm shocked that he's actually agreeing to this, "But Eli, it's just an interview. I'm not making any promises before I talk to her and see what her skills are for myself."

"Understood." I nod as I get up, eager to go share the news. "Thank you, Mav," I tell him genuinely before heading for the door.

"Eli," He calls out before I can make it out the door, "I'll work on being a brother to you both and step back from acting like dad." He doesn't offer anything else, but he doesn't need to; he's telling me that he hears me, and that's enough for now.

"Thanks, Mav," I tell him warmly before I'm on my way.

10

~Charlotte~

I wake up in discomfort. My head is pounding like a kick drum against the sides of my skull. And I'm hot, drenched in sweat, overheating, I may as well be in the Sahara Desert.

Peeling my eyes open, I'm immediately assaulted by two things. One: The light in my dorm is blinding. The curtains over the window are still pulled open from yesterday. Two: a tanned and tattooed chest rests just beneath my cheek, seeming to be the source of at least some of the heat that I'm feeling.

Memories from last night flash through my brain. Myth, Kai and Eli, dancing, playing music in the car to piss off Maverick.

Shit.

I had a lot of fun last night, but now I think that drinking may not be for me, given how I feel after, and how much of a fool I feel like for how I was acting last night. I don't dance, but that didn't stop me from dancing on the guy's last night. I definitely don't act like a brat towards people that I know hate me...but that's exactly what I did to Maverick. I can almost guarantee that my behavior in the car didn't win me any points with him.

Embarrassment washes over me, and I want to just burrow under the blankets and hide from the world. Kai's raspy, sleep-filled voice pulls me out of my mental spiral.

"Lottie girl, I can hear your brain working overtime from here."

Hearing his voice and feeling the vibrations of his chest has me quickly remembering that my face is currently plastered to it. Shuffling up, I shuffle to the far side of the bed, needing to have some space to think and wallow in my embarrassment some more.

"I-I-I-I'm sorry a-about last night." It's a struggle to force the words to come out, but I know that I need to apologize for him having to take care of me last night. I don't like the guilt that sits on my chest, making me feel like a burden once again in my own life. My parents spent my entire childhood yelling and screaming at me, throwing it in my face every day that they made so many sacrifices to be my parents. The truth is that they were emotionally neglectful, not fit to be parents, and they were more often than not angry at the responsibilities that fell on them to take care of me in the most basic ways. Throw in the fact that I was different than other children, and that only heightened their rage towards me.

So much yelling and screaming at me to 'be normal' or 'grow the fuck up already'. I learned at a very young age not to ask my parents for anything, only to bother them if I was dying. Yet even that didn't seem to be enough to stay out of their hateful fits of rage. And when I got older, and they realized that I acted differently from their friends' kids, they took that as their cue to 'fix' me.

This is why it's easier to keep myself isolated. To stay in my own little bubble away from people. I always do the wrong thing and anger those around me. Or I end up causing the people around me to try to fix whatever I made wrong. When I'm by myself, I don't have to worry about this feeling. If something gets messed up, then it's on me; if I can't act like a normal person, then who cares? If I'm alone, then I'm the only one affected by my actions.

Kai, seemingly more awake now, sits up. Thankfully, staying on his side of the bed, he shifts so that he's propped against the headboard. His shirt still lies open, his picture-perfect chest on display for me to see. And I do because that's where my eyes stay fixed, not able to bring myself to look at him.

"Lottie, can you look at me?" he asks softly. I shake my head quickly, not ready to see the annoyance in his eyes. I twist my fingers harshly as he sighs, probably readying himself to berate me for acting like such a fool last night and having to go out of his way. "Lottie. You have *nothing* to apologize for. Last night was awesome, we all had fun, and it was absolutely fucking amazing to see you enjoy yourself. So, whatever is going on in your head right now, I need you to try and tell it to shut the hell up so you can hear what I'm telling you."

His voice sounds sincere, but the noise in my head is louder than him, drowning out everything he's trying to tell me. Logically, I hear what he's saying, but in my brain, I can only hear the words 'disappointment' and 'burden' being shouted through a bullhorn. Suddenly, everything feels wrong. I'm already overheating, but now the hoodie I wear is too much, scratching at my skin like ants crawling all over me. Even my sheets brushing up against my legs feel like thorns poking and prodding at me and tearing away at my skin.

Pulling at the hoodie, I try to keep it from touching my skin as I jump from the bed, making a beeline for the bathroom.

"Lottie." Kai's voice calls me from the bed, but I need to get this off, now. I need to wash away all the feelings that are overwhelming me.

"Shower," I call back as he tries again to get my attention.

Locking the door behind me to ensure that Kai can't try to come and check on me, I strip the clothes off like they're on fire, reaching in to turn the shower as hot as it will go. I only give it a few moments to warm up before jumping under the spray, the still chilled water feeling like needles on my skin. It doesn't feel good, but it does distract from the crawling sensation a bit. The water heats up quickly, turning to molten lava as it pours over me, plastering my hair to my skin, while I scrub my arms vigorously, trying to rid myself of the feelings. Grabbing the soap, I use it a few times, the discomfort easing with each rinse.

I'm not sure how many times I scrub and rinse before the feeling finally subsides, letting me take a full breath for the first time since waking up. I give myself a few moments to breathe and calm down, and to give Kai plenty of time to leave before I shut off the water and step out of the shower to dry off.

My arms are red from the constant scrubbing and hot water combined, and although the mirror is fogged up, I don't need it to know that my face and chest are in the same state.

I mentally slap myself when I realize that I didn't bring a change of clothes in here with me. Securing the towel around me, I quickly brush my teeth before going in search of something to wear.

Knowing that Kai probably ran the second I closed the door earlier, I don't think twice about swinging the door open and stepping back into the room. I almost jump out of my skin when I'm greeted with matching startled expressions from the island in the kitchen in the area. Kai and Eli stand on either side, a takeout bag on the counter between them. All three of us just stare at one another in silence for a few moments, but Eli is the one to break it.

"Good morning, Charlie." he stops to clear his throat, "Um, I brought over breakfast." He keeps his eyes on mine, not straying to the towel I have strangled in my grasp. A quick look at Kai, though, shows me that he doesn't have the same restraint, his eyes trailing over me from head to toe, zeroing in on the towel and where it clings to me.

I stare dumbfounded at the two of them. Eli glances at Kai before rolling his eyes, slapping him in the head, and shooting him a look.

"Why don't you get dressed, and we'll get the food laid out?" Eli suggests, giving me a reassuring smile.

Spinning on my heel, I rush into the closet at the reminder of clothes, shutting the door firmly behind me. I can hear muted whispers through the door, but not enough to make out what's being said, so I focus on finding clothes for the day.

I keep it simple, wanting something to make me feel secure without bothering me too much, as the hoodie did earlier. I throw on a pair of old leggings and a faded band tee, then tuck my wet hair into a messy bun, so it's out of the way.

I'm not sure why Kai didn't cut and run the second I left the room; I fully expected him to bolt. Seeing that Eli is here only makes me feel embarrassed again. Facing one of them was enough to send me into a spiral. I don't know how to face both of them.

It's clear that neither of them is going to leave until they've said their piece, so I just need to go out there and get it over with. Then I can wallow away for the rest of the weekend alone.

Preparing myself, I take a deep breath before slipping out. They both still stand on either side of the island, their whispers cutting off as I come into view. The food containers are now out of the bag and open, revealing a wide spread of pancakes, eggs, bacon, hash browns, grits, and fruit. It looks like Eli brought a whole dinner with him and laid it out in my kitchen.

Their eyes are glued to me as I cross the space to stand opposite them at the island, keeping it between us as a buffer.

"Feeling better?" Kai asks as I look over the spread up close.

Avoiding their stares, I nod.

"Well, let's dig in. I got one of everything since I wasn't sure what you would want to eat." Eli says cheerfully, but I stay frozen as they both sit down and start making plates.

Not wanting to drag this out, I decide to just bite the bullet, "I'm really sorry about last night. You guys shouldn't have to take care of me." I blurt out.

They both stop grabbing food and look my way, waiting for me to say more. I wait in nervous anticipation before

Kai speaks up, realizing that I'm not going to say anything more.

"Lottie. I already told you that you have nothing to apologize for. Eli and I had a great time last night and we absolutely enjoyed ourselves." I say nothing but a quick peek at Eli and I see him nodding in agreement. "Now, this morning when you woke up, you were freaked out. Was that just because you thought we'd be mad that you had a good time? Or was it something that I did that made you uncomfortable?" Again, I don't answer. "I just need to know if I did something so that I don't do it again by mistake."

His concern for me is so sweet, I don't want him thinking that he did anything to upset me because that's the furthest thing from the truth.

"You can tell us, Charlie. Just be honest if either of us did something." Eli gently urges.

"I just thought that you two would be annoyed that I got drunk, and you had to get me home and stay with me. I really didn't mean for you two to have to worry about me while you were having a fun night out as well." Twisting my fingers I recall more of last night's events, "And then you had to call your brothers to get us and I was rude to Maverick, and I'm not usually like that and I feel bad. I need to apologize to him. But I get it if dealing with me is too much and you guys don't want to. You can go, no hard feelings. I get it." I try to offer them an easy out now so we can get it over with.

Silence fills the space around us as they soak in my words.

Eli's hands are on mine, stopping me from pulling at my fingers, "Charlie, neither of us is mad at you. Seeing you let loose made us so happy, almost as happy as seeing you sass Maverick. We all know that he deserves it."

"You don't need to apologize; we had a fantastic time. Getting you home safe and staying with you was not and is not a burden." Kai says firmly, "Neither of us is leaving and we're not *dealing* with you. We enjoy being around you and unless you tell us to leave, we're here to stay so you may as well get used to it." Shrugging, he turns back to his plate and starts digging into a pile of eggs.

I feel a weight lifted off my chest at their insistence that they want to be here, even if there is still a small seed of doubt that they're going to tire of me and leave. For now, I'll just have to try and push that doubt away.

Looking at them for the first time since sitting down they give me matching smiles and I feel a small smile of my own tugging at my lips.

Eli lets go of my hands and starts moving the food around, "Now that's settled, let's eat. I'm starving."

We eat in a comfortable silence, only sharing small comments about the food here and there. I pick at a small selection of food while they happily devour everything else that's left over. As we finish eating, I gather all the trash and scoop up any crumbs to toss.

Eli sits back, stretching while Kai checks his phone.

"So, I spoke to Maverick this morning." Eli tells us, we're both instantly curious about what they could have talked about. "And I know I should've asked first, but he agreed to interview Charlie for a job at GLS."

Kai's brows shoot up, the surprise clear on his face.

"Why would I interview at GLS?" I ask, confused at how this came about. I thought Maverick's biggest concern with me was being too close to the guys and the work they do for the family business.

"Well, apparently he's been keeping tabs on the leads we've been following for the case recently and so he knew that you've still been helping us with the software, so originally he wanted to scold me for that," He rolls his eyes, clearly over the many lectures they told me Maverick has delivered about me. "So, my suggestion was to hire you to work with us. That way you can help out and do something you enjoy while also keeping him off our back. It seemed like a good idea at the time."

"Holy shit, that's brilliant!" Kai's excitement is evident as he looks between the two of us.

I want to be excited to actually have a job opportunity, like Eli said it would be something that I would enjoy. And it would take the stress off of me to find something to do after graduation, but why the sudden change in Maverick?

"Are you sure that's a good idea?" I ask them.

"It's a fantastic idea." Kai says.

"You don't have to if you don't want to do it." Eli reassures me, "It was just a spur of the moment idea that I threw out there. But the more I think about it, I think it'd be a good thing. You like the work you've been doing for us, right?" he asks, "Now you can get paid to do it. And it's steady work so you would have something to do for as long as you like after we graduate."

I mull it over for a few moments, considering what it would be like to work with them. I've already been helping them for weeks now, and I have had fun. Having something lined up for work would mean that I wouldn't have to go back to living with my parents once school is over, eliminating a worry that's been sitting in the back of my mind since I started at Oceancoast.

"It's not a horrible idea..." I start, "But what made Maverick change his mind? I was pretty sure he hated me. He's really on board for this?"

"He doesn't hate you." Kai is quick to assure me, but it lacks conviction because we all know that while he may not hate me, he definitely isn't fond of me, from the moment he locked me in that room.

Eli thinks about for a minute, "I think he just agrees with me that having you help us is a lot easier than fighting with Kai and I anytime he finds out we're going behind his back. Honestly, it's a win for all of us as long as it's something you want to do."

"I'm not against it," I admit, "What do I need to do then? First, I need to apologize to Maverick for how I acted in the car last night." I remember my little stunt with the music, and if I'm going to work for him then I need to start off on the right foot.

They both laugh at the reminder of the car ride home, "Trust me, you don't have to apologize Maverick deserves a lot worse than some melodramatic songs aimed his way." Eli assures me as Kai nods his agreement, "But I told him we'd come by GLS this afternoon so he could interview you, officially."

Nerves fill me at the mention of an interview, thinking of what kinds of questions Maverick will ask me and what I could show for my work experience. I know I have a folder on my laptop of references from freelance jobs I've done over the past year. Is that enough? Can I take my laptop to a job interview? What do I even wear for an interview?

Too many questions flow through my mind, I've never sat down for a formal interview before always having worked jobs that were posted on freelance sites.

Kai interrupts my mental breakdown, "This is awesome Lottie! You're going to crush it."

Eli on the other hand seems to notice that I'm freaking out in my own head, "We have time. Why don't you guys queue up your game to kill some time. Then we can help you pick out something to wear before we have to head over?"

I'm thankful for the distraction, this is what they're both good at. Kai has an easy going, carefree attitude that makes everything feel lighter while Eli is his calmer counterpart and seems to know what to suggest to bring me back into the moment. They're the perfect balance when they're together, keeping me from getting lost in my mind.

We spent a couple of hours getting lost in Dragonlight, taking turns playing multiple rounds before they help me pick out something to wear. We settle on a simple pair of jeans with a blue and white striped button-up blouse, comfortable for me but nicer than my usual leggings and t-shirt combo.

Piling into Kai's truck for the drive to GLS the nerves slam into me full force once we're on the way. Kai offers to let me play some music, but I get lost in my thoughts.

Both of them try to pull me into conversation with no success as I silently worry the whole way there. By the time we pull into the parking lot I'm ready to have a full breakdown at the thought of having to see Maverick.

Before I realize it we're standing in the lobby, a girl that wasn't here last time stands behind the front desk batting her eyelashes at Kai and Eli.

"Hey guys, I didn't know you were coming in today." She greets them as she twirls her hair between her fingers. She's very pretty, her blonde hair sitting in perfect curls with makeup looking fresh and ready for a runway show.

Her cleavage threatens to spill out of her baby blue top as she leans over the counter to eye up the guys.

Kai barely looks her way as he greets her, "Hi Sasha. We're just here to bring Lottie to meet with Maverick."

Disgust fills her features as she takes me in from head to toe, quickly turning back to talk to Kai.

"He doesn't have a meeting scheduled and he told me he's very busy today, so your little *friend* will have to come back another day I'm afraid."

Eli, who was already looking annoyed, is grinding his teeth to my right as he narrows his eyes at her.

"That's not really your place to tell us our brother's schedule seeing as we weren't asking. And I would check your attitude with our friend here." His tone is venomous, leaving no room for argument. I don't ever see Eli upset… it's pretty hot. I feel myself flush from the excitement that sparks through me at hearing him.

"Eli, I'm just doing my job," she pouts. "Maverick doesn't have time to be bothered with some little girl. He's very busy."

Kai's head quickly snaps around to glare at her now.

"Watch your mouth, Sasha." he glares daggers at her.

Shit. Both of them are upset and at my defense now. I think I may melt into a puddle on the floor if they keep this up.

"I don't know what you think your job here is, but I can tell you it's not being a bitch towards someone that we brought here." He points out.

She gasps, holding a hand to her chest in outrage and looking like she may cry at any moment. Before she can say anything, else Cooper comes out from the hallway leading towards the back.

"Hey Charlotte," he smiles brightly at me before looking between Sasha and the guys, confusion flashing on his face. "What's going on?"

Sasha quickly turns to him, fake tears brimming her eyes as she sniffles, "I was just doing my job and telling Kai and Eli that Maverick doesn't have any time to meet with their friend today and then Kai got angry and called me a bitch."

Cooper's eyes widen as he looks to the guys for an explanation. Kai just rolls his eyes while Eli runs a hand down his face looking annoyed at the situation.

"Yeah, only *after* she was rude to Lottie and tried to dismiss her while we were trying to explain that she has an interview scheduled with him." Kai explains to him. "Sasha seems to think his schedule is too busy for Lottie."

"Maverick told me that he doesn't have time for any meetings today!" Sasha exclaims, "I'm just doing what I was told, Coop."

Ew. Hearing her use a nickname for Cooper just feels… gross. Maybe it's her fake tears, or the way she's trying to push her cleavage towards him while defending herself. It could be the idea of confrontation making me feel sick, though it's probably just her blatant lying about her actions that really grosses me out. Either way I'm not sure I like Sasha.

Cooper tries to shift so that Sasha can't brush up against him,

"Okay, I'm sure it's just a misunderstanding. Charlotte, why don't you go back. Maverick is in his office." He motions for the hallway while Sasha shoots a look my way, if looks could kill then I'd be six feet under. I'm thankful for him diffusing the situation but nerves still fill me at the mention of going to see Maverick.

Eli gently brushes my shoulder, waiting for my attention before passing me my bag with my laptop. Giving me a reassuring smile, he motions for me to go ahead so I make my way slowly down the hallway.

Making my way through the hall I quickly come to the door of the room that I was locked in weeks ago, my breath catching at the memory. I try not to let my mind wander to the panic I felt in that moment, quickly turning my back to that room and focusing on the door with Maverik's name on it.

Taking a moment, I push down the nerves rushing through me. I take a deep breath and straighten my spine before I knock on the door.

Maverick's gruff voice calls out from the other side.

"Come in."

11

~Maverick~

"Come in." I call out after the timid knock sounds through my office. The door pushes open slightly as Charlotte slips inside, closing it quietly behind her.

I watch from behind my desk as she stands just in front of the door, not coming any further into the space.

Raising a brow, I look from her to one of the chairs in front of my desk.

"Have a seat." I offer, she stands for a moment pulling at her fingers before shuffling over to the chair closest to the door and sitting, clutching her bag in her lap.

She looks just as timid as she was the first time she was here, though she seems to have tried to dress up from the last time. Rather than swimming in a hoodie, she wears jeans and a button-up blouse, showing more of her petite frame.

She doesn't seem to be suffering from a hangover which is a bit of a surprise after how drunk she was when we drove her home last night.

We sit in silence as I observe her. She looks at everything in the room but me, giving me plenty of time to catalog every detail about her. Like how the tiny gold ring in her septum matches the rose gold color of her glasses. Or how her waist length dark hair has some light streaks sprinkled throughout, looking to be lightened from the sun. And then there's the finer details, like how her nails are bitten down to the quick and her fingers are red from how much she seems to twist and pull at them.

She's a ball of nerves sitting before, looking ready to bolt at any second. She's cute, but I'm not sure what it is about her that has Kai and Eli falling all over themselves for her.

I don't know anything about her, and I'm trying to go into this with an open mind. Remembering my conversation with Eli earlier this morning, it still stings knowing how he feels I haven't been a brother to him. That's why I'm going through with this interview, and I'm doing my best not to be judgmental right from the start. It's been difficult since our parents died. I'm the oldest, and I feel I have a responsibility to protect everyone. The unknown that comes with Charlotte is what makes me so hesitant to allow her to get close to my brothers. I don't know where she came from or what her intentions are. She could break my brother's heart, hurt them, do something to drag them into trouble with her, I just don't know. To me, that lack of knowing – lack of control is daunting.

She's clearly not going to speak first, so I decide to get the interview started so we don't have to sit in silence any longer.

"So, I assume that Eli filled you in about how we discussed the possibility of you coming to work for GLS?" I ask to confirm that she knows why she's here. Her eyes meet mine for a brief moment before she gives me a small nod. "This will benefit me in that I don't have to worry about you knowing sensitive information regarding our cases or clients behind my back." I give her a pointed look, "But, Eli also had great things to say about your abilities and said you would be an asset to have here with us."

Leaning back, I give her a chance to respond, but she just shifts nervously in the chair.

"Eli mentioned that you have some work experience?" I ask.

She quickly nods her head, "Y-yes. I've done some freelance jobs when I can find them. Mostly bookkeeping and basic background checks." She fidgets with her glasses before continuing, "But I've also done a few jobs writing code for different businesses for security reasons or just basic functions like websites."

I wasn't expecting much in the way of any work experience considering she's still in college, so I'm not too worried about her resume. I'm trusting Eli's judgement considering he's trusted her to work with them for the last couple of weeks, but I still need to see if her skills would be useful to us in the long run.

"I understand that you helped Eli with the program to hack into the security footage from our friend's bar and facial recognition?" She nods, "Did you happen to bring your laptop with you?" Again, she nods so I tell her to get it out and pull up the program.

Once she has the laptop set up on the desk she looks to me expectantly.

"I want you to use the program that you sent Eli, see if you access the security cameras for Myth from last night." If she was able to pull the footage from the bar where Ivy went missing back to two years ago then she should have no issue pulling the feeds from the club last night. If she's able to do it then she's going to figure out who slashed Eli's tires for us.

I already spoke to Tyler, my friend and the owner of Myth, to discuss the fact that someone was able to get to Eli's car while they were there. I also forewarned him that I'd be trying to access the feeds to check it out. Eli and I set up the security system for them, and theoretically Charlotte shouldn't have any way to gain access to them without our help. How far she's able to get will definitely shed light on how good her skills are.

She taps away at the keys, her brow furrowing in concentration as she works, and I wait patiently for her to admit that she can't get into the feeds. I scroll through my phone for a few minutes before responding to emails while she continues to work.

About twenty minutes in, the clacking of the keys stops. Looking up I see her sitting back, chewing on her bottom lip and staring thoughtfully at the screen.

I'm about to give her a simpler task when she speaks.

"It was one of the valet members." She says quietly, still studying the screen intently. "I'm still waiting for the software to pull a name, but his picture isn't matching any of the ones that are in the staff file for the club."

What. The. Fuck.

Not only should she not have been able to even access the feeds, but it was a valet that slashed Eli's tires?

Standing up I round the desk to look at the screen myself. Sure enough she has the security footage from the back parking lot of Myth with a time stamp showing last night, Eli's car right in the frame and a shadowed figure wearing a valet coat standing at the front end of the car.

"How?" I ask, mostly to myself.

"The feeds were hard to get into, but there was one small opening that I was able to find. Then, from there I went ahead and pulled all the footage that's stored into this window here," she pulls up another window with codes filling the screen. "It's still pulling, but from what I can tell it looks like there's at least a year of footage that's stored. Now I'm trying to run the facial recognition software on the valet, but it's hard because the image is so dark. Over here I'm pulling frame by frame to see if I can get a clear shot of his face, then I'll move that over here to see if I can lighten it any to get a better match." She explains all of this while clicking through different windows, pointing to different features as she goes. "Over here I have the files that are stored for the club's employees, all of their applications and profiles for people who work there now, and then there's people who have applied, it looks like they are keeping those on hand in case they need them. You can see that none of the valet's profiles match the guy in the frame there."

Everything she's saying makes sense, but I'm absolutely dumbfounded as to how she got this far. The software we put in place had one small, encrypted access point that no one else should have ever been able to find, and Charlotte just found it in less than twenty minutes.

Sitting in the chair to her left, I watch as she keeps clicking through screens, running more searches.

"Did you check the entire staff's profiles to see if maybe they had someone from a different section filling in for valet for the night?" I check.

She doesn't look my way, but she makes a face like I'm an idiot for even asking.

"Yes. He's not anywhere in the system as being employed there." she tells me distractedly while moving to a different window. She has a new image of the guy now and is adjusting levels to adjust the brightness and contrast until we can finally see his face. The kid looks no older than seventeen but is clearly wearing a valet jacket.

I lean in closer to get a better look, Charlotte stiffening next to me, still typing. I pull back some so I'm not in her space and she seems to relax slightly.

Another window populates on the screen, and she reads it over.

"Timothy Davis." she reads out loud, "Looks like he's a senior over at Bartram High School. Eighteen years old. No criminal record, juvenile or adult, not even a speeding ticket. It looks like he plays football for the school, has a scholarship waiting to attend the University of Florida and he drives a black Mustang." She reads it off as if she's reading the Sunday paper, no infliction to her voice and no interest in what she's saying while I sit back in my chair, at a total loss for words.

Questions fly through my head, wondering where Charlotte was able to learn how to do any of this. I'm almost certain that Oceancoast isn't teaching hacking and surveillance in their general curriculum.

"Was Timothy the valet that took the car from Eli when you got to the club last night?" I ask, needing to know where this kid came from before I can start to look into why he did it.

"No, it was an older guy when we got there." She barely pays me any attention as she answers, still clicking away at the screen. "Short, dark hair, looked terrified of Eli." She pulls up another image from when they arrived at

Myth, "Him." She shows turns the screen towards me and I see Steve, one of Tyler's longest employed staff members.

I need to call Tyler, see if he knows anything about this kid and why he was there. Charlotte seems content to keep working away at what she's doing so I decide to leave her here while I try to work through this.

"See if you can run Timothy's face in the feeds, let me know if he's been there any other night." I tell her, making my way to the door.

"Obviously." she whispers under her breath just as I get to the door. Freezing, I turn to look back at her, but she isn't looking my way, still clicking away at the laptop.

"What was that?" I ask, daring her to say it again.

"I said o-o-okay." she sputters nervously, her cheeks flushing a dark shade of pink at being caught. Deciding to leave it alone I head down the hall to Cooper's office, finding him and the twins sitting around talking.

Kai instantly perks up at seeing me, "Hey how'd Lottie do? Did you give her the job?"

"Were you nice to her?" Eli asks, doubt lacing his words, causing me to roll my eyes at his theatrics.

"I was pleasant." I tell him shortly, turning to address Cooper, "I need you to call Tyler and tell him we need him down here now. I need him to look at something we found from Myth last night."

145

Cooper wastes no time getting on the phone to dial Tyler while Kai impatiently badgers me with more questions.

"You had Lottie break into Myth's feeds? Did she find what you wanted? Did you give her a job? Don't leave us hanging bro, tell us what happened!"

"Kai." Cooper chides him, shooting him a look like an errant toddler before going back to his phone call.

He's like a damn puppy, all excited and has too much energy for his own good. Eli just sits beside him, silently waiting for what I have to say, looking deep in thought.

"Yes, I had her hack into Myth's feeds," I tell them once Cooper is off the phone, looking to Eli to gauge his reaction. "She was able to get through in about twenty minutes. And she found out who slashed your tires."

Surprise shines in Eli's eyes when he hears how quickly Charlotte was able to do it. He, like myself, knows the ins and outs of that security system so he knows that it should've been damn near impossible to do.

"Damn, didn't you two build that system up like Fort Knox?" Cooper asks, surprise and pride ringing through his words.

Eli grins, "We did." Looking at me he adds, "Told you she was good."

"Soooo, she got the job?" Kai asks again, looking between all of us impatiently.

"Yes, she got the job."

"Yes!" he jumps out of his seat, fist pumping the air.

"But-" I quickly try to bring him down from his ridiculous victory dance, "There are going to be rules in place. Just because you're working together doesn't mean you two can spend all your time hanging out and cutting the shit with her. You are still going to have your own assignments, as will she and things you have to get done. This isn't a free for all to just have fun with your friend." I level them both with a hard stare, trying not to go full dad mode on them as Eli just called me on this morning, but trying to remain serious so they know that I mean business.

Eli nods his agreement and we both look at Kai, waiting for the same from him.

"Bro, no worries. This is going to be awesome! We told you she was great." beaming with pride over being right for once and rather than crush his spirits I decide to just let him enjoy the moment for now. I will crack down on him later if he tries to ignore my rules.

Kai starts to head for the door, but I reach out to stop him, "Where do you think you're going?" I raise a brow at him.

"To go see Lottie, you're done with the interview, right?"

Pushing him back towards the chair I roll my eyes, "No I'm not done. I'm going to have her check a couple more things out for me and then I still have to go over the job offer with her and get her set up in an office. You two go find something to do, I don't need you hovering over her while we do this." I say, looking between the two of them.

"Like what?" Kai looks exasperated at the thought of not going to see Charlotte.

"You two can go cover the front desk and work on some filing since I had to send Sasha home." Cooper raises a brow at the two of them, implication heavy in his words.

Eli rolls his eyes, and Kai just looks annoyed at the suggestion while I try to silently ask Cooper what they did that meant he had to send our receptionist home but he just gives me a subtle shake of his head.

Eli caves first, sighing as he drags himself out of his chair, "Fine. Let us know when Charlie is done for the day." He tells me as he grabs Kai's shoulder to drag him out of the room after him.

Cooper sits back, looking at me and waiting for me to fill him in on the day's events and probably wondering why we needed to call Tyler down here.

"So, twenty minutes to crack your little security program huh?" he's fighting to hold back a grin, seeming to find this whole scenario amusing.

Narrowing my eyes, I fire right back at him,
"That *little* security program is the same one that we implement with every business we sign contracts with. There's no way that she should have been able to hack into it that easily." I rack my brain for how she could have done it with that much ease, the only possibility that I can come up with is she may have seen Eli working on it before. I don't want to doubt Eli like that though, he surely wouldn't have coached her for that prior to coming

148

here. Hell, he didn't even know that I was going to ask her to look into Myth so that just doesn't add up.

Cooper shrugs, not seeming to be concerned. "Maybe the twins were right and she's just good. You already told them you were offering her the job, just give her some more work to do and see how far her skills stretch."

"You seem very relaxed about this whole ordeal." I note.

He holds both his hands out in a 'what can you do' manner. "Why shouldn't I be relaxed? The way I see it we all benefit from this. I don't have to listen to you and the twins argue about Charlotte, she has a safe space to hack and code without ending up arrested for digging into the wrong things with no cause, and we all get some help that can benefit us in our work. What's there to stress about?"

"I just don't understand it. Where could she have learned to do all this?" I shake my head.

"Here's a thought," he starts, and I already know I'm not going to like where he's going with this. "Talk to her." he says simply.

I just stare at him, waiting for any other explanation he can offer that doesn't involve talking it out, but he doesn't offer anything.

"She's literally in your office right now. Just go ask her. You have to get her information to hire her here anyway, just ask some general background questions while you're at it to satisfy that little nagging voice in your head that we both know won't stop until you have it figured out."

149

He rolls his eyes before turning his attention back to his computer, ready to move on from the conversation.

I'd rather dig into this myself, not knowing Charlotte means I don't trust her. Employee or not, she could easily lie to me if I outright ask her. Letting out a breath I head back for my office, knowing that I will have to ask her either way, so I can catch her in a lie later if she's trying to feed me any bullshit now.

Making it back to my office Charlotte is still working on the laptop, barely sparing me a glance as I settle back behind my desk. Once I'm seated, she clicks a few buttons before turning the screen my way.

"Timothy has been outside of Myth every Friday night for the last month. Never going in the club, always standing across the street in front of the convenience store. He usually sits there for about three hours before leaving, but last night he was out of frame for about a half hour after Eli and I got to the club. It was another hour or so before I can see him in the car lot with a valet jacket on. He came in through a hole in the fence in the corner of the lot." She gives me a play by play as I watch the videos play on the screen.

Studying the feeds I think it over for a moment before asking her, "So why do you think he snuck in the lot to slash Eli's tires?"

She considers it while looking out the window, twisting her damn fingers again. It shouldn't annoy me, it's harmless. But seeing her take all her energy out on herself just seems to grate on my nerves.

"I don't know, maybe he's just a stupid teenager pulling a prank?" she guesses, but her brows furrow so I wait. "It just doesn't make sense. It seems like he's been waiting for Eli specifically, but I don't know why. They aren't close enough in age for him and Eli to have crossed paths that would cause him to seek him out. So maybe someone else put him up to it?"

I have to smother my reaction. I'm a bit shocked at her assessment, considering that's where my mind would go given the information she's been able to pull up.

"Who do you think would put him up to it? And why him? He's just a high school kid." I ask, wanting to hear more of her thought process.

She just shrugs. "I have no clue; I don't know who you guys have dealt with in the past. But high school kids are eager to make a quick buck so he'd be easy enough to convince, and he's obviously much more under the radar than someone that Eli may have dealt with before."

She's not wrong. And her logical assumption makes irrational irritation spark inside me, here I am looking for any indication that she wouldn't be good for this job and yet she offers me reasonable explanations for everything I throw at her. It's infuriating and impressive all at once.

"So, what would your next move be from here, given what you've found?"

She mulls it over, sitting back in the chair and actually looking relaxed for the first time since stepping into the office.

"I'd probably try to dig through traffic cams to see if I could find out if he went to someone before or after he slashed the tires, maybe go back further to see if I could find him meeting with someone prior to last night to try and figure out who put him up to it."

"You can do that?" I can't keep my brows from quirking as surprise fills me again at her answer. I tried giving Eli a shot to hack into traffic cams before to track movement for a kidnapping case we worked on last year, even he wasn't able to get more than a single shot of a license plate.

It's not like we don't have any experienced employees on our payroll that are able to do this stuff. But they all work in different locations. Having someone in house that we could turn to for quick answers certainly would be beneficial.

Charlotte rolls her head back and forth, considering it. "It would definitely take some time to try and work it out, but I don't see why not. It's the same idea as logging into the feeds for the bar, as long as I can find an access point, I should be able to."

If she could pull that off, then I'll be utterly speechless. But for now, I need to get her set up in an office and get her employment sorted, which also means getting some information out of her. Unlike the last time I spoke to her, this time she can't deny my questions.

I can't contain myself any longer, the more she says the more confused I am.

"Where in the hell did you learn all of this?"

She's startled, her wide eyes locking on me before she drops them to the floor, never maintaining eye contact. She almost looks embarrassed as she thinks about her answer.

"I-I didn't have a lot of friends growing up..." she hesitates, and I wait. Vulnerability rings through her words and I'm interested to know where she's going with this.

"It got lonely, so I started learning about computers. Once you start, it's addictive and so I just kept trying to learn everything I could about them." Her nerves ease the more she talks, morphing into fascination. "Once I learned everything I could find in books and online I moved onto more... creative platforms. I've talked to a lot of people over the last couple years who have taught me a lot." She shrugs.

I'm almost positive that 'creative platforms' translates to the dark web, but I really don't want to get into that right now. She's at least given me some information that I can catalog for later if I need it.

"Right, well consider that your first project. I'll show you to an office where you can set up, that will be your space so do with it what you want. But first we have to fill out some forms for your employment." I tell her, pulling up GLS's employee portal that we use to store all the employee profiles and payroll information on my computer.

As I wait for it to load, I glance up to see her wide-eyed expression staring back at me.

"I got the job?" she asks, surprise lighting up her face, and she's clearly trying to tone down the smile she has forming.

I snort at her shock, her question reminding me of Kai earlier in Cooper's office. "Yes, you got the job. That is if you would still like one?"

She nods her head enthusiastically, "Thank you." She blurts out, obviously trying to compose herself and remembering her manners.

I only offer a simple grunt in response as I pull up a new profile.

"Full name?" I ask her, typing her responses as she gives them.

"Charlotte Lynn Woods."

"Age and date of birth?"

"22. May 6th, 2001"

I ask a few more basic questions, including her address, parents' names for emergency contacts, which she seemed reluctant to give so I make a mental note to remember that, and contact information, filling it all in fairly quickly. It goes smoothly until we reach one question in particular.

"Any medical conditions that we should know about or medications that could affect your job performance?" as I ask, I'm met with silence. Looking up Charlotte now seems tense, and she's pulling at her fingers more violently than she was before.

"Charlotte?" I raise my voice, trying to draw her attention away from whatever's going on in her head. She startles at my voice but doesn't immediately respond. "We just have to have it on file for legal reasons with the type of situations we can end up in, we just need to be aware. It's not going to affect your job if there is something to note." I try a gentler approach, not wanting to cause her any worry over her answer to the question. Clearly there is something, but I'm not a complete dick. I wouldn't hold it over her head.

She mumbles something, her eyes downcast and focused on the carpet under her feet but it's so low that I can't make out what she said.

"Say again?" I wait while she closes her eyes and takes a deep breath before repeating herself, louder this time.

"I have Asperger's. I take medication to help manage my behaviors and to help my anxiety."

Her face fills with shame as she tells me, before she catches herself and wipes her face of any emotion, staring at the floor and waiting for me to say something. I meant

155

what I said, this won't affect her job except in the sense that knowing this I probably won't be likely to send her to interrogate someone or have her on scene for any tense situations. But it's clear to me that this is a bigger issue to Charlotte than it is for any of us, and I respect her honesty.

Realization washes over me, thinking back to locking her in the room for how she acted cagey last time she was here. I'm officially an asshole. I did send her into a panic attack for acting the way I did towards her, not that I would've known that upon meeting her but still, I'm a dick.

Part of me wonders why it's such a big deal to her, but deep down I know that there are people who are bigger assholes than me, and she's probably been made to feel like less just because she's a little different. Given how her interview went today, it's clear that it doesn't affect her ability to do the job that we need her to do. So, I'm going to stick with the knowledge that she's got skills that we can use, fuck the rest of it.

The twin's protectiveness over her makes a lot more sense now too. They've both always been good, caring kids, but knowing this sheds more light on their anger towards me after that first meeting with her.

"Okay, if you want to follow me then I will show you to the office that you can take over. You can work off your laptop, or if you want there are some monitors laying around that you can take to set up in there." I tell her, gesturing for her to follow me.

She looks surprised that I didn't comment on her telling me that she has Asperger's, but I give her nothing in return, flashing my own emotionless mask. She throws her laptop into her bag and follows me down to the end of the hall while I push open the door for our spare office.

It's pretty bare inside, having just a desk and two chairs. The walls are completely empty, one wall being filled mostly with a large window that looks out to the St. John's river. Aside from the desk and the filing cabinet the room is a blank slate.

Charlotte slowly steps around the room, looking at it wide-eyed and staring at the window for a long time as she drops her bag onto the desk.

"Like I said, it's yours to do with what you want. I'll leave a folder on your desk with your compensation information for you to look over on Monday, you can come here after school, and we'll iron out your schedule then and get you set up with direct deposit and all of those details." I tell her from the doorway, she abandons the view to nod, a small smile pulling at her lips. I'm about to leave when I remember that to be fair, I should give her the rules, same as I did with the twins.

Making sure her attention is still on me I tell her, "Charlotte, I know your friends with the twins but they're not your boss. You take directions from me, or from Cooper if I'm not available. This is a job, and we all have to take it seriously. As you already know, I take our client confidentiality seriously, before you head out today I need you to stop by to see Cooper. Sign the forms saying that you understand that you can't discuss any of our cases or clients with anyone outside of GLS, and that you can't use any of the information you access for your own personal reasons." My voice is firm, leaving no room for discussion on the rules and she offers no objection. Having said my piece, I leave her to get acquainted with her new office, knowing the twins will be coming back to sit with her while she gets the paperwork signed before going to enjoy the rest of the weekend.

 Sitting back at my desk I find that Charlotte has already sent me an encrypted email with the screenshots of the kid that slashed Eli's tires. Perfect, with everything going on I'd forgotten that Tyler should be here anytime to discuss the mishap and having the images will help us with informing security at the club, so it doesn't happen again.

As much as I wish I could find a reason to think that hiring Charlotte is a bad idea, nothing this afternoon has given that indication. I'm still going to look more into Charlotte, but for the time being I'll just have to benefit from her skillset.

Hopefully it doesn't come back to bite me in the ass.

12

~Charlotte~

After Maverick hired me, Kai and Eli spent the rest of the weekend doing things to 'celebrate' with me. From playing Dragonlight with a pizza feast, to taking me out for the biggest ice cream sundaes I've ever seen.

They were both so excited for me, and as much as I feel awkward about them making such a big fuss for me getting the job, it did make me feel all warm and fuzzy inside.

They finally had both gone home last night after we finished all of their celebratory ideas, to get some rest before we all had class today. While I'd had a great time with them, I also loved the time I got to myself once they'd left.

Only having one class today, I'm eager to get over to GLS for my first official day. Kai had told me to hang around until they were done with their classes for the day so that we could all ride over together, but the nerves and excitement won't let me just sit around and wait.

I rush back to my dorm once my class lets out to quickly change before starting the walk to the office. I figure the fresh air should give me a chance to reel in all of my anxious energy. Plus, I enjoy being active. Before I officially met all the guys, I had been religious about getting in a run every day, mostly to quiet the noise in my head, but also because it just felt good, and free. So, the walk to GLS is quite peaceful for me.

Even with Thanksgiving quickly approaching, the Florida heat hasn't let up much, and the humidity is still awful so I'd opted for a loose-fitting band T-shirt with my leggings and vans, knowing that one of my hoodies would be likely to give me heat stroke on the long walk.

Just around the corner from the office, I pick up my pace, eager to get settled in and work. I'm not paying much attention to my surroundings, focusing more on what I can do to get a head start on the search for Timothy that Maverick already assigned me on Saturday. I hear footsteps a second before I feel a wall of muscle crash into me, the force knocking me flat on my ass right there on the sidewalk, sending my glasses flying off my face in the process.

My head is spinning from the impact, and I can't see more than a foot in front of me without the assistance of my glasses.

"Charlotte?" The deep voice rumbles above me, but I can't look up to see who it is. It wouldn't matter anyway since I can't see their face. I'm doing my best Velma from Scooby-Doo impression as I scour the ground, reaching out to try and make contact with my glasses.

The voice above me mutters a curse just before a hand appears inches from my face, my glasses thankfully in their grasp. I slide them on before tilting my head back to see who I collided with. I'm greeted with none other than Maverick's deep scowl staring back.

He's wearing nothing but a loose pair of black basketball shorts, his chest on display for the world, glistening with sweat. He has a black ball cap turned backward, covering his buzz-cut hair, and a pair of wireless headphones hanging around his neck. Taking him in, my eyes zero in on his mid-section, seemingly free of ink; unlike the rest of his upper body.

Holy abs.

I didn't think people actually had muscles like this in real life. But the proof is staring me dead in the face in the form of a perfectly sculpted 6-pack. Little beads of sweat roll down into the grooves of his defined muscle, occupying all of my attention.

A demanding urge snakes through me, begging me to *lick his abs*, but I shake it away because even dazed and confused I can comprehend enough to know that's insane.

Maverick huffs before reaching down, sliding his arms under mine to lift me to my feet. I can feel the hardness of the muscles in his arms as he does, and I know for a fact that his muscles are not just for show.

"Hi." I greet him once I'm steady on my feet, currently at a loss for any other words.

Unsurprisingly, he doesn't look happy to see me, his scowl staying firmly in place as he narrows his eyes.

"Hi?" he questions, stupefied. "What the hell are you doing out here?"

Looking around at the 'here' I take in the empty street leading up to GLS, confused at his question.

"Coming to work?" I say as though it should be obvious.

His eyebrows shoot up as he shifts to rest his hands on his hips, his face showing a mixture of annoyance and confusion.

"I thought you had class. Kai said that you'd be riding with them later this afternoon." My own annoyance sparks briefly at the fact that he seems incapable of thinking that I can find my own way to work without the help of his brothers. I quickly dismiss it when I remember that I might not have told Kai that I'd be finding my own way here rather than waiting on him.

I try to ignore the guilt that I feel about not telling him by reminding myself that I'm an adult and I can make my own decisions. If I want to walk to work, then I can. I just hope he isn't mad at me.

"Change of plans." I offer with a small shrug of my shoulders, making a mental note to text Kai and tell him once I get to my office. "I got out earlier than him today, so I decided to just head over and get started early." I'm proud of how sure my voice sounds as I speak, not letting any of my true emotions show.

Maverick, however, looks as though he can see right through me, doubt written all over his face.

Crossing his arms, he continues to stare me down, "And Kai was fully on board with you walking thirty minutes from the school by yourself?"

"Yes." I nod once, "I am an adult. I can walk by myself; I have been for over twenty years now." I remind him.

His eyes close and he pinches the bridge of his nose. I wonder if he has a headache, his forehead is scrunching up like mine does when I start to get a migraine. But he steps to the side and gestures for me to continue walking.

"Just go and get to work. We'll talk later." He dismisses me quickly, not allowing me to ask what we need to talk about before he takes off down the sidewalk.

My excitement builds again as I finally reach the front door. Making my way into the lobby I deflate a bit when I'm faced with Sasha behind the front desk, looking just as bitchy as she did last week.

Dropping my gaze to the floor I head towards the hallway that leads to my office, hoping to avoid any interaction, her high-pitched voice calls out before I make it.

"Where do you think you're going?" she demands just before I get to the hallway.

Looking up I find her standing from her seat, leaning halfway across the desk, shooting daggers at me with her eyes. The same disgust she looked at me with last time evident in her eyes now as she waits for an answer.

"M-my o-o-office." I curse my stutter for coming out at the most inopportune times.

"Y-y-your office?" she mocks me with a nasty sneer, "You don't work here, you freak. Get the fuck out of here before I call someone to throw you out."

I'm rooted to the spot, unable to move. I hate confrontation, absolutely loathe it. I don't understand her anger or malice towards me, but I do understand that it makes my skin crawl with discomfort.

"I d-do w-work here. Maverick h-hired me." I try to explain as I violently pull at my fingers, urging myself to not avoid her vicious stare.

She snorts, "Yeah, nice try. Like Maverick would hire an idiot like you to work here." Amusement rings through her words as her insult cuts through me. "Like I said. Get. The. Fuck. Out." Each word is emphasized as she steps around the desk, coming to stand inches away from me, looking down at me as her heels give her a good 5 inches to tower over me.

Not sure what to do, I stay stuck in place. Before she can say anything else Cooper comes from the back hallway like a guardian angel sent to watch over me.

"What's going on out here?" he asks, looking between the two of us, "Hey, Charlotte. You're early."

At Cooper's approach, Sasha takes a step back. Plastering a fake and what I'm sure she considers flirtatious smile on her face she bats her eyelashes at him.

"I was just showing her out." She pouts at Cooper, "Poor thing must be confused. She thinks she works here." She adds in a mock whisper that I'm clearly able to hear.

I grit my teeth at her malice attitude. He just shoots her a look as if she's grown a second head before offering me a friendly smile,

"Charlotte, go on back. I left some paperwork on your desk, I'll be in a minute to go over it in case you have any questions."

Sasha shoots me another deadly glare as he dismisses me but quickly recovers as he turns his attention back to her.

I can hear him talking to her as I practically sprint to the safety of my office. Shutting the door behind me I drop into the chair situated behind the desk, holding my head in my hands I focus on trying to calm my erratic breathing and force her seething words from my brain.

I was so excited to get here today, to put my best foot forward and hit the ground running. But the interaction with Sasha has me rattled, flashes of memories of my parents' disappointed faces as they screamed at me to be normal assault me. I rock in my chair, gripping my hair by the roots as I mentally try to scream at the figments of my imagination to shut the fuck up, but my parents' faces just morph with Sasha's disgusted sneers, my brain throbbing in protest.

A knock on the door startles me, halting my movements. I wait for something else but am met with the silence of the room and my labored breathing.

As I wait, it sounds again, Cooper's muffled voice filtering through the door.

"Charlotte? Can I come in?"

I jump up from the chair, rushing to the door. My nerves are too shot to have him in my space right now, I want to intercept him before he comes in. I pause with my hand on the knob, taking a deep breath to steady myself before gently opening the door.

Cooper's smile greets me again, though his features are pinched, and his concern is evident on his face.

"Hey, everything okay?" He looks me over head to toe as I nod, "It took you a minute to hear me knocking."

"J-just trying to get my stuff set up." I tell him as I force a smile to my face, though it feels more like a grimace.

He eyes me for a moment, "Riiight." his eyes flick to my empty desk behind me before quickly focusing on me again. "Well, I just wanted to say I'm sorry for the misunderstanding with Sasha. I've explained that you'll be working here so you shouldn't have any other issues, and I left that paperwork for you to sign on your desk. Let me know if you have any questions, otherwise, just drop it off in my office sometime today before you leave."

I'm lost in thought, my mind still reeling from the last hour. Cooper's striking appearance and friendly smile before me aren't helping my mind get back on track.

"Charlotte?" Cooper is staring at me expectantly, telling me that I've zoned out while cataloging his features.

"Got it." I tell him, just wanting to get him out of my space before I embarrass myself further.

He stares at me skeptically but ultimately must decide to let it go as he nods and backs away from my door. "Well like I said, just come see me if you need anything."

Shutting the door quickly behind him as he walks back towards his office, I lean my head against the door, taking a minute to collect myself before finally sitting at my desk to throw myself into work. Nothing works better for getting over an episode like distracting myself.

I'm lost in my work, trying to figure out the best way to track Timothy's movements to know where he's been going when my office door flies open. I nearly fall out of my chair from the scare, reaching over to silence the music I had playing – which was admittedly just one song on repeat. Looking up I find Kai and Eli standing in my doorway staring at me, eyes narrowed and not looking happy.

"What the hell, Lottie?" Kai exclaims.

I look to Eli, confused at his brother's irritation but he just looks back, eyebrows raised.

"I thought you agreed to wait for us to drive you over after school?" Kai crosses his arms, looking both irritated and hurt that I didn't follow his plans for the day.

My gut reaction is to bow my head and apologize, but after the discussion I had with Maverick on the way here I remind myself that I'm an adult and I'm capable of getting to work without having to wait on anyone and I want to stand by that. I love spending time with them both, but I don't want to become dependent on them.

"I got out of class early and wanted to get started on my work. I never actually agreed to that, you made that plan." I tell them both simply, only able to look them each in the eyes for a fleeting moment before I settle on looking at the wall next to them.

Eli sighs, "Charlie, you shouldn't be walking from campus over here by yourself. You didn't even text us to let us know."

Crap. I had forgotten to let them know when I got here after the interaction with Sasha. Regardless, I still don't think it's as big of a deal as they're making it out to be.

"I'm sorry, I forgot." I tell them, "I'll try to remember next time."

"Lottie, there shouldn't be a next time." Kai retorts, "We can bring you to work. You shouldn't walk here on your own. Just please wait for us next time, or hell, call Cooper if you really want to get here early."

Frustration bubbles up within me. They're not listening to me, I don't want to rely on anyone to get to my job. And I don't want to inconvenience anyone to get here either.

"It's not a big deal." I tell them, trying to keep my composure as my pulse starts to throb in my head and my palms start to sweat, the stress from today starting to get under my skin.

"Lottie, it's a big deal to us. We want to make sure you're okay and walking across town to get here is just not safe." Kai starts in on a rant, Eli chiming in to add his agreement every so often, but I can't hear them as sounds start to become muddled.

Overwhelmed with all of the attention from both of them, not to mention Maverick's judgment and Cooper's concern, I just can't process it all.

My whole life I've only had to worry about myself, my parents didn't share that concern, and I was never one to have friends, so their constant companionship and all the socialization is threatening to suffocate me.

Their muffled voices continue to swirl around me as I begin to struggle to take in a full breath, everything hitting me full force. I close my eyes to try and block them out, grasping at my roots, trying to center myself with the pain when that seems to be ineffective.

I focus on counting in my head, rocking with the counts to try and settle the storm of emotions bombarding my brain. Too many thoughts are bouncing around in my head today. *It's too loud.* I just need it to stop. I need them to stop. I need to be alone. I need to scream. I need to cry. I just need *something* to break me out of this spiral.

"Hey!" The booming voice breaks through the noise, part of my brain can hear it while the rest is still stuck in the spiraling vortex of noise. It's dizzying, I try to ignore the voice and go back to fighting the rest of it but now that my brain has registered it I can't ignore it.

"What the hell are you two doing? You can't just barge in here to try and throw your weight around at Charlotte." The voice sounds pissed, even if their volume has softened significantly. "I get she's your friend, but when you're in this office you all are co-workers. That means you leave your shit at the door, and you don't interrupt work to solve your grievances."

If there's any response to the voice, I can't hear it. Still fighting in my own head, I try to focus back on counting, hoping that it can block everything else out.

"I don't care. Go find Maverick and see what he needs help with. I better not catch you two in here again uninvited." The voice filters back in before disappearing again.

Without the voice I can focus on the numbers in my head and timing my rocks to match the pace of my counting.

I feel a hand gently touching my shoulder and I jerk away from the foreign touch, not expecting it. More muffled sounds filter around me but I just push them away, not having the energy to try and decipher them right now.

Usually, I can pull myself out of an episode by now, but I can't seem to shut down my brain, I'm stuck spinning.

I feel warmth wrap around me, pressure closing in against my back and pinning my arms to my side.

Panic instantly seizes me; I fight and struggle to break through whatever is holding me. The more I fight, the tighter the hold on me is. I feel the sweat coating my forehead and I'm gasping for breath before I hear Cooper's voice, calm and low behind me.

"Charlotte, you're okay. Just try to breathe for me. Everything's okay, I got you. Just breathe."

Knowing it's Cooper, I feel slightly more relaxed but still eager to break the contact with him. I struggle for a moment while he only tightens his hold, repeating his mantra.

I take a moment to pull in a deep breath, trying to ignore his hold.

"Good job. Now, another: just focus on taking deep breaths. Try to hold them in for 3 seconds and let them out for 3 seconds," he encourages.

I focus on his voice and his instructions. Taking a breath in and out while he counts. I'm not sure how long we do this before I can finally breathe easily again. I even find myself relaxing in his hold, not panicking at the contact any longer, almost enjoying the warmth coming from him.

Feeling more clear-headed I finally take stock of my surroundings. I no longer sit in my chair; I'm now on the floor with Cooper behind me. His chest is pressed to my back with his arms wrapped around mine, pinning my arms to my side and his legs are over mine.

The relaxed feeling is quickly replaced with mortification realizing that I'm sitting in Cooper's arms. And he just watched me have a breakdown. Not only that, Kai and Eli were in here, so they watched that too until Cooper kicked them out.

Great. Now they all have another firsthand account of how crazy I am.

I stiffen, trying to pull away from Cooper's hold but he doesn't let up, pulling me in tighter.

"Just relax for a minute, Charlotte. That was a long one." He urges me.

I try to block out everything that just happened, closing my eyes with the hope that when I open them none of this is real.

Opening my eyes I let out a long sigh, still seeing my office.

"You okay?" Cooper asks gently.

172

A sharp laugh escapes me before I can keep it in. "O-oh yeah. I'm great, I always love starting a new job by having a mental breakdown and letting my crazy out for everyone to see."

"You're not crazy." He's quick to reassure me, "And you didn't have a mental breakdown, you had a panic attack because of my shithead brothers," he says that as if that makes it any better. "They shouldn't have been in here bombarding you, this is on *them*, Charlotte, not you."

Trying to avoid the topic, I decide to ask him about something else. "Um, why are you holding me?" His arms tighten around me, I'm not sure if he even notices.

He snorts a laugh, "I took a lot of behavioral psychology classes in college, one of the things we frequently debated in class was how to help someone with anxiety attacks. Distraction is the typical tactic, which can be a lot of things, but some research showed that bear hugging someone is supposed to suppress their parasympathetic nervous system. It was a controversial topic, and most people suggest you shouldn't touch someone when they're having an attack but, I wasn't sure how else to break through to you so, I gave it a shot."

"Oh," that was a lot of information to answer my question, "Do you k-know about my A-asperger's then?" holding my breath I wait for him to confirm that he, along with his brothers are now all aware of my issues.

"Yeah, I talked with Maverick last night." he confirms. Clearing his throat, he continues, "I know it's not my

173

place to ask, so you don't have to answer, but when were you diagnosed?"

I'm confused by his question, but he quickly explains his thought process before I have a chance to answer.

"I only ask because Asperger's is a very outdated diagnosis, it's not really referred to anymore. Now, people are usually diagnosed as autistic, or they have ASD."

My eyes go wide at that, having no clue that my diagnosis isn't technically even real anymore.

"J-just before high school. My parents took me to someone, and they told me I have it. I-I've been on m-medication ever since." I shudder at the memory of my parents trying to 'fix' me, tired of having to deal with my 'weird' and 'annoying' behaviors.

Cooper's quiet for a few moments, "Hmm, you haven't had any follow-ups since they put you on medication?"

Shaking my head I start to wonder why it matters. I clearly have something wrong with me, so, even if the diagnosis isn't completely accurate anymore it doesn't change the fact that I'm a freak.

"It'd probably be worth it to see someone for a new perspective." Cooper is gentle with his suggestion, not demanding, but rather just trying to make sure I understand. "Going to see someone now, they could give you a more accurate diagnosis, see if anything has changed and even check to see if you need a different prescription to help you out with your anxiety more."

My chest tightens at the thought of having to see another doctor, having to answer all their questions while they sit and watch me with all their judgmental looks. I don't even want to take the pills I have now, they don't do anything substantial for me. I don't want to add anymore to my daily routine.

"You don't have to," he reassures me, "But would you at least consider seeing someone for a follow-up? I have a few good friends from college in the field. I could get you set up with one of them whenever you want. I really think it could help you manage your anxiety."

"It's n-not that bad." I weakly protest, my voice shaking giving me away.

"You know yourself better than anyone else, Charlotte. I just notice some of your anxious habits, and those are pretty frequent. Like pulling at your fingers or picking at your nails." he points out, taking my hands in his, halting my fidgeting that I didn't realize I was doing. He doesn't sound judgmental, just observant. "There's nothing wrong with it, but I just think it would be beneficial for you."

I don't like that he notices so many details about me. I appreciate his concern, but I'm not sure that I can handle discussing it with anyone right now.

"I'll think about it." I offer, not willing to make any promises that I can't keep.

"Okay. Just let me know if you ever want to talk to someone." He lets his arms fall from mine, shifting behind me to stand before offering a hand to help me off the floor.

Steady on my feet, I can't bring myself to meet his eyes. "Thank you." I tell him quietly as I focus on a spot on his chest.

"No thanks necessary." he tells me simply; I can hear a smile in his voice.

I need to get back to work but my brain is fried after all of the events from the day, for the first time since I can remember I almost dread having to sit behind my computer trying to focus.

My face must show my dread because Cooper is quick to speak up.

"I think you've had enough work for today, why don't we head out. I can drive you back to the dorms, just have to make one quick stop on the way there." He offers as he leans down, ducking his head to meet my eyes, smiling sweetly.

Normally I would decline, eager to jump into whatever projects I have waiting for me. But today has taken a toll on me, and I really just want to curl up in bed with a book and silence. Before even realizing it, I'm nodding my head.

"Great, let's get out of here." He moves to the door, swinging it open and looking back at me, waiting for me to join him.

I quickly throw my laptop into my bag. Stepping out into the hallway, Cooper shuts my door behind me, gesturing me ahead of him.

Leaving the office I don't see any of the other guys and I feel a brief stab of guilt for how Kai and Eli must feel. But my mental exhaustion quickly shoves that to the side to be dealt with later.

Stepping out into the afternoon sun I soak it in, letting it warm me to my core. I follow Cooper to his car, ready to get back to my dorm and just forget about the shitshow that was today.

13

~Cooper~

I watch Charlotte as she steps out of GLS, tilting her face to the sky with her eyes closed, soaking up the afternoon sun. For the first time today, she looks relaxed.

I should smack some sense into my bone-headed brothers for how they were talking down to her when I walked into her office earlier. I know they both care about her, and they both tend to be a little protective – it runs in the family, but they had no right to bombard her like that.

I'm sure it didn't help that Maverick told me that he ran into her before she got to work - literally. And then there was Sasha, who swore whatever was going on between them was just a silly misunderstanding, I'm not convinced.

It was a lot of shit for one afternoon, I'm not surprised that it was too much for Charlotte to handle. I also wasn't really surprised when I'd talked to Maverick last night and he filled me in on her...differences. Having studied psychology, I knew the signs for certain things, I knew she had some of the traits of someone on the spectrum but wasn't sure. Not that it matters either way but knowing helps avoid situations such as the one that occurred today. Or it would, if my brothers took a second to think about how to handle any situation rationally.

I lead Charlotte over to my cherry red Jeep. My pride and joy, other than our business of course, but a close second.

She's so short that it takes her a lot of effort to haul herself up into the passenger seat. Once she's in and buckled I shut her door, rounding the front to get in the driver's seat.

Charlotte stares out the window, mindlessly fiddling with the strap of her bag. Reaching over I turn on the radio, quickly pairing my phone and turning on some Taylor Swift. She looks over shyly, a small smile spreading across her face. I shoot her a wink, catching the blush on her cheeks before heading in the direction of the campus.

We drive in a comfortable silence, me tapping out the beat to the music on the steering wheel and Charlotte humming along to different songs, a stark contrast to the last time we were in the car together.

I pull into the parking lot for the department store that I was looking for, finding a spot close to the front to park.

Looking over to Charlotte I see confusion written all over her face.

Jumping out of the car I round to her side, opening her door and offering a hand to help her out.

"What do you need from here?" she finally asks as we make our way through the lot to the store.

"We need to get you some stuff for your office at GLS. Since I'm taking you home anyway it seemed like the perfect time." I tell her, shrugging. "Plus, shopping is a great way to unwind. Two birds, one stone, and all that."

She stops walking abruptly.

"I-I don't n-need anything." she argues wide-eyed, her stutter slipping out hinting that she's anxious.

"Your office is completely empty." I turn to face her, slipping my hands into my pockets to keep from reaching out and touching her to comfort her. "We set up all of our offices to be more comfortable since we spend so many hours there, it's no big deal."

She just stares back at me as if the idea of getting anything to decorate is the most absurd thing she's ever heard.

"Look, if we don't find anything that you like then we don't have to get anything. Let's just take a look." I compromise.

She chews on her bottom lip, considering. Finally, she sighs and nods her agreement, and I can't help my triumphant smile as I lead her into the store, grabbing a cart on the way in. She looks between the cart and me, clearly thinking that she just won't pick anything out. But either way, we're getting something for her office. It's a nice space but it's terribly bland, no one should have to sit inside an empty box to work for hours on end.

I like this store, it's typically where the guys and I shop when we need to decorate the house, and we all found stuff for GLS here too back when we opened. They have a wide range of decor options, office supplies, nick-nacks and really, anything you could want.

We stroll down a few aisles, Charlotte walks beside me, taking in all the offerings, not seeming drawn to anything. After another two aisles it's apparent that she's not going to pick out anything, so I start making suggestions as I see them.

"What about a cool lamp?" I ask, pointing to a shelf of at least twenty different lamps in a range of colors and sizes.

She scrunches her nose while looking them over.

"Okay, no lamp. What else…" I trail off, looking for the next option when I see her eyeing a set of fairy lights. They're all on a long strand that can be looped around, they're dim and dainty, but cute. And it's the first thing she's shown interest in so I quickly grab the box and toss them into the cart.

Her wide eyes look from the lights to me, then back again.

"W-why did y-you get those?" she asks frantically.

I shrug, "I like fairy lights."

Her brows curl in confusion but I just usher her down the aisle, "Come on, let's keep looking."

Next is a set of blackout curtains that have little star cut outs scattered throughout to let a small amount of light shine through. Into the cart they go. Then there's a retro-styled, mint green mini fridge just big enough to hold a few drinks. Into the cart. Essential oil diffuser? Don't mind if I do. Fuzzy under the desk mat? Give me five. Giant, over-sized bean bag chair? No brainer, into the cart.

"Are you just picking up stuff that I look at?" Charlotte asks, looking shocked as her eyes dart between the cart and me after I throw a pair of rose gold noise-canceling headphones into the cart.

"Of course not, I happen to like all of this stuff." I tell her innocently; I can't help the shit eating grin on my face that now that she's finally caught on.

Her eyebrows shoot up in surprise, her suspicion quickly replaced. "Really?"

I nod once, composing myself. "Absolutely. This is all going in my room at home as soon as I drop you off." I say matter-of-factly.

Her mouth forms a cute little 'O' as she turns to continue looking and I try my hardest to smother my laugh at her bemused surprise.

We've just about made it through the whole store, picking up a few other small items when I see a shelf full of stuffed dinosaurs.

"Hey, look at these."

She looks over the shelf before looking at me expectantly, not understanding my enthusiasm. I pick one up, feeling the weight in my hands under the soft material.

"They're stuffed animals, but they're weighted. Check it out." I offer it to her.

She looks uncertain but takes the offered toy anyways. Shifting it from hand to hand she looks intrigued, but a small crease forms between her brows.

"You like it?"

She looks at me with a small grin, nodding while pulling it closer to her chest, squeezing one of its arms in her hand.

"Awesome, now you won't leave empty-handed." I wink and she quickly averts her gaze, focusing on the dinosaur, shifting the beads in its stomach that give it the weight. I don't miss the blush on her cheeks as she turns away.

While she's distracted, I quickly grab another and sneak it into the cart before we finally make our way to the checkout. Charlotte offers to pay for her one item but quickly relents when I give her a look.

We make it back to the Jeep; Charlotte waits in the front while I load everything into the back.

Charlotte seems lost in thought as we drive back towards campus. "Penny for your thoughts?" I offer a chance for her to talk if she wants to take it.

Her gaze stays fixed out the front window as she thinks it over, fidgeting with the dinosaur absentmindedly.

"I just don't want Kai and Eli to be upset with me, or have their feelings hurt because of me." She admits quietly.

"Charlotte, I can almost guarantee you that neither of them will be upset with you." I keep my eyes on the road as I speak. "And you can't worry about their feelings before your own, having them in your office with their attitudes was overwhelming, right?"

A quick flick of my eyes shows me her small nod.

"You're allowed to tell them that you need space. If that's what you need in the moment then you need to say that, don't disregard what you need just for the fear of hurting their feelings." I try to keep my tone light but my words are firm, trying to make sure she hears me.

A tiny huff of frustration comes from her, "They've just been so nice to me, and they're my first real friends. I love spending time with them I just, I don't know. I get tired but I feel bad pushing them away and it feels like I need to reset." Her words trail off as she just sounds tired.

Taking a chance, I reach over and rest a hand on her leg. She doesn't seem off put by it so I leave it. "You can still value your friendship without giving up your own boundaries. And believe me, I've lived with the twins for most of my life, their feelings will be fine. Take a break from them whenever, just try giving them a heads up so they don't go crazy worrying. Or don't, it would be fun to watch them squirm." I joke with her as a grin pulls at her lips.

***

After dropping Charlotte off at campus I head back over to GLS. As I'm carrying in bags of stuff in from the store I find Kai sulking behind the front desk. He perks up when he hears me come in but quickly deflates when he realizes it's just me.

"Where's Lottie?" he asks with a frown.

"Back at her dorm. I drove her back." I tell him, struggling to carry the bags loaded in my arms.

"You should've told Eli or me so we could take her. We could've stayed with her after what happened earlier." He follows me as I take the hall down to Charlotte's office. Dropping the bags onto her desk, I start taking things out of the bags, taking off tags and wrappings.

"What the hell, Cooper?" Kai grunts from the doorway.

Eli comes to join him, never far behind. He raises a brow, looking between the two of us. " What's going on? Where's Charlie?"

"Alright, enough." I snap as I drop the curtains to the desk, leveling them both with a glare. "Both of you need to cool it. I get that Charlotte is your friend and that you both care about her but that doesn't mean you can bombard her like you did today."

They both start to argue but I hold up a hand to stop them.

"I also talked to her, she said sometimes she just needs a break. She loves being around you both, but it gets exhausting for her. She was too afraid to hurt your feelings and tell you, so today was too much when you two came in here like neanderthals and demanded answers from her about not following *your* plans." They both at least look somewhat chastised at the new information.

"She never said anything." Eli comments softly, looking hurt while Kai just stares blankly as the wall.

"Like I said, she didn't want to hurt your feelings. She's upset about today so just give her some time to decompress. And in the future just check in with her to see if she needs space or not." I say, looking between the both of them.

Neither of them says anything as I get back to unbagging the items on the desk.

"What is all this?" Eli suddenly asks.

"I took Charlotte by the store on the way home to get some stuff to decorate her office."

"She actually picked out all of this?"

"She let you buy her stuff?"

They talk over each other, both sound shocked at the prospect as they start picking through the selections.

Snorting I recall Charlotte's reluctance to pick anything out. "No, but there were certain things that clearly caught her attention. So, I just grabbed anything I noticed her looking at."

Kai picks up a paper weight, rolling it around in his hands. "So, she doesn't know that you're setting up her office?"

"Nope." I tell them simply as I work on untangling the fairy lights. "I told her all of this was for my room at home."

Eli snorts a laugh at that.

"You want help?" Kai offers.

We spend a few hours setting up the office with everything I bought, moving the desk around to give the office the best layout and most relaxed vibe. It looks fantastic once we're finished. The curtains fit the window perfectly to either block out the sunlight or to be pulled to the sides. The bean bag chair sits in one corner and the desk in another with all the little trinkets and items I grabbed. Everything that I brought from the store blends together nicely throughout the space, giving it a warm feeling rather than the sterile feeling as it was.

It was a nice afternoon, getting to spend quality time with both of them that we've lacked lately. Our lives are so busy now that everything seems to center around work, so this was a good change of pace.

We all finish out the rest of the day before heading home and going about our nightly routines. I go through the motions, my mind straying to the shy little brunette who seems to have captured my brother's and I under her spell.

I can't say that I hate it.

14

~ *Charlotte* ~

The next few days pass by quickly, the guys all give me a wide berth, giving me the space I wanted. I throw myself into my work to try and avoid the guilt I feel at keeping them at arm's length after my meltdown on Monday.

Eli and Kai spoke with me briefly, apologizing for how they barged in on me. Neither of them gave me a chance to apologize for my reaction, saying that I had no reason to but that didn't make the guilt in my chest lessen any. Other than that, I've not seen them more than in passing this week. They've both been out on different projects from Maverick.

I was also shocked to see my office when I came in the day after Cooper dropped me off. The once plain office now looked amazing and cozy, filled with things that I loved and that made the space more comfortable. I tried to argue with Cooper that it was all too much when I walked in to see the changes but he had shut me down quickly, telling me to just say 'thank you' and enjoy the stuff.

I spent the weekend in the office doing just that, enjoying the space while doing everything I could to try and track Timothy's movements. I loved the setup, that didn't mean that I was just going to accept it all though. I looked up everything that Cooper bought at the store and wrote a check to cover the cost of everything, leaving it on his desk for him. As expected, he tried to give it back to me, ripping it up when I refused to take it. So, naturally I may have looked up his bank information and made the deposit into his account myself. It was fairly easy to do and honestly, I wasn't sure he'd even notice with the amount of money he had stashed away. But I knew that I paid him back and that made me feel better so I left it at that.

The office is quiet today, with Thanksgiving being two days away I'm not surprised. I don't expect to see any of the guys in the office, which is fine since Maverick gave me my own code to get into the building when they're not here.

Since I've been at Oceancoast, I've spent every holiday alone. My parents didn't normally celebrate anyways but with me being out of the house they didn't have any excuses to even pretend. I can count on one hand the number of times I've gone home since leaving, and none of those were under the guise of a holiday visit. This year would be no different, I'd spend the holiday in my dorm with a bowl of noodles and some crappy movie channel playing all of the holiday classics.

Not having the interruption of the holiday was good for working on this case, I'd tracked very minimal movement from Timothy and wasn't happy with my lack of progress. I knew it wouldn't be easy, but I had hoped that I'd have more to show for it. It was also good that no one was around because I was pretty sure that I was coming down with something. My head pounded in time with my pulse and I shivered in my multiple layers despite the warm temperatures outside. I wanted to fall into bed and sleep whatever this is off, but more than that, I wanted to take advantage of the quiet office and find something to show I was worth keeping around. Taking a sick day when I'd only been here a short time didn't really give a good impression, so I will power through with the promise of a hot shower and a soft bed later tonight when I make it home.

"Charlotte!" Cooper's voice yells from the hallway, sounding less than thrilled and scaring the crap out of me. I didn't think any of them were coming in today considering its already lunch time and I haven't heard anyone until now.

A quick knock sounds before the door to my office opens and Cooper walks in, standing before my desk with his arms crossed, his brow arched expectantly, waiting. For what I'm not sure. Maverick is close behind him but leans against the door frame, crossing his arms as well with his impassive stare, just observing.

I look between the two of them, trying to figure out where they're here. But they give nothing away as they both stare back at me.

"Um, hi." I offer, waiting for either of them to say something.

Neither of them responds, so I sit and wait, pulling the blanket I brought with me tighter around my lap to fight the chill that seems to be seeping into my bones.

Cooper moves from standing in the middle of the office to sitting in one of the chairs that's positioned just on the other side of my desk, taking a deep breath like he's trying to compose himself as I just watch.

Propping his chin on his clasped hands he looks at me calmly, "Charlotte, can you tell me why I just found a deposit into my bank account for the same amount as that check that I ripped up a couple days ago?"

He waits patiently as I look to Maverick, who tilts his head, brows raised awaiting my answer.

Looking back to Cooper I shrug, "You wouldn't take the check." It's pretty self explanatory so I offer nothing more.

Maverick snorts from the doorway as Cooper rubs his temples.

"Charlotte, you can't just hack into my bank account. I told you that you weren't paying for the additions to the office because we set up all of the offices here." He speaks slowly, trying not to get angry. But I hate owing people, and he bought a lot of stuff for the office so of course I'm going to pay that back.

"I have the money, I wanted to pay for it." I argue back.

"Regardless, you can't go around hacking into our bank accounts." he argues back, "That's an invasion of our privacy and it's technically against the rules." He seems to have dropped the issue of me paying for my stuff for now, thankfully.

"Isn't a lot of the stuff we do against the rules?" I ask, my eyes flicking to Maverick while remembering his little interrogation weeks ago. His eyes narrow back, obviously knowing what I'm referring to.

Cooper shoots a look Maverick's way as well, "Technically, yes." Looking back to me he adds, "Just please don't hack into our personal stuff okay? It's a trust thing." he explains lamely.

"Got it." I agree to get this conversation over with before falling into a coughing fit while they both stare at me. When I can breathe again I ignore both of them, turning back to my computer to continue working, hoping they'll both leave now that Cooper's said his piece.

No such luck.

"What are you doing here? We gave everyone the week off for the holiday." Cooper asks.

Not looking at either of them I continue typing away. I've overheard them all talking about their holiday plans, picking up on the fact that holidays are a big deal to them.

I don't want to get into a conversation about why I don't celebrate.

"I had some work to get done." I tell them, focused on the screen before me.

"You should go home, take some time off to enjoy the holiday." Cooper offers, "Aren't you going to see your parents?" he asks, hesitant with his words.

I ignore the question completely, avoidance is the best thing when we reach a subject I don't want to discuss.

"I'm fine here." I tell them, cringing at the raspy quality of my voice.

They're both silent, the only sounds filling the room are typing and quiet sniffles that I can't seem to avoid if I want to breathe.

"You look like crap." Maverick tells me bluntly, still not moving from his spot at the door.

My typing falters for a moment before I pick it back up again. I know Maverick is upfront but that was rude, even for him.

"Mav," Cooper sighs, rubbing the bridge of his nose. Clearly, he's in agreement that the comment was rude.

"What? Are you just going to ignore the fact that she looks like she's ready to fall out of her chair at any moment?" Maverick shoots back, talking as if I can't her them. "She needs to go home."

194

"I'm fine." I try to sound firm but the effect is ruined by another coughing fit. I avoid looking at both of them, still hoping they'll both go away.

I hear Maverick shift from his spot but I don't look up.

"*Fine.*" The word is clipped as I hear him moving, thinking that he's left.

My attention is pulled away from my computer as I catch him in my peripheral, settling into the beanbag chair in the corner. He shifts around making himself comfortable, pulling out his phone and ignoring my confused look.

"What are you doing?" I ask, my attention firmly on him rather than my computer.

He shrugs, not looking up from his phone. "If you're staying, I'll stay too. That way when you fall out from exhaustion or that fever you're clearly running then someone will be here to make sure you don't die." He looks up, eyes narrowed "It's bad for company morale." he adds with an arrogant smirk.

"Company morale? What does that have to do with anything?" I ask, confused as to what he's talking about. "And I'm not going to die, I'm fine."

"He's being sarcastic." Cooper explains, "But you really don't look good, you should go home and rest."

"I'm fine." I argue again, my irritation building as they both look at me with disbelieving looks.

"You're wearing a hoodie and huddled under a blanket when it's 86 degrees outside." Maverick points out, still staring at his phone.

"I'm always cold." I counter.

"Regardless, your face is flushed, you can't stop coughing and sniffling and you've been here for at least twelve hours everyday while school's been out. I highly doubt you've slept much when you've gone home since you log into the employee server to keep working when you're not here." Maverick goes down the list, still looking disinterested in the whole conversation. "You either go home and rest, or Cooper and I will stay here with you. Those are your options." He shrugs, looking nothing but comfortable where he sits.

Cooper shifts to get comfortable in his chair, telling me that neither of them are bluffing about staying here while I work. I want to ignore both of them but I know their presence will be blatantly obvious to me no matter how hard I try to focus on my computer. Their eyes on me will feel like tiny ants crawling all over my skin.

"Fine. I'll go home." I give in. Besides, I can just log into work from my dorm and be alone while they go about their personal business.

"Great." Cooper sounds happy, clapping as he stands and waits for me by the door.

I get up from my chair, holding onto the desk as a wave of dizziness washes over me before folding up my blanket and cleaning up my space so everything is organized the way I like for when I come back.

"Leave your laptop." Maverick barks out just as I'm reaching for my computer to throw it in my messenger bag. He stands up from the bean bag chair with so much ease, it's irritating. I shoot him a look now that he's finally not looking at his phone and instead is watching me, waiting for an argument. I don't have the energy to fight him so I drop the laptop, throwing my bag over my shoulder with an eye roll at his high handedness.

It's not like I can't log into the server from my computer in my dorm.

They both follow me out of the office, telling me that they'll drive me home. I don't have the energy to argue and walking back to campus right now sounds awful with how tired I feel, so I settle into the back of Maverick's SUV without a complaint.

I drift in and out of sleep for the entire ride back to campus, Maverick and Cooper not making any attempts to fill the silence.

Cooper offers to walk me inside once we pull up to my dorm but I wave him off, telling them both to have a good holiday and that I'll see them on Monday, making my way to my dorm on shaky legs.

The halls are quiet, most of the students having gone home for the holiday break.

Making it into my room I take a moment to soak in the silence. Enjoying the calmness that it brings me, not having to stress about anyone around me.

I settle in at my desk, making quick work of logging into the employee server so that I can continue working on my project, getting lost in the different threads that I have open to check on Timothy's movements.

Day turns to night before I realize it and my eyelids droop with the setting sun. I take a break to take my meds and to try and drink some water, though I'm not very successful as the irritation in my throat has only increased from this morning. I'm tempted to go to sleep but I've finally found a lead to follow, tracking Timothy to a dive bar on the far end of town where he met with some shady looking people just nights before he started waiting outside of Myth every night. I throw all of my focus into the lead, trying to distract myself from how crappy I feel. Before I know it, the sun is rising again, shining brightly through my open curtains.

I work through most of the day, only taking a break in the afternoon when my eyes refuse to focus on the screen any longer. I stumble into the shower, hoping that the boiling water will ease the ache in my muscles, before falling into my bed and huddling under the covers, trying to hold onto the warmth from the shower.

It's still early in the evening, and my phone keeps pinging from my desk, but I don't have the energy to keep my eyes open, let alone go check who it is.

My muscles convulse as I shiver under the weighted blanket, causing more aches to plague my entire body. I blindly reach across the bed, dragging the dinosaur that Cooper got me under the pile of blankets. Tucking it against my face to try and feel warmer I succumb to the exhaustion, letting it drag me under and enjoying the sheer nothingness that welcomes me with the darkness.

15

~ Maverick ~

Thanksgiving has always been one of my favorite holidays. I've always enjoyed the food, and the time spent with family. Once our parents died I took on the role of cooking a huge spread for the guys and I to enjoy. It started the first year because I didn't want to see my brother's feel the void of our mother not being there to cook all of our favorite dishes, then from there it just became our new tradition.

It's a great day for all of us. Unlike traditional Thanksgiving dinner, we cook a spread of all of our favorite dishes. Cooper's pick is lasagna, Kai's is pierogis and mac and cheese - homemade not from the box, Eli's is Pad Thai and mine being meatloaf and mashed potatoes. It was a disgusting spread when all laid out together honestly, but it made each of us happy and it was how we still managed to enjoy the holiday when it became just us.

I love Thanksgiving, but I'm about ready to punch Kai in the face if he doesn't stop blowing up my phone while I try to cook.

"What?" I growl into the phone, finally picking it up on his sixth try calling me. The twins and Cooper were on their way to Gainesville as they insist on having homemade pie and cheesecake from a mom and pop shop that we found years ago. Part of their tradition was driving down to visit them and pick up dessert every year while I cooked for us.

"What has your panties all in a bunch?" he asks, entertained by the irritation coloring my tone. "Isn't this like your favorite day of the year? Shouldn't you sound happy?"

"Usually, I have peace for a few hours while you all go to get your sweets." I bite out as I work on mashing potatoes to make them smooth the way I like them, "Instead, I have you blowing up my phone and interrupting that peace."

He huffs a laugh, clearly amused at the situation. "Well, you didn't respond to my texts or any of my calls, I wouldn't hound you if you just replied."

I shift the phone to hold it with my shoulder as I add cream and butter to the pot. "I'm not going to check on your girlfriend."

"But you said she was sick! And none of us have heard from her since you and Cooper dropped her off." He argues.

Covering the potatoes, I leave them on the stove top to be reheated later, moving to check the meatloaf in the oven, "She's an adult, I'm sure she can take care of herself. Maybe she just doesn't want to talk, or she's probably working since I told her not to." I offer dryly.

"Eli said she hasn't been online since mid-day yesterday, and we're trying not to barge in there again and freak her out," his voice is filled with concern, not that I think it's completely warranted, but I know both the twins have been feeling guilty about Charlotte's episode last week.

"And you think she'll be fine with me stopping by to check on her?" I ask, a laugh of my own slipping out.

"Can you please just check on her? We don't have time with going all the way to Gainesville and back before dinner." he pleads, sounding more and more desperate.

"I'll look into it." I tell him shortly before ending the call, focusing on the food.

I work for a while, putting together the rest of the food so it only needs to be heated up when they guys are back home before I head into my office, Zeus following closely behind me.

Thinking about what Kai said, I pull up the log for the employee server. Confirming what he said, I see that Charlotte worked overnight after we dropped her off the other day until about mid-day yesterday when her progress stops.

Pulling out my phone I click on her contact, listening to it ring until it finally sends me to voicemail. I send a text, telling her to respond so that we at least know she's alive.

I flip through some emails on my computer while I wait for her to respond, but after a few minutes the message still shows that it hasn't been opened.

Zeus sits up at my annoyed sigh as I open the phone finder app, I never did tell Charlotte that I synced her phone to mine while she was in the office one day but the way I see it is if she can track Eli and hack Cooper's bank account then I should be able to check on her location.

The little blue dot immediately lights up, showing her in her dorm over at the college. I think about what to do, I could just tell Kai that I got in touch and that she's fine since I know she's in her dorm. But then he's going to be depressed that she's ignoring his messages, and he'll never shut up. Knowing her, I'll drive all the way over there and she'll be hunched over her computer, doing whatever it is she does with her free time.

Zeus lets out a whine, pawing at my hand holding the phone. As if he's begging like Kai for me to check on her.

Rolling my eyes I head towards the garage, checking that the oven is off before locking up and jumping into my SUV. I'll go check on her so I can tell Kai that she's fine, maybe tell her to stop ignoring the twins so they'll shut up with all their worrying while I'm at it.

The drive to the school is quick, no traffic given that everything's closed today. The campus is a ghost town, no students lingering around and no cars in any of the lots. It doesn't take me long to find her dorm considering Kai sent me thorough directions in addition to the dorm number. I knock lightly on the door, not wanting to scare her. Waiting, I don't hear anything coming from inside, so I knock again, louder this time. Still nothing.

Testing the handle the door opens with no resistance. Peeking my head into the room I don't see much as the curtains are drawn shut, no lights on anywhere inside. I shut the door softly behind me and feel for a light switch along the wall. Finding it I flip it on, a light above the door and the small kitchen illuminates the space, allowing me to see the room in its entirety.

It's not a large space by any means, but it's still much nicer than any college dorm room I've ever seen. My dorm in college had been more like a closet and was filled to the brim with takeout boxes and textbooks at any given time. Charlotte keeps her space immaculately clean, much like her office at GLS. I look around the space, even looking into the closet and bathroom but it's apparent that she's not here. Just as I go to head out the door wondering where she could be, I hear a muffled groan.

Looking behind me at the bed off to the right side of the room I realize that what I thought was a pile of blankets is actually Charlotte. Calling her name, she doesn't acknowledge me as I approach the bed.

I sit on the edge, not wanting to startle her. Even just sitting next to her I can feel the heat radiating off her, she's burning up. I pull the blanket down from over her head, her usually neat long hair is a jumbled rats nest piled on top of her head, strands of hair sticking out in every direction. Her cheeks are flushed a deep shade of red, the rest of her skin pale and covered in a thin sheen of sweat. I reach out to feel her forehead and just as I thought, she's burning up. She groans at the contact, pulling her head away and trying to bury it into the pillows without opening her eyes.

"Charlotte." I try to catch her attention as she just burrows further into the pillows. Moving from the bed I leave her while I go find a bottle of water in the fridge, among the many cans of energy drinks. I also search the cabinets and find some Tylenol to give her to help with the fever before settling down next to her again.

"Charlotte, wake up." I shake her shoulder, trying to rouse her from sleep. She grumbles a response, but I can't make out what she says, other than the word 'no'.

Taking a breath to keep myself calm I remind myself that she feels like shit. That's the only reason that I try to be gentle as I drag her up to a sitting position, supporting her back against my chest.

"Charlotte, you need to take these pills and drink something." I hold both out in front of her while she shakes her head.

"No. Just wanna sleep." Her voice comes out slurred, more like a whine than an actual statement.

Uncapping the water, I hold it to her mouth, trying to tip her head back so she has to swallow some of it.

"Just take the pills and some water and you can sleep." I make the false promise hoping that she'll do what I say, if anything, so she thinks I'll leave her alone. I roll my eyes at the fact that I'm trying to negotiate with a half-conscious woman who doesn't even know what planet she's on right now.

"Charlotte." My voice comes out firmer this time as she tries to roll her head away from the water, a warning not to test my patience.

She grumbles something else but takes a sip of the water and swallows the pills as I offer them before turning away again.

I lay her back on the bed as I take a second to consider my options. She's clearly sick and not coherent enough to look after herself. God knows how long she's been laying here with a raging fever. All three of the guys will literally murder me in my sleep if they knew I left her here like this.

Not having any better options, I leave her on the bed while I walk into her closet, finding a duffle bag on the top shelf, I throw some clothes at random into it before stepping back into the main space. Looking around I find her glasses on the table next to the bed and toss those in, along with the small pill bottle on the counter and her phone.

She hasn't moved an inch by the time I'm done. Completely dead to the world. I sling the bag over my shoulder before reaching down to scoop her up, not struggling at all to hold her tiny frame in my arms.

She doesn't stir the whole way back to the SUV, only coming to when I sit her in the passenger seat.

"What are you doing?" she grumbles, her eyes still firmly shut against the afternoon sun shining brightly.

"You're sick." I tell her, pulling the seatbelt over her before jumping in behind the wheel.

Charlottes slumped over, leaning her head against the window looking anything but comfortable. A frown taking over her face.

"I'm fine." she slurs again.

"Yeah, tell me that again when you can sit upright or keep your eyes open for longer than five seconds." I tell her with a snort.

She blindly tucks one of her legs up close to her chest, resting her head on it. Eyes still closed.

"You're a dick."

My eyes shoot to her, waiting for her usual look of surprise at insulting me out loud rather than in her head but it doesn't come as she struggles to stay conscious. Her eye lids flutter but stay shut.

"Maybe so," I tell her as I pull out of the lot back onto the main road. "But at least I'm not so much of a dick to let you turn your brain into scrambled eggs with a fever."

I don't expect her to respond, thinking she's asleep again so it surprises me when she mumbles a few minutes later.

"Gross."

"What is?" I ask, nothing better to do during the drive than have half a conversation with her.

It takes her a minute, looking over I see her brow scrunched up either in confusion or concentration before she finally answers me.

"Scrambled eggs. So gross." her slurred speech trails off as she falls out of consciousness again.

I don't respond this time, just shaking my head at her half responses.

She doesn't wake again before we make it back to the house, I consider trying to wake her up to walk inside but I decide to save myself some time and carry her so she can't argue with me that 'she's fine'.

Zeus is immediately on alert as I step inside, not recognizing the scent of Charlotte. I order him to his bed while I lay her on the couch before going to find the first aid kit.

Finding the kit is easy and when I return with the thermometer Zeus is sitting on the floor by her head, whining softly. I go to step towards her when he bears his teeth at me, growling out a warning.

Great, my own dog is taken with her seconds upon meeting. What is it about her that has everyone acting like putty in her hands?

"Zeus, stand down." I tell him as he just stares back at me. Snapping at him and pointing at her feet he huffs at me before moving down the couch to sit by her hips, watching me closely.

Kneeling next to Charlotte I run the thermometer over her forehead, she barely notices as the numbers flash bright red across the screen.

103.4

Well shit, she has to cool down or her brain really will start to scramble. It's no wonder she's not coherent.

Lifting the bottom of her hoodie I see she's wearing a t-shirt underneath, so I make quick work of stripping the hoodie off, tossing it onto the far end of the couch.

Zeus lets out another growl as she grumbles her protest to being left in her sweat soaked shirt, but I just ignore him as I get a wet washcloth to lay on her head. Turning the TV on low I settle onto the other end of the sectional to let her sleep and hopefully let the Tylenol bring her fever down. Zeus stays rooted by her side, on guard and not willing to leave.

I give it about 45 minutes before I check her temperature again.

103.7

Damnit. It's not going down, and if it gets any higher then she'll have to go to the hospital. I try shaking her awake with little success.

Carrying her upstairs I shut the door behind me so Zeus can't follow, sitting her on the vanity in my bathroom as his whines filter in under the door.

"Charlotte, you need to get in the shower to cool down, I can help you, but I need to make sure you're okay with that." I tell her as she finally starts to open her eyes, confused at why she's sitting on the counter.

Looking around groggily she shakes her head then sways at the dizziness that probably causes her.

"No."

"Your fever is too high, you have to get in. I don't think you can stand on your own." I try to hold onto my patience as I explain, trying to get her consent to help her here. Putting her in the shower in her clothes isn't productive to cooling her down, I don't want to make her uncomfortable, but this fever has got to come down.

Her eyes fall shut again as she shakes her head.

"No, I'm cold. Just want to sleep." she whines.

"That's not an option." My patience snaps and I lift her by the waist to slide her leggings down before grabbing the shirt to lift it over her head, dropping both to the floor leaving her in her matching baby blue bra and boy shorts. I keep one hand on her to keep her from falling as I strip off my own shirt, leaving me in my gym shorts and kicking off my shoes.

Picking her up again I walk us both into the shower, closing the glass door before reaching over to turn on the spray, making sure it's cool before moving her under the spray.

Her eyes fly open as soon as the water hits her skin, fully alert for the first time since I found her.

I have to set her on her feet as she struggles against my hold, not wanting to drop her. I keep my arms around her, so she doesn't collapse on her trembling legs.

"C-c-c-cold." she mutters, reaching for the knob to adjust the temperature.

Wrapping her up tighter in my arms I keep her from turning the temperature up as she struggles weakly against my hold.

"It has to be cold; it's the only way to get your fever down." I tell her as I keep her under the spray, turning her to face me so she'll stop reaching for the knob. She struggles more as I tighten my hold, trying to break away from me but not having the strength to move me even an inch.

"N-n-n-n-no m-more." she struggles to speak as her teeth start to chatter violently, chills racking her body and goosebumps taking over every inch of her smooth skin.

"Shhh" I try to soothe her, "Just breathe." I support more of her weight as her legs continue to shake, threatening to collapse.

She doesn't argue any more, just shudders in my arms as her teeth continue to chatter.

We stand there for some time, shivering under the spray. The longer we stand, the more relaxed she becomes. Her head rests against my chest as she fights nodding off every couple of seconds. I gently reach up to release her hair from the matted mess it was tossed in, letting the water smooth away the tangles and cool her down.

Once her skin is no longer burning where it touches mine I reach over to turn off the water, grabbing a towel to wrap around her trembling frame. I quickly throw one around my waist and take her into my room, sitting her on the edge of the bed while I grab clothes for both of us.

Her eyes have fallen shut again as she sways on the edge of the bed, still shivering from the shower.

"I'm going to help you get dressed and then you can sleep." I tell her, not knowing if she's hearing me since she doesn't acknowledge me either way.

Careful not to let the towel slip, I keep that pulled around her as I blindly reach to unclasp her soaked bra before sliding one of my shirts over her head. I make sure it's pulled down before letting the towel go and pulling her arms through before repeating the same routine with her lower half and a pair of my boxers that I have to roll up a couple of times so they don't fall off her hips.

She lays back on the bed once I have her dressed and I leave her there while I step into the bathroom to quickly dry off and throw on some clothes.

I contemplate leaving her in my bed but decide against it, figuring that it will be easier to check on her if she's on the couch. I carry her back downstairs and lay her on the couch again, Zeus taking his spot watching over her while I get another bottle of water from the kitchen.

She argues with me the whole time I try to get her to drink, seemingly more alert this time around, though that's not saying much given the state I found her in.

I end up sitting behind her on the couch, my legs thrown over hers pinning them down with her back pressed against my front.

"Drink. Then you can sleep all you want." I tell her firmly, my patience nowhere to be found now.

"Your bossy." She grumbles out as she weakly tries again to push my hand away and move from my hold, but even if she weren't weak from being sick she wouldn't fare much better.

"Not exactly breaking news, hate to break it to you."

"I'm c-cold. Can I just h-have a b-blanket?" her voice is raspy, either from her sore throat or being dehydrated, or both.

"No. You can have water." I force the water up to her lips, leaving her no choice but to swallow it or have it run down her chin. She drinks about half before I let her push my hand away. Giving in for now as I continue holding her against my chest.

"Can you let me go now?" she asks, her voice clearer now but heavy with exhaustion.

"No."

"Why not?" her eyes are closed, she's half asleep and still questioning me.

"Because if I do, you're just going to go look for a blanket. That's not productive to resting or to keeping your fever down."

"You're such a dick…" her voice trails off at the end, telling me that she's falling into sleep again.

I just chuckle at her insult, not the least bit offended. "So I've heard."

I hold her for a while, making sure she's completely asleep before I grab the thermometer again to check her fever.

101.8

Still high but at least not close to needing to take her to the hospital.

I carefully shift out from behind her, laying her back onto the couch and sliding a pillow under her head.

Telling Zeus to keep watch I leave her there to rest while I go to work on the food for dinner.

I try to feel annoyed at the way my day has been thrown off the rails by the tiny little spitfire that's barreled into our lives but for some reason I can't find it in me.

I just find myself trying to bite back the laugh that's threatening to come out at the whole situation as I pick up where I left off this morning.

16

~ *Charlotte* ~

My body aches. Every muscle in my body feels as though they've been sent through a meat grinder as I start to come to.

I'm hovering in that moment between being awake and asleep, I can hear sounds around me though I'm not sure where they're coming from. I shift onto my side, trying to get comfortable and allow sleep to pull me back under when I hear voices.

"Wake her up and I will throttle you into next week." A deep voice growls. I feel my brows scrunch in confusion because that voice, it sounds like Maverick. What would Maverick be doing in my dorm room? And who would be trying to wake me up?

Pulling my eyes open they're immediately assaulted by bright light. Squeezing them shut I try blinking a few times to get them to adjust.

My vision is blurry, as to be expected since I don't have my glasses on. I turn my head, and a small scream escapes me as I find myself face to face with a bear. Or at least I think it's a bear. It's big and brown and furry and its hot breath is covering my face. I don't know what it is, but I don't want to get any closer to it to find out.

I shoot up, feeling lightheaded as I shuffle back, almost falling off the couch I find myself sitting on.

Where the fuck am I?

I try to make myself smaller so the animal won't come any closer, I can't see clearly to figure out where I'm at, but I can at least see that the thing isn't coming any closer. I can see its head tilt as it stares at me, probably trying to figure out the best way to attack as my heart pounds in my chest.

Can it hear my heart? I bet it can, it's probably loving the sound of my fear as it plans the best way to attack me, the quickest way to devour me.

"Lottie." Kai's voice breaks through my panic, squinting in the direction of his voice I can make out his shape leaning over the back of the couch I'm on.

"Kai?" I ask. How is he here? Where is here? I have so many questions and no answers and I still can't see.

"Yeah, it's me." I feel his hand on my shoulder squeezing. "You alright?".

Squinting, I look between him and the bear.

"There's- that's a-" I stumble over what to tell him, shouldn't he be able to see the animal sitting feet away waiting to eat me?

Another voice comes from the other end of the room, "Shit, she can't see. Where are her glasses?" That sounds like Eli.

Shuffling sounds fill the silence before another hand hovers just before my face, my glasses in their grasp.

I slide them on, taking a moment for my vision to adjust so I can finally see, "A dog?"

Eli drops down onto the couch next to the massive German Shepard, rubbing his head as the dog looks over at me affectionately.

"This is Zeus. He's Maverick's."

I stare dumbfounded at Zeus, mentally slapping myself for thinking he was a bear. I take a quick look around at my surroundings, finding an open plan living room with dark couches and matching armchairs facing a giant TV, minimal furniture and a couple pictures of the guys hanging on the walls. Over to the right the space leads into a massive kitchen with a huge island dominating most of the space, Maverick stands with his back to us at the far end of the kitchen. A small dining area sits to the left and a set of stairs sits behind me. I can just barely see the entry way from where I'm sitting as well as a couple of doors leading to different areas of the house.

"Is this your house?" I ask stupidly.

"Yup. Welcome to our casa." Cooper's voice answers just before I see him rounding the bottom of the stairs before he flops down into one of the empty chairs.

I take in all three of them, looking more relaxed than I've ever seen in sweatpants and T-shirts as opposed to their usual everyday office attire.

Twisting my fingers I try to figure out how I got here before I finally just ask them, "Why am I here?" Looking down I take note of my own attire, "And w-where are my c-clothes"

None of the guys answer as Maverick walks into the room, leaning against the island where he crosses his arms as he answers.

"I brought you here when I found you in your dorm burning up with a fever barely conscious. You're in my clothes because I had to put you in the shower to cool down before you ended up at the hospital with brain damage."

I feel heat rush to my already flushed cheeks.

"O-oh." I answer lamely.

Cooper, per usual breaks the awkward silence, "You feeling any better then? You've been passed out since before we got home over an hour ago."

I take quick stock of myself; I feel like utter garbage. My body hurts, I'm freezing, my head is pounding, and I feel like I swallowed glass. But not wanting to cause them any more worry I stick with my usual answer,

"I'm fine."

Maverick huffs at my response, rolling his eyes before retreating back into the kitchen.

Looking at the other guy's Eli shakes his head, "Don't mind him. How are you really feeling?" he asks with an eye that's too critical for my liking.

I'm about to repeat myself when Maverick stalks back in, holding a bottle of water and something else in his hand.

"She's fine, Eli. She could literally be on her death bed and her response would still be 'I'm fine'". He seems angry, though I'm not sure why as he holds the bottle of water out for me to take, I accept it with shaking hands as he waits.

I'm not sure what he's waiting for, but he keeps looking from the water to me, so I decide to uncap it and take a sip. Only then does he stop staring, moving to swipe a thermometer against my forehead.

"101.4 so you're not fine, you need to drink the rest of that water." he orders before stalking back to the kitchen.

"I don't think I've seen someone be so caring while being such a major prick before." Kai says from the back of the couch.

Caring? Is he talking about Maverick? I'm not sure caring is in his vocabulary, more than likely he just loves bossing people around. Why else would he come drag me out of my dorm other than to get to order me around?

Zeus moves forward, nudging my hand with his nose as I jump back in surprise. I didn't grow up around dogs, never allowed to have a pet as a child and for that reason I'm skeptical around them. Growing up my parents only ever told me that dogs like to attack people, and their only purpose was security. Zeus is huge, probably half my size, while part of me is curious and wants to pet him the other part is terrified that he'll lash out against me.

"You can pet him." Eli offers, watching me closely. "He won't hurt you; he was guarding you while you slept. He's taken on a protective role with you."

"Really?" I'm skeptical of that because from where I'm sitting he seems to be eyeing me up like I'm his next meal.

"Oh yeah," Kai laughs, "He was growling any time Maverick came near you. I thought he was going tear his hand off."

My eyes widen at the mental image, only ramping up my apprehension.

"Kai." Cooper shoots him a warning glare that even I can decipher means to shut the fuck up, before smiling at me, "Go ahead, he won't hurt you." He encourages me.

Slowly I reach out a hand, avoiding the dog's mouth as he keeps turning to smell me. Settling my hand on the top of his head between his ears I pet him gently, feeling his coarse hair tickle my fingers. He stays still, only moving to lay his head on the couch next to me so I can reach him easier. It's actually kind of cute.

221

Looking up, I see all three guys watching, small smiles on their faces.

Kai ends up quietly going into the kitchen and Eli looks to me, "Can I get you anything?" he asks quietly.

I shake my head, but a shiver racks through me, "Are you cold? You want a blanket?" he asks, never one to miss the smallest detail.

Before I can respond and practically beg for a blanket Maverick call out from the kitchen, "No blanket."

Eli rolls his eyes. "Maverick she's cold, she can have a blanket." he gets up to go look for one and Maverick shoots him a look across the island.

"Not while she has a fever, the whole point is to keep it down." looking at me he adds, "Unless you want another cold shower?"

Not able to keep his gaze, I study Zeus's fur, shaking my head.

"Didn't think so." Maverick mutters, and he must return to whatever he was doing because Eli settles onto the couch next to me again.

Kai rejoins us in the living room and the four of us sit in a comfortable silence, them watching the TV and me petting Zeus while Maverick works in the kitchen. I'm not sure how much time has passed when Maverick calls out to let everyone know that dinner is ready.

"Come on, Maverick cooks a huge spread of all our favorites for Thanksgiving." Kai explains, offering me a hand off the couch.

Guilt seizes me, it's Thanksgiving. Maverick just spent the holiday taking care of me, and the guys are sitting around with me when they should be doing…whatever families do on the holiday.

"Oh, no. Y-you guys eat. I'm just g-going to h-head out." I brush off his offer and stand on shaking legs, trying to steady myself after laying down for so long.

"Go where?" Eli asks from my other side. "It's thanksgiving, just have dinner with us. It beats being alone."

Little does he know that I spend it alone every year, not knowing anything different. But I already feel horrible that I crashed the day for them, I don't want to stick around for dinner and offend Maverick when I don't eat any of the food, for my own reasons and for the simple fact that I feel like utter shit.

"N-no, thank y-you. I don't w-want to crash your d-dinner." I sidestep both of them, heading towards the direction of the front door. I'm not sure how far we are from campus but hopefully the walk isn't too far. Maybe I can order a ride, I just need to get out of here first.

Maverick steps out of the kitchen, effectively blocking my path. I try to step around him as well, but he just matches my side steps, continuing to block my way.

"E-excuse me." I try to be polite, but my stutter is slipping out and I'm honestly just exhausted.

Maverick though, doesn't move, standing wide and crossing his arms while looking down at me.

"Where do you think you're going?"

"H-home." I state, it should be obvious. And of all people he should be thrilled, after having to look after me all afternoon. He's the last person I'd expect to argue that I stay.

Maverick locks one of his hands around my bicep and steers me back through the kitchen towards the small table in the dining area.

"Yeah, I don't think so," he says, sitting me into one of the chairs. "You weren't even coherent a couple hours ago, you haven't eaten in God knows how long and you still have a fever. You're staying here."

"I'm f-fine." I argue, gripping my fingers to cover their shaking and to calm my nerves at going toe to toe with the eldest Locke brother. "T-thank y-you for looking after m-me but it's just a fever. I'll g-go home and sleep it off, I don't n-need to crash your d-dinner."

"No."

That's it. His response is one word. He doesn't even look my way as he says it, turning back to the table to plate up food as his brothers settle into their respective seats around us.

What the fuck does he mean no? He's not the boss of me. Well, I guess he is but that's at work. He can't tell me what to do outside of the office.

I turn to get out of the chair but before my butt leaves the seat his hand is on my shoulder, keeping me rooted in place.

Nervous energy flows through me, adrenaline causing me to shake at the thought of being trapped.

"Y-you can't k-keep me here." I argue weakly.

"You don't have anyone to look after you, you're staying here before you get yourself hurt." He sets a plate of food in front of me, "And you need food. Eat."

I look to the others but they're all seemingly on his side holding me hostage.

Twisting my fingers harshly I try again, "You're not the b-boss of me here. I c-can leave if I w-want to." Something cold and wet roughly nudges my hands, glancing down I see Zeus nudging my hands with his nose. He continues to poke at me until I release my fingers.

Looking back to Maverick I see him staring thoughtfully at my lap before meeting my eyes with a bored expression, "I am your boss, so we'll call this protecting my assets. You're staying." He starts digging into his food and the others follow his lead, devouring their shares of the food laid out on the table.

There's a weird variety of food before us, everything consisting of a weird texture and nothing that I eat. I sit quietly, petting Zeus as they all eat.

Maverick looks up, noticing that I haven't touched any of the food.

"Charlotte, eat something." he doesn't ask, he only demands.

"I'm n-not hungry." I take a moment to be proud of controlling my stutter but I'm really not hungry. Even if I was, I wouldn't be able to eat anything on the table. It's why I don't like to eat around people, texture is a huge thing with food for me. Something can taste great but if it has the wrong texture then it will make me sick. It used to infuriate my parents; they'd force me to eat whatever was served for dinner and I'd just throw it up. Finally, one day they just gave up, we stopped eating dinner together and I made whatever I could tolerate. That just happened to be a variety of instant noodles, chicken nuggets, pizza, and a few select items.

"You haven't eaten in a day; you have to be hungry." Maverick counters.

Cooper chimes in, a much calmer approach than his brother, "Charlotte, just try to eat something. You're shaking and I don't think it's from being cold."

I clench my hands in my lap, trying to push aside my feelings of frustration at all of them. I remind myself that they care, and I'm not used to that, that's what makes me feel uncomfortable and that's why I feel angry when they keep pestering me.

Taking a few breaths to calm myself I look at the food again.

"If I eat c-can I go home?" I ask, no one in particular but I know Maverick will be the one to answer.

Just as I guessed, all the guys look to Maverick who shrugs, "Sure."

I ignore the guys gawking at him and pick up the fork next to my plate. Scooping up some of the macaroni, the only thing I think I can handle I take a bite. It doesn't taste bad, but it's slimy and gooey, it takes everything in me to swallow it. I don't look at any of them as I choke a few bites down, having plenty of practice as a child at just getting it over with.

Before I can swallow the last bite though, I feel the churning sensation in my stomach. Saliva fills my mouth, and I can't stomach the food any longer. I look up frantically, finding Eli's stare across the table.

"Bathroom?" I choke out, already standing from my seat.

He rushes to tell me, trying to get out of his seat to lead me there but I don't wait. Bolting around the corner, I barely make it before I drop down to my knees, throwing up all seven bites I took along with the water Maverick made me drink earlier.

I continue to dry heave over the toilet until there was nothing left, then I finally fall back onto my butt, the wall behind me the only thing keeping me up.

I let my eyes fall shut and try to breathe through my raw and burning throat, hurting worse than it did before. I hear some shuffling, letting me know someone is in the room with me but I don't open my eyes to see who.

It was only when I felt a damp cloth being placed on my forehead that I startled out of my dozing state, finding Cooper sitting on the floor next to me.

"Hey, you okay?" He asks, grinning kindly.

Closing my eyes against my embarrassment, savoring the feeling of the cloth on my flushed skin, I answer him.

"You all are asking me that a lot today," my voice is raspy and just over a whisper, but his chuckle lets me know he heard it.

"We just want to look after you, I know you might not be used to it, but we care about you." His voice is calm.

Cracking one of my eyes open I study him for a moment as he stares back.

"Why do you assume I'm not used to it?" I venture to ask, wondering if my shitty childhood is that easy to recognize.

He breaks my stare to focus on running the cold cloth over my face, clearing it of any sweat from throwing up.

"Well, for one you suck at letting any of us take care of you." He tells me bluntly, but he smiles as he says it so I think he's joking. "But you don't talk about your family, and you didn't go home for the holidays. I just kind of figured that you aren't close to them and maybe haven't been for a long time."

The mention of my family makes my stomach tighten, apparently it is obvious to them that I had a crappy home life. But I also remember telling Cooper about how my parents forced me to see someone about 'being different' so I suppose it's not a stretch to connect the dots.

"I'm g-grateful," I tell him slowly, not wanting to offend him or his brothers after all they've done for me. "But I c-can take care o-of myself.".

"We know that." He tosses the cloth into the sink, setting a hand on my knee stretched out in front of me. "But we do care about you, and one way that's easy to show that is by taking care of you when we can. Wouldn't it be nice to not have to take care of everything on your own?" he asks gently.

I think about it for a minute, not having to take care of myself sounds great in theory. But from my experience, being taken care of just leaves something for others to hold over your head later down the line. I've already had my parents throw being a burden back in my face more times than I can count, I don't think I could take someone else doing it.

"It's n-not taking care of me. I'm just b-being a b-burden to you guys." I admit my fear softly, hoping he doesn't hear me.

He leans forward, locking his eyes with mine, "You're not a burden, Charlotte. And we wouldn't offer to do any of the things we have or take it upon ourselves to do anything if we thought that." Conviction fills his words, so much that I'm almost inclined to believe him. But Maverick's irritation this afternoon about taking care of me flashes in my mind, pushing Cooper's words to the side.

"Maverick seems fairly decided that I'm just an asset to be looked after, that sounds like a burden to me."

"Maverick is complicated, I'll give you that," he huffs, leaning back to rest against the cabinets behind him. "But I can promise you that he doesn't do anything for anyone that he doesn't want to. And he definitely wouldn't go out of his way to take care of someone with a simple fever if he didn't care for them."

Cooper makes everything sound so simple. They care for me. They want to take care of me. I should just accept it with open arms. Everyone will be happy.

Sounds great, but reality is a bitch, and it doesn't work the way he's laying it out. What would I do if I let the guy's care for me and then they decided that I was too much to handle? Too weird, too different? How would I fight through the disappointment of that?

"I'm not saying you're going to instantly become okay with us looking out for you or doing things for you." Cooper interrupts my thoughts, "I'm just saying, try to take a chance and let us do some things for you. It lets us show you that we care for you and it makes us feel good."

Chewing my lip, I consider it. Giving him a small nod to let him know I'll think about it a huge grin spreads across his face, lighting up his mood.

"Good." He stands, helping me up as well before giving me a serious look, "So no more hacking into my bank account to pay stuff back."

I giggle at the reminder, and he can't keep a straight face, losing his fake seriousness.

"Come on babe, let's go back out there before the twins send out a search party for you."

I try to tame the butterflies in my stomach at him calling me 'babe' as he leads me back to the kitchen. The other three are still sitting at the table waiting.

Settling back in my chair I try to give the guys a smile to let them know I'm okay, but Kai and Eli just look concerned and Maverick stares at his plate, still picking through his food.

Looking at the table for a distraction I notice that one of the dishes is missing from the spread.

"What happened to the macaroni?" I ask, my voice still raspy and Cooper passes me a glass of water to soothe some of the irritation.

"Threw it out." Maverick says, not looking up from his food.

He threw out a full pan of food?

"Why?" I ask, utterly confused.

No one answers me and I look around at all of them as they look at me as though the answer should be clear.

"Because it made you sick." Kai finally tells me, biting back a smile and shooting a look at Maverick that I can't decipher.

Maverick threw out an entire dish just because he thinks it made me sick? Is this what Cooper was saying about him showing he cares? Great, now I feel awful for making him think that.

"T-that's not what made me sick. I mean it is but n-not because the food is bad. It's a texture thing. I h-have a hard time with textures. I thought that macaroni would b-be okay because I've had it b-before but I was wrong. You s-shouldn't have thrown it away. I'm s-sorry." I've gone from actual vomit straight to word vomit, all the guys just stare at me blankly.

"Good to know." Eli finally says, putting me out of my awkward misery.

"Why did you eat it if you knew it was going to make you sick?" Maverick asks suddenly, his wide-eyed stare locked on me.

I'm confused by his question; he told me to eat. I was just doing what he said.

"Y-you said to eat something."

His jaw clenches and he lets out a breath, looking ready to yell at any moment.

"Next time, just call me a dick again and tell me." He says, clearly holding his frustration back.

I offer a small nod before catching on to one smaller detail,

"Again?"

"Yeah, you told me I was a dick at least twice today," he snorts, gathering his plate and taking it to the sink to rinse.

The rest of the guys burst into laughter at that.

"Oh man, I would pay to see that!" Kai hits his fist on the table in between his laughs.

I just hold my hands to my cheeks, trying to cover my blush at the thought of telling Maverick that.

"Charlotte, can I make you something else to eat?" Maverick asks from the sink, sounding kinder than I've heard him before.

"No, thank you." He doesn't look happy with my answer but doesn't push me on it this time.

I sit with the guys as they finish eating, offering to clean up when they're done but they all brush me off. I end up sitting on the couch with Zeus's head in my lap, savoring all the pets I'm giving.

One by one the guys all trickle in to settle in different spots around the room. Eli and Kai sit on either side of me on the longer couch, Cooper stretches out on the shorter sofa while Maverick takes one of the oversized chairs in between.

They all ask me what I want to watch but I tell them to choose, they settle on a football game at my insistence that I'm fine with that. I have the urge to ask one of them to take me home, but I don't have the energy to move and having gone toe to toe with Maverick already I don't have the energy to argue when he inevitably tells me no. Settling between Kai and Eli I try to soak in their warmth, letting it chase away my chills.

At some point I must drift off because the next thing I know I feel myself being lifted. Opening my eyes the room is covered in darkness now, the TV no longer lighting up the space. Looking up I see Maverick is the one carrying me, looking around I don't see any of the others.

"Where are we going?" I ask, fighting to keep my eyes open.

"Bed." he answers simply, offering nothing else.

I pull against his hold, trying to get down. "I can sleep on the couch, let me go."

"No, just go back to sleep."

I'm prepared to fight him, but I don't want him to drop me on the stairs, so I'll wait until he puts me down to come back to the couch. If I'm staying here then I will not be taking over anyone's bed.

I quickly lose the battle with my eyelids though, just before I feel him lay me down on to a soft mattress that completely envelops me, wrapping me in comfort all around.

I try to remember what I was going to tell him, muttering nonsense as I feel him pull my glasses from my face and tuck a soft comforter over me.

Sleep continues to pull me under as I settle into the softness around me, I know I won't be able to sleep much without my weighted blanket, but my body is past the point of caring it seems and I fall deeper and deeper into the darkness.

Just before I fall completely under I feel a shift behind me and a heavy weight settle across my waist. Maverick's soft command is the last thing I hear as I drift off,

"Sleep."

17

~ *Charlotte* ~

The rest of the weekend has been fairly uneventful. After falling asleep with Maverick, I'd woken up alone, wondering if I'd imagined it, but his side of the bed was still warm and I'd been left confused and alone to dwell on it all.

I thought about how since I'd met Kai and Eli I've been trying to deny to myself that I was attracted to them. Now, the more time I spent with Maverick and Cooper I'm having a hard time trying to push down the attraction I felt for both of them as well. As much as Maverick pissed me off and pushed me, or how much they all smothered me now and then, that couldn't dissolve the warmth they all made me feel and the butterflies that seemed to live in my stomach when they were around.

The thought of it is equal parts amusing and terrifying. I've never felt an attraction to anyone, yet now here I am attracted to four men at once. Cooper said they all cared for me, and Kai and Eli all but said they had feelings for me. But how would I know how they felt unless they told me. And if they did have feelings for me then would I just choose one? Wouldn't that hurt one of them, or both of them? How would that even work? How could I cope with that, knowing that I hurt any of them.

Eli found me in Maverick's room drowning in my thoughts and dragged me down for breakfast with everyone which was fairly relaxed and conveniently missing any scrambled eggs, courtesy of Maverick I'm sure after I'd expressed my dislike for them.

Once Cooper had mentioned the little things that they do because they care the night before, it was like my brain was zeroing in on every little thing and was taking note of each of the things that they did for me that weekend.

I ended up staying with them the whole weekend, Maverick not deeming me well enough to go home even though I'd insisted I was fine. But he didn't budge, and I relented, deciding to take Cooper's advice and *try* to let them take care of me.

I'd spent Friday napping on the couch with Zeus over my lap, each time I'd woken up one of the guys was there with me. It was different each time, like they were taking turns. That night we all ended up in the living room together, with a spread of pizza watching some show about an office. The guys seemed to love it, laughing at all the jokes. I didn't really get it but was content to sit tucked between Kai and Maverick with Zeus at my feet.

By Saturday I felt a lot better, but with Maverick still deemed me not able to leave until I was fever free for twenty-four hours, I'd spent the day playing videogames with Kai while Eli watched on. We'd offered to teach him to play but he said he was just happy to watch us and see our teamwork play out.

Then today, Cooper taught me how to make pancakes, after we spent a couple hours baking cookies and brownies that I left with the guys when I'd finally been released from Maverick's house arrest after dinner.

Eli and Kai offered to drive me back when I decided that I wanted to go back to my dorm. The three of us ride in a comfortable silence back to campus in Kai's truck. I sit next to Kai with Eli in the back as we listen to some today's hits playlist filter through the speakers.

When we arrive, I ask them both if they want to come in and stay, before I can talk myself out of it.

I have the itch under my skin to take it back and enjoy the silence and solitude my room could offer me, but I'm actively trying to ignore it. Pushing the feelings down into a vaulted box to be forgotten. I don't want to push the guys away, don't want to hurt their feelings. After this weekend with all of them, I want to work out the feelings I have for each of them, and I'm not going to do that by avoiding them.

I was tired of being weird, and different. I want to feel normal. I want to let myself explore these feelings rather than force them down for once.

I try to remind myself that as I stand awkwardly at the counter while the two of them make themselves comfortable, settling on the couch and kicking off their shoes, tossing their jackets onto the floor. The items look so out of place. They don't belong there.

Shaking myself, I try to ignore it, if I start organizing their stuff they're really going to think that I'm insane. But I would feel so much better if I just moved it. It wasn't that weird to like things tidy all the time, was it? It clearly didn't belong there, I don't understand how each of them can see their stuff just sitting there in the middle of the floor and feel nothing. I envy that carelessness towards such unimportant things that I clearly lack, like kicking shoes off in the middle of the floor.

"Lottie?" I look up to see them both looking at me with confused, slightly concerned eyes and realized that now I'd made myself look weird by just standing here doing nothing.

"You want to come sit? I can sit on the floor if you want some space." Eli offered kindly, but I'm still distracted by the mess.

Sighing I march over and quickly gather their shoes and jackets. Not acknowledging either of them, I try to quickly go about lining the shoes by the door and hanging the jackets on the back of my desk chair while quickly putting my own shoes away.

A quick glance around the room shows nothing else out of place, so I drop into the space between them on the couch, refusing to look at either of them.

Rather than point out my quirks though, they both just settle in as Kai scrolls through the TV for something to watch.

A small knot of tension in my chest seems to loosen as I realize they aren't going to comment on my need to have everything in order. They both seem perfectly fine with my need to go and move their stuff, not a hint of judgement to be found.

Even as I feel relieved, that doesn't stop my mind from wandering, recalling how my parents used to yell at me over things like that. They'd get in my face and scream while throwing anything within arm's reach around the house at random, knowing that it would only upset me further.

Kai settles on some quirky sitcom, knowing that I won't care what's playing on the screen. As we watch the show, both of them shift on either side of me, moving closer and touching me lightly, almost as if they're both trying to test me and see if I'll shy away from them or not. It almost seems to become a game between the two of them as I remain still and pretend that I don't notice them taking turns getting closer to me and moving their hands once they make contact with any part of me.

Eli appears to win their little game, at least that's how it seems to me from the smirk on his face and the pout on

Kai's as Eli's arm settles lightly over my shoulders, tucking me into his side.

I bite my lip to stifle a groan when his hand slips to the base of my neck and starts to gently knead my tense muscles, almost instantly I feel a rush of relief as the tension is slowly forced from my muscles.

Kai though, doesn't hold back and lets out a low groan next to us. Looking over, his eyes are hooded and half closed as he watches us. His hand rests lightly on my thigh while the other runs through his hair, fisting it and causing it to stand wild out at different angles.

"You can't bite your lip like that. I'm already dying to put my lips on yours, but that just makes me want to do so much more." He tells me, his eyes zeroed in on my lip as I quickly release it.

Wait, he wants to kiss me? I've never kissed anyone, never really understood the appeal of smashing your face against someone else's. I am intrigued to know what other things he could be thinking about though.

I'm sure it was just a figure of speech; he wouldn't actually want to kiss me let alone do anything else with me. Not to mention, his brother is currently sitting with his arm around me.

Kai sits up so suddenly it causes me to jump in my seat, he angles so he's facing me. Both his hands rest on my thighs, gently squeezing to keep my attention while sending shivers through me.

"Please say I can kiss you, Lottie Girl?" He half asks and half pleads, but doesn't demand, leaving the choice completely in my hands.

I'm torn, wanting to say yes, to experience something new. I've come to trust all of the Locke boys, so I really can't think of anyone better to try with, but the weight of Eli's arm on my shoulder reminds me why kissing Kai is a bad idea. Why would he want to kiss me in front of his brother? Was that some male territorial stuff like I'd read about in books before?

Either way, I didn't want to hurt Eli by kissing Kai in front of him. I think I have feelings for both of them...possibly both of their older brothers as well, which I know is wrong and I should not have feelings for four men at once, but since I clearly do then I shouldn't announce that, it'd make things weird between us.

If I haven't told any of them that I have feelings then was it wrong to kiss Kai?

What were the rules here? I need a guide to how to navigate this because all of the dark romance books that I've read have given me nothing to reference since none of my guys are stalkers, criminals, or demons.

Shit, *the* guys. Not *my* guys, they're not mine. They're just the guys.

Kai squeezes my thigh again, bringing me back to the present. I realize he's still waiting for an answer.

"W-what about E-Eli?" It seems my brain has completely forgotten about the need to know why he wanted to kiss me in the first place and instead just wants to focus on the logistics of kissing with his brother in the room instead.

Eli's chest bounces, shaking me as he laughs on my other side.

"Oh, I'd love to kiss you too. But I won't force you into anything" His voice is low and gravely, sounding much like he did at the club a couple weeks ago.

Kai's expression remains hopeful as I continue to try and filter through the questions rattling my brain.

"But you guys - Why would- I don't get it." I stumble through the words, not even knowing what to ask. This is weird, right? Not all brothers go around kissing the same girl in front of each other. Or did they? Do I need to get out more?

Kai must see my inner turmoil and he takes pity on me,

"I promise you; Eli won't have any problems with seeing us kiss. He would probably fucking love it to be honest," he explains, "We don't date a lot but in the past, Eli and I have been happier when we've shared."

"Share what?" it's a relief to know that I wouldn't be hurting Eli's feelings, but I'm more confused now than before this conversation started.

"Girls, Charlie." Eli chuckles lightly as he answers me this time.

Girls? They share girls? How does that even work? I've never heard of such a thing. I've only ever overheard conversations from classmates who freaked out if their significant other even looked at another person for too long in passing but now they're telling me that they share girls. Don't they get jealous?

"H-how does that w-work?"

"Pretty good usually, we've never gotten any complaints." Kai winks as a grin tugs at his lips.

"What about Cooper and Maverick?" I can't help but ask, though I'm not sure why when I had just resolved in my head minutes ago that I wasn't going to mention my feelings that were building for all four brothers.

"What about them?" Eli asks, sounding curious.

"Do they share too?"

"They have before," Kai thinks about it for a moment, probably trying to recall, "But neither of them have dated in quite a while. And we haven't ever shared with them before."

Before I can dwell too much on why I asked that or Kai's response he speaks again.

"We can explain all the logistics to you at some point if you're ever curious, but for right now I really want to kiss you. Will you let me?" he asks patiently, but I can see the eagerness bubbling just under the surface.

I think it over; I want to try it…but what if I suck at it? Or what if I hate it?

I just don't want to do the wrong thing and offend him, either of them really.

"I've never…" I try to explain to them that I haven't done any of this before, but the words are stuck in my throat. The blaring message in my brain reminds me that I'm different. Different than any other 22-year-old away at college. I haven't ever kissed a guy, and I had a strong suspicion that most people in college weren't virgins. It was just another thing to add to the list of things that made me weird.

Realization dawns on Kai's face but he doesn't pull away, instead he leans in closer. Slowly, raising a hand to cup my cheek as he looks at me, waiting.

He isn't pushing me away in annoyance at my lack of experience, he isn't belittling me for not having done this before. Instead, he's leaning closer, waiting to give me this new experience, to let me try something new.

That acceptance that I feel from him is the reason that I take a chance, nodding slightly.

That's all it takes for him to close the distance between us, his lips soft and warm against mine, my eyes falling shut on instinct. For a split second I worry about what I need to do or how to move with him as his head angles to the side, but that washes away as a wave of something sweet and dizzying washes over me. I can feel my heart hammering against my ribs as he continues the sweet torture, I both love it and dread when it will end all in the same breath. But for once my racing pulse isn't from anxiety, it's from excitement and satisfaction.

Slowly though, it comes to and end, my eyes open as Kai pulls back before leaning in to kiss me quickly once more, looking me over and studying my face closely. He's checking to see if I'm going to freak out. I'm not though, I was surprisingly calm, no worrying thoughts forcing me into a spiral of panic as it normally would.

Inside my head felt different, I look around the room half expecting it to look different as well. But it didn't, it was just the usual noise in my head was muted, still there but like someone turned the volume down several notches.

I was calm.

Eli wastes no time once Kai pulls away, turning me to face him before leaning in for a kiss of his own.

Though they were identical, the way they kissed was anything but. Kai was soft and sweet, taking things slow with me whereas Eli's kiss was firm and frantic, like he was trying to devour me.

I don't think about what to do as I just follow his movements, I can feel myself leaning back as Eli pushes forward but rather than the couch, I feel Kai's chest pressing into my back as his hands grasp my waist tightly, sending more of those little shivers rolling through me.

Eli pulls away, grabbing my bottom lip between his teeth as he retreats. I can't hold back the moan as he does it.

My eyes widen in shock at the sound, not having expected it. But Eli just shoots me a smirk as I feel Kai's hands tighten even further.

Then as if nothing had happened, they both settle back in their respective spots on the couch and resume watching the show still playing on the T.V.

They each hold one of my hands, slowly brushing their thumbs over the backs of my hands and acting unaffected. But I catch the smile on Kai's face, looking like a kid on Christmas morning, even Eli looked satisfied.

Maybe part of me should be worried about the fact that they weren't talking about what just happened, but a much larger part of me was just thrilled at the feelings that it gave me. And the satisfaction at feeling normal, between my first kiss and the calm that enveloped me.

I still had a lot of questions, and a lot that I would dwell on later, of that I'm certain, but for right now I am perfectly content to sit and soak in the silence, even with the two of them sharing my space with me.

The rest could wait.

18

~ *Charlotte* ~

A week went by, and I still found myself thinking about the kiss that I shared with Kai and Eli. I tried to forget about it since neither of them had mentioned it, but my mind continued to take me back there.

I have to admit, it was nice to have flashbacks to something other than my parents' cruel words and my shitty childhood.

But right now, I was at work, so it was proving to be a problem. I have things that I need to do that don't involve thinking about the guy's lips, or the feelings that shot through me from Kai gripping my waist.

I had finally made some progress on tracking Timothy, and my work had led to me finding out that other than regularly hanging out in front of Myth he had been meeting with some guys in a rundown bar on the north side that were known to be affiliated with the Vipers, a well-known gang that ran half the city.

That information had been enough for Maverick to want to question Timothy, so through some strings that he had with his buddies at the police department he was out getting a warrant for suspected gang activity that would allow him to bring him in for questioning to try and figure out what was going on.

Kai and Eli were out on another short trip to Atlanta to snoop around the bar where Ivy Gilbert went missing, the case they were working when we'd first officially met. I had now become privy to the details of that case, and Maverick was having me continue to work with the software that I'd given Eli to try and comb through the security footage from that night to try and get something to work off of.

Much like tracking Timothy's movements, trying to find something from the night Ivy went missing was proving to be a very tedious task. It seemed every time I thought I had an image to work with it got corrupted somehow before the profile could ever fully generate or the software could clarify it for me. I have no clue why it was happening, the software worked great, but it was like someone was literally snatching the images away from me anytime I was able to pull one from the security footage.

It was frustrating, to say the least.

Ivy's case was obviously our top priority but with the trouble I was having with it, I needed to take a break and work on something else before I smashed my computer. So, I found myself looking into the gang that Timothy had seemingly been reporting to, trying to find any motivation for them targeting Eli's car specifically at Myth.

Their gang wasn't the largest by any means, but they did have deep rooted ties to other, more powerful gangs around the country from what I could tell. They seemed to deal a lot in drugs and had their normal routines that they followed, which is how I was able to track Timothy there with some work. None of it was adding up, it didn't make sense why they would send a high school kid to slash some tires when they were more than capable of doing it themselves, and I couldn't figure out the motive behind it no matter where I looked.

Looking down at the time, I realize that I missed lunch by about an hour, so I push away from the desk, taking the excuse to get up and step away for a bit to reset.

A glance at the overcast weather outside made me decide to forgo lunch for a run instead. It would give me a chance to clear my head of all the dead ends I'd been hitting today, and I haven't been on a real run in a while and my muscles were aching to feel the usual pull and burn from exerting myself.

I stop by Cooper's office to let him know what I'm doing so he won't freak out later if he can't find me, then I sneak past Sasha at the front desk as she stares at herself in her phone's camera. I'm still not convinced she actually works while she's here but it's not my place to say so I keep my mouth shut. I just try to avoid any interactions with her because she always seems to go out of her way to be rude to me.

The overcast weather is perfect as I run along the river walk, the water a dark grey, as violent, choppy waves splash against each other creating an eerie sight. But the wind that comes off the river is perfect for keeping me cool in my leggings and oversized shirt without having the sun beat down on me like most other days.

My phone starts ringing through my ear buds about halfway through my run. I stop off to the side of the river walk, catching my breath and taking in the view as I answer it without a second thought.

"Hello?" I pant out a greeting, still trying to steady my breathing.

"Charlotte, what on Earth are you doing? That is no way to answer the phone, you sound like a dying animal." My mother's sharp critique blasts through my ear buds, the disgust clear in her tone.

If I were smart then I would've checked the caller ID, because if I had then I would've sent my mother to voicemail. She hardly ever calls me, and at this point I almost prefer it that way. She only ever calls when she wants to demand me to do something for her, or when she was in one of her particularly bad moods and wanted someone to blame for her lack of success in whatever endeavor she was currently trying out.

"S-sorry, I was o-out for a r-run." I force my breathing to slow down, so as not to be heard through the phone but I could do nothing for the stutter that choked me. It always came out when talking to my parents, and it was one of their favorite jabs to throw at me when they wanted to hurt me.

"Oh, good. Wouldn't want you to be gaining weight while you're away at your little school, I know you're incapable of making proper meals for yourself."

I stay silent, the best way to act when she started to throw digs at me was to just shut up and take it. The sooner she got them out, the sooner the call would be over.

"Well anyway, I was calling to tell you that you will be needed to attend the party that we're throwing on New Year's Day. So, you'll need to find a way to get home. You'll also need to book a place to stay for the night since your room is no longer available."

Yes, my room. Well, no longer my room as my parents waited exactly one week after I left for college before they turned it into a storage space for their extravagant holiday decorations and extra closet space for my mother.

"What p-party?" I ask simply, as far as I knew they usually only threw parties on Christmas Eve. On New Year's Day they usually got drunk or went to a friend's house, more often than not they did both.

My mother sighs like the thought of having to explain anything to me is some specified form of torture.

"The party that we're throwing to announce your father's campaign to run for mayor," her voice is clipped, "You are expected to be there so we can promote his family image. I will have your dress picked out for you and it will be sent to your dorm, do try your best to look presentable."

As if I would intentionally try to look like crap?

"Yes, Mother." I agree quietly, "Just send me the details, p-please."

Having said what she needs she ends the call quickly, there is no casual conversation, no asking me how school is going, no sharing with her that I got a job. We didn't talk about that stuff, she only talked at me, and never more than necessary. I was used to her ways at this point.

Now that the calm from my run had been snatched away by my mother I turned back to loop towards the office, deciding to jump back into work to avoid thinking about having to sit through one of my parents' parties.

Entering the office its obvious luck isn't on my side today as Sasha immediately notices my presence.

"Why do you think you have free reign to leave the office whenever you want?" She sneers from her perch behind the desk. "I'm sure Maverick would love to know how you abuse your work time while he's away." The threat lingers between the two of us as I try to ignore her and head back to my office, but she's doesn't seem happy to not get a reaction out of me.

"Hey, freak! I'm talking to you" She stands now, "I could get you fired, you know. I practically run this place, and the guys will listen to anything I say, so if I tell them that you suck at your job then they'll be happy to throw you out on your ass."

Freezing at the entrance to the hall I turn to face her, taking in her evil smirk and typical barely there outfit. She seems very satisfied at the thought of getting me fired.

"I told C-Cooper that I was g-going out. Not that it's your b-business but it w-was my lunch break." Aside from my normal stutter I manage to keep my voice fairly even while responding to her ridiculous threats.

"Sure, but you know that they're looking for any excuse to get rid of you. So watch yourself, because I have no problem getting rid of you. What do you even do here? I can't for the life of me figure out why they would hire a freak like you, they must really feel sorry for you." She laughs, but there's no humor to it. "I mean that has to be it, because I know you're not sleeping with any of them. No one wants to sleep with the slow girl, especially when they already have me."

I don't expect her words to hit me as hard as they do. Have the guys really slept with her? Do they really like her? I just had a really good weekend with all of them, and that night with Kai and Eli. They really convinced me that they cared about me, but was it all just superficial? Did they only care about me as a friend?

"Hey, Charlotte can you come in here for a minute?" Cooper's voice startles me from his office door just inside the hallway where he stands halfway out the door.

Taking the excuse to get away from Sasha and her smug smile I quickly shuffle into his office and sit while he closes the door behind him.

Taking a seat behind his desk he studies me for a moment, making me feel uncomfortable at what he's trying to see. He's looking at me like I'm a complicated math problem that he's trying to solve, trying to get a read on my emotions. But I keep everything I'm feeling locked down tight, so he won't catch a glimpse of the inexplicable hurt that I'm feeling.

"What were you and Sasha talking about?" he asks casually.

"Just a-about my run, and when the g-guys will be b-back." I lie easily. Being around the guys more has given me a lot of new perspectives and goals, one of those being that I want to stand up for myself. I might not be quite there yet, but running to Cooper anytime Sasha is rude to me isn't going to help me reach that goal. I would figure this out myself, especially if any of what she just said is true, he wouldn't take my side anyways.

Cooper's eyes narrow, making me think that he may have heard part of the conversation and is just waiting for me to say something so he can address it. After studying me for a few moments he tries a different approach,

"Everything okay? You look a little upset."

"I'm fine." I assure him before remembering my mother's phone call. "I will n-need to go home on New Years though."

"I thought you didn't go home for the holidays?" He starts clicking on his computer and a glance shows me the schedule that he keeps for the guys and myself.

"I don't. My parents are having a party, and I have to be there." I explain, "My father is running for mayor."

Suprise flickers on his face, "Oh, how long will you need off?" He asks as he starts typing.

"Just two days. T-they live in Atlanta, I'll c-come back the next m-morning."

"I didn't know you were from Georgia." He stops, trying to look at me. I just nod, not having anything to say about the town I grew up in seeing as it doesn't hold a lot of happy memories for me. "Well you can take off more time if you want to stay with your family for a few days since you're going up there."

"N-no." I quickly refuse that idea. "I'll just stay the n-night."

He goes back to typing, "Okay, I put it on the calendar so you're good to go. How are you getting up there? Do you even drive?"

More questions I wish he wouldn't ask, only because I know him and his brothers aren't going to like the answer, with their overprotective tendencies that have come out over the last few weeks.

"I usually take the b-bus." He stops typing abruptly and I avoid his gaze this time, opting to study the wood grains in the desk. But I can feel his eyes burning a hold into my face as he mulls over my response.

"Charlotte -"

"The bus is good. It's comfortable, affordable and I take my laptop with me so the eight hours really flies by." I quickly interject, "And it's t-totally s-safe." That last one may be a stretch, last time I took the bus home someone tried to steal my bag when I had dozed off in the last few hours of the ride. Not to mention the questionable passengers that were along for the ride as well, but Cooper didn't need to know that.

Cooper sighs heavily, looking up like he's begging the heavens for the patience to deal with me.

"You know we would have no issues driving you up there." He points out. And I know they would do it, but I would never ask and I really don't want to drag any of the guys back home with me to deal with my parents because as much as they aren't involved in my life, bringing a guy home would stir up way too many questions and way too many insults at my expense. I just couldn't deal with all of that on top of going back home to my own version of hell.

Another thought strikes me, when did I get used to the idea that the guys would do whatever I needed if I just asked? I mean they do things without me asking, but when did that stop freaking me out?

"Will you at least consider letting one of us drive you up there?" Cooper asks when I don't respond.

"Mhmm." Another lie. I won't consider it but for his sake and for ending this conversation I will try to appease him.

"Okay." He continues to tap away at his computer, and I take that as my sign to leave, but just before I get to the door he stops me again. "Maverick texted to let me know that he got the warrant for Timothy, and he was on his way back here with him to do some questioning, you can sit and observe if you want."

The thought of the interrogation room across the hall makes my blood turn to ice, the feeling of being trapped in that room hitting me full force. I fight to keep myself calm and not let the thoughts of it overtake me.

"No, thank you." I tell him before darting from the room before giving him the chance to say anything else.

I will look into whatever is needed for the case, but as far as Timothy and questioning goes, Maverick can just give me the cliff notes.

Getting back into my office I settle in to continue working, texting with Kai and Eli for a while as Eli lets me know how things are going while Kai just complains about motel showers and crappy fast food.

Hours pass with me making no progress of any of the information I try to pull from the footage and my frustration grows with each failed attempt. I blindly reach for one of the notebooks on my desk and chuck it towards the door just as it opens. The book hits the door just as Maverick comes into view.

He steps halfway in, looking behind the door to see what I threw, giving the book an unimpressed look before looking at me with raised brows.

"S-sorry." Embarrassment crashes over me at him walking in on my mini meltdown and I look anywhere but at him as he comes to sit in one of the chairs before me, sitting something on the desk.

A steaming hot bowl of my favorite noodles sits before me and one sits before Maverick as well. When I don't make any moves to take it he nudges it forward and nods, indicating that I should take it.

I pull the bowl closer, and the smell immediately overwhelms me, I start devouring the noodles, inhaling them. I recall that I skipped lunch and haven't had anything to eat since dinner yesterday, which explains my hunger.

Maverick eats his with much less gusto than me, looking almost offended at the noodles as he stirs them around the bowl.

"You really eat this crap every day?" He asks suddenly.

I pause mid-bite, noodles hanging out of my mouth. How dare he insult the food of the Gods.

"This is the best thing ever invented." I say around my mouthful of food.

He snorts a laugh, grabbing another mouthful and looking thoughtful as he chews.

"This is literally sodium coated garbage. It's horrible for you."

Swallowing, I aim to give him one of his own unimpressed looks,

"Then don't eat it." I tell him simply; I wouldn't mind finishing off his bowl if he thinks it's so awful.

"So, why were you assaulting a notebook when I walked in?" He changes the subject.

I go back to stirring my noodles, picking through the bowl.

"Just frustrated." I mutter, my earlier embarrassment coming back to me.

He nods, understanding on his face.

"So, no luck with the footage?"

"I have images to pull from but it keeps getting corrupted." I huff. "No matter what I try I can't seem to figure it out."

We eat in silence for a few minutes, Maverick waiting until I finish my food before standing from his seat.

"Come on." He commands with no explanation.

"W-Where?"

He looks back from the doorway, impatiently. "Just come on."

I'm obviously not going to get an answer from him, and rather than sit and try to argue I get up to follow him. Shutting my office behind me I follow him down the hall to Cooper's office.

"Cooper, come on. We're going for a drive." He calls to Cooper before heading towards the front of the building.

Cooper comes out of his office only looking slightly confused but going along with Maverick's demand.

"W-where are we going?" I ask, following him out into the parking lot as he locks the doors behind us.

He shrugs. "With Mav, there's no telling. But it will be fine, let's just go see what he wants to get up to." He gestures for me to go ahead to Maverick's SUV.

Cooper opens the door for me but I feel weird sitting in the passenger seat and leaving him in the back, so I sidestep him and jump into the back seat. Cooper looks offended and I catch Maverick rolling his eyes and huffing a laugh in the rearview mirror.

We drive for a few minutes, only the soft music coming through the speakers to fill the silence before I finally ask again.

"Where are w-we going?"

"Rage room." Maverick answers simply.

Cooper though seems excited, cheering from the front seat.

"What is that?" I've never heard of a rage room, I don't even know what that could possibly entail.

"You'll see." Maverick says evasively, not putting me at ease any.

"You'll love it, it's going to be fun." Cooper tries to assure me, but I still feel anxious with the lack of information. I don't like not knowing anything about where we're going or what we're going to be doing.

I twist my fingers in my lap for the rest of the drive, looking out the window to watch the passing scenery. None of us talk, content to just ride in silence until Maverick finally pulls into a small strip mall that looks mostly abandoned. One shop in the whole strip looks open. A bright sign lights up the lot, "RAGE" in full, blood red letters and darkened windows that prevent anyone from seeing in.

They both get out of the car and having no other choice, I follow.

The lobby is pretty dingy when we walk in, the rubber floors are covered in dirt, looking like they haven't had a good sweep in years. The walls are covered in broken glass windows made up to look like art pieces as well as wire fencing and graffiti.

Maverick talks quietly with the guy sitting behind the counter, signing forms and paying for something as I stay rooted in place, taking everything in.

Cooper's excitement is evident as he bounces on the balls of his feet looking around the space.

"W-what is this p-place?" I ask him.

"This is the rage room, it's awesome." He smiles at me, brimming with eager energy, "We come here when we get too caught up in work and need a break. It's a great stress reliever."

Before I can ask any more about this 'stress relief' Maverick comes over and leads us into another room. He doesn't say much as he hands me a jumpsuit and helmet to put on, grabbing one of his own as Cooper does the same. The jump suit barely fits Maverick, looking ready to rip at the seams as he slides it over his muscular frame. He ignores my questions as he goes about, handing me a baseball bat and then weighing different crowbars before picking one out of the bunch, along with a golf club and sledgehammer. Cooper settles on a wooden baseball bat and a shovel? Then Maverick is leading us down a hallway to another room.

He holds the door to usher me in first and looking around I see we're in a room with cement walls on all four sides, red LED lights cast a glow over the whole room, just enough to see but not bright. The walls have tables lined in front of them with various breakable items, from dishes to vases, picture frames, mirrors and glass ornaments.

Scattered throughout the room are traffic cones, computers, TVs and even a washing machine?

Spinning around I look to both of them, still utterly confused at what we're doing here.

Cooper rushes around me though, going to set small glass jars on top of all of the traffic cones. I look to Maverick for some sort of explanation.

"Coop, here." he calls as he tosses a pair of safety glass to him before handing me a pair. "Put these on."

I do as he says before asking him again, "What are we doing?"

He pushes on the final pair before opening his arms to gesture at all the items around the room.

"We're raging. Pick something out and break it. You can use one of the tools we brought in here, or if you want you can throw it at that wall over there with the target on it," He explains.

He wants me to break all of this stuff? I don't understand why anyone would pay to come and break stuff. How is this a real thing?

"But, why?"

"Because the work that we do can tend to have us running in circles and it's exhausting and frustrating." He spins the crowbar in his hands. "We need a way to get the frustration out from time to time. Seeing you throw your notebook at me earlier let me know that you need to let some rage out."

"I w-wasn't throwing it a-at you." I protest.

"Cooper also said that you seemed upset after your run today. I'm not going to sit around and talk about your feelings, so this is the next best thing. Plus, you've been at the office non-stop for over a week now, you need to take a break now and then before you get burnt out or sick again." He adds before moving to pick out a mirror from the items table, taking it and throwing it forcefully against the wall.

I jump as I watch the mirror shatter into hundreds of tiny pieces and rain down to the floor. Cooper hoots in excitement, hitting a jar with a baseball bat and watching the shards fly.

I sit and watch them destroy a few items, both intrigued and startled at the violence. I don't really get the appeal, I know I throw my stuff when I'm frustrated but I don't see how destroying all of this pretty stuff would be stress relief.

They destroy a few more things before Cooper grabs some wine glasses and sets them up on the edge of a table before calling over to me.

"Charlotte, come on! Try these, they break easy. It's so much fun!" his child-like enthusiasm is too hard to ignore so I shuffle over slowly, trying not to step on the broken glass everywhere even though I have shoes on and stand before the glasses.

I contemplate the best way to break the glasses sitting there while Cooper and Maverick stand and watch, pausing their destruction to see what I'll do.

I tighten my grasp on the baseball bat in my hand, lifting it over my shoulder before swinging it sloppily at one of the glasses.

It shatters instantly on impact, tiny shards of glass flying through the air before dropping to the floor. A burst of excitement and adrenaline rush through me and I quickly swing at another and Cooper cheers me on.

As I move down the line I start to label the glasses with different things that frustrate me. One for the stupid footage files that keep getting corrupted, one for Sasha and everything she said to me today, one for my mother's phone call and so on.

With each glass, a weight lifts off my chest. I feel excited but strangely calm, like when I was kissing Kai and Eli. Then I smash another glass at the thoughts of the kiss popping into my head.

I keep moving around, grabbing small items and slamming them to the floor and throwing them at the wall. My happiness builds with each broken item, and all of my thoughts continue to get banished from my brain the more I break.

I forget about Maverick and Cooper in here with me as I take and destroy anything that my hands touch. I hear punk metal music pumping through speakers somewhere in the room but I'm too distracted to really focus on it.

Turning, I catch sight of the washing machine again. I look to the bat in my hands and back at the machine and only think for a split second before I bring it down hard on the top.

Shockwaves shoot up my arms at the contact, but a small dent forms on the lid and satisfaction fills me.

I start swinging without thought, hitting from every angle. I ignore any pain that I feel from the bat making contact with the metal and just focus on destroying the machine and with it, all of my negative thoughts.

All of the stressful situations and meltdowns from the last few months become a spot on the washer and I continue to beat on them. Sweat starts to coat me, making my hair stick to the back of my neck and I can feel the dark flush of my skin but I don't care.

Even as I start to feel exhausted from the exertion, I keep going. Not wanting to give up this freeing feeling of attacking my own emotions.

Who knew I would love a rage room?

19

~ *Cooper* ~

Who knew destruction could be so hot?

All of the blood in my body has rushed straight to my dick as I watch Charlotte completely annihilate a washing machine. Sweet, innocent Charlotte has some serious anger inside her, begging to come out and play.

Of course, Maverick would notice that and think of bringing her here, I'm not sure the idea would have ever crossed my mind. But as much as Maverick wants to act like Charlotte is just a nuisance or 'just an employee', he has a soft spot for her. I'm not sure if he's attracted to her in the way that the twins and I are, but him bringing her here tells me that he probably is.

Maverick doesn't do things for other people outside of family. Yes, he works cases for people and does all he can to help them and take care of what they need but he doesn't go out of his way to take care of people. But with

Charlotte now, he took a whole weekend to take care of her when she was sick and dropped his evening plans to help her get her frustrations out. He's not slick, I also caught sight of him taking her dinner earlier, because he noticed that she hadn't eaten.

He was definitely attracted to Charlotte, whether he admitted it or not. Knowing him, he'll deny it until his dying breath.

Even now, as I stand back to watch Charlotte go full she hulk on the washer Maverick stands next to me with the same awe-struck expression.

She really does make destruction look angelic. Granted, her cheeks are beet red, and her hair is a sweaty matted mess sticking to her neck and forehead, but still, she is stunning.

She seems to be getting exhausted so I'm about to pull her away from the destruction but Maverick beats me to it.

He gently grabs her from behind, avoiding the wild swing of the bat that she wields and immediately her shoulders drop, heaving from the exertion of destruction.

No one says anything for a moment, we all just stand there looking around while Charlotte catches her breath.

"Well spitfire, I think you killed it." I finally break the silence, "Didn't know you had that in you."

Maverick ignores me, turning her to face him as he looks her over,

269

"You alright? Feel any better?" He asks.

She breathes heavily for a moment, looking around at all the broken debris before turning to him with a blinding, albeit somewhat manic smile taking over her face.

"That was awesome!"

Maverick and I both let out a laugh of surprise and relief at her reaction, seems Charlotte gets a kick out of destruction. And fuck if that doesn't draw me to her even more.

Having destroyed nearly everything in the room in the 45 minutes we've been here Maverick decides to call it and leads Charlotte from the rage room.

Back in the car, she seems much more relaxed and content in the back seat than she did on the way over here.

"So did you have a good time?" I ask, though I know the answer. I just want to talk to her on the drive back.

"I did, thank you both for taking me there." She meets Mav's eyes in the mirror as she says it, making sure he knows that her appreciation is directed towards him.

"Sure." He at least makes some effort to acknowledge her and not ignore her, but she seems to take it as a win if her beaming smile is anything to go by.

It doesn't take long to drop her off at her dorm where Maverick tells her to avoid working for the rest of the night, even though we all know she won't. She's been nothing but determined to do a good job and show her worth since we hired her on. Always coming into the office on time, on days off, she stays late without complaint and if the office is closed then she works from her dorm.

We only have about 20 employees that work under us, none of which are usually in the office since they take care of the private security for events and personal details and things of that nature, but none of them show anywhere near the work ethic that Charlotte has in the last month or so.

It's really admirable, and just another one of the things that draws me to her. She is very soft-spoken and quiet, afraid to stand up for herself but in the last few weeks I've noticed that shifting slightly. She's becoming more upfront about her needs or her boundaries and she's kicking ass at work.

I don't know when my attraction for her took root, but all I know is that I can't deny the feelings I have stirring up inside for her. I know my brothers all feel the same way; I just have to wonder how she'd feel about that? We are all no stranger to sharing between one another, granted usually the twins share together and Maverick and I share together, we haven't all shared the same girl...but if we all have feelings for her would all of us be willing to try? Would *she* even be willing to try? I make a mental note to talk to the others about it soon before any of us make any type of move with her that could jeopardize the friendships and working relationships that we have with her.

Maverick is quiet on the drive back to the house, seeming to be lost in thought.

"So, that was fun." I break him from his trance, "What made you want to take Charlotte to your favorite hideaway?"

He just grunts in response and for a moment I don't think he's going to answer, but finally he grumbles out a response.

"She was clearly frustrated with her work, almost assaulted me with a notebook when I went into her office earlier."

I laugh at the thought of Charlotte being violent with Maverick,

"I would have loved to see that. Did she get at least hit you?"

"No." He glares at me before returning to look at the road, "She threw it across her office when I was coming in. The Gilbert case is proving to be as difficult as we were hoping it wouldn't be." The Gilbert case was going nowhere it seemed. Every time we thought we had something to grab onto that would lead us somewhere, it ended up being a dead end. We were unfortunately no closer to finding out what happened to Ivy than we were weeks ago. It was frustrating for sure, but I tended to get lost in a lot more of the administrative work for the other jobs that we completed as a company, so I definitely didn't feel the stress as much as Mav did.

"Did you find anything about Eli's car while talking to that Timothy kid that you brought in today" I think to ask after recalling Maverick's interrogation.

"Nothing that we didn't already know. Seems he's just some high school kid that was offered cash by the Vipers to slash the tires." Maverick seems more annoyed by that than the dead end on the Gilbert case.

So we solved the issue of who slashed the tires, though Charlotte found that out fairly quickly but that still left us with the why. Why did the Vipers have some type of grudge against us that they needed to vandalize Eli's car?

"You think it's anything to be concerned about that we have a gang targeting one of our cars?" I ask.

"Probably not. We've worked on a lot of jobs that have resulted in some of their guys getting time, so it's probably just an old grudge that they wanted to act out on." Maverick says, though he doesn't seem completely convinced. I decide to let it go for now, seeing as we haven't had any other concerning activity happening around us.

"What are your thoughts on Sasha?" I ask, catching him off guard from the looks of it, he does a double take, shooting me a confused glance before answering.

"She does her job and answers the phones. What more do I need to think of her?"

His reaction to hearing Sasha's name versus Charlotte's is night and day. He has absolutely no interest in Sasha other than her ability to work as our receptionist. It doesn't mean much, but for the matter of discussing his potential feelings for Charlotte later, it bodes well for me at the moment. But I do have other intentions for asking about her right now.

"I just think it may be time to look for a new receptionist, she's always on her phone and distracted when she's at work. And I have to remind her multiple times to get the smallest tasks done." I tiptoe around my real concerns, hoping he doesn't ask. But this is Mav, so of course he sees right through me.

"She's been that way since we hired her when she needed a job in college." He points out, "What's your real issue here?"

Sighing, I tell him my real concern.

"She seems to have not taken kindly to Charlotte being around. She's honestly been kind of a bitch to her. I walked into a situation with them and the twins the day she came to interview and didn't think much of it other than a misunderstanding but since then I've overheard a couple different interactions between them. None of them have been nice."

I definitely didn't mean to eavesdrop on any conversations that happen in the office, but with only four of us there and my office being right off the lobby it was hard not to. I had wanted to step in each time I overheard any of the encounters between the two of them, but I also didn't want to overstep and have Charlotte think that I was being too overbearing. Also, I just really wanted to see her stand up for herself, and she wasn't going to do that if I stepped in. But Sasha's comments were really uncalled for and she only had the intention to hurt Charlotte, and the closer that I got to her, the more I personally took offense to that.

"Has Charlotte come to you about any of this?" he asks.

Ah, I knew where this was going. And I wasn't going to like it.

"No, she hasn't." Even I can hear the petulance in my voice, knowing what his response will be.

"Then leave it alone, she's a grown woman and she can fight her own battles. We don't need to disrupt our office because of some catty drama."

There it is. I knew I wasn't going to like that.

We arrive back to the house, sitting down to enjoy a beer and talk about nonsense for a while before we go our separate ways. Maverick goes on a run with Zeus and feeds him dinner while I reheat some leftovers and settle in for the night. I'm not ashamed to admit that I definitely rubbed one out in the shower to the thought of Charlotte in the rage room completely destroying everything in her path. She was a hellcat under her anxiety and shyness, I want to figure out a way to bring that out of her more, and it will no doubt be my undoing if I can get her to show that side of her on a daily basis.

I wake up early the next morning to get in a workout in our gym before heading into the office. The twins arrive home as I'm whipping up some breakfast and settle at the island with matching cups of coffee and Maverick comes in to make his usual concoction with Zeus right at his heels.

We all make small talk, discussing the lack of leads that the twins were able to find in Atlanta, and what we having coming up in the next couple weeks. Finding a lull in the conversation, I decide to finally just address the nagging question in my mind.

"So, what do we all think of Charlotte?"

All of them look at me with varying confused expressions, stopping in the middle of whatever they were doing to stare motionless at me.

"What are you asking?" Eli bites out, breaking the silence.

Taking a breath, I ready myself for the impending meltdown from the twins and just bite the bullet.

"Well, I'm finding myself attracted to her and think that I may want to pursue something with her eventually, just wanted to know if we're all on the same page with that." I drop the bomb casually and wait for the explosion, which takes approximately 6 seconds.

"Oh hell no, not happening." Eli declares.

"Yeah, screw that! I've had dibs for like 4 years now!" Kai adds as Maverick stays silent, watching all of us.

"Oh I'm sorry, I wasn't asking permission. I just wanted to make it clear so there was no confusion." I tell both of them before looking to Kai, "And you can't call dibs on a person, she's not the last slice of pizza."

He crosses his arms, looking anything but pleased.

"No, she's not a slice of pizza, she's a really great person. A person that Eli and I have formed a really good connection with and have known for years might I add. You just met her."

"Okay, I assume you and Eli are going to try and pursue your usual type of relationship with her," I say shrugging, "Throw Mav and I into the mix."

Kai looks stunned and Eli drops his glasses to the counter to drag his hands over his face.

"Don't drag me into this, I'm not a part of this." Maverick states firmly.

"Yeah and while we're at it, how about we don't include you Coop. No offense, but three's a crowd." Kai is quick to build off Maverick's statement.

Narrowing my eyes, I shoot him a look.

"There's already three of you. And like I said, I'm not asking. Besides, it's Charlotte's choice." I point out before spinning to Maverick, "And don't act like you aren't attracted to her. Just admit you want to be a part of this if we all do pursue something with her."

He crosses his arms, not budging.

"I'm not a part of this. She's my employee and 10 years younger than me. I have no interest in a relationship with a *child*." He spits back.

"She's 22, that's hardly a child." Eli points out and Kai slaps him on the shoulder.

"Don't try and encourage this!" Eli rolls his eyes at Kai's outburst.

"I'm not. But Coop's right, it is her choice in the end. That's if she wants anything to do with any of us."

"Like I said, leave me out of it." Maverick interjects again, raising my irritation.

"Don't bullshit yourself. I've seen how you are with her; you have feelings beyond boss and employee," I argue, "And you took her to the rage room yesterday, that's your place and you hardly ever even take any of us there. You notice things about her, and you love to take care of her. And don't try to say anything about sharing because you and I have shared plenty of times." I add.

"You took Lottie to the rage room?" Kai asks, his frustrations seeming to have disappeared.

"She was frustrated," Mav answers curtly, looking back at me he adds, "And I don't need to justify myself, I'm not interested. End of story."

He stalks off to his office, leaving no room for any more arguments and leaving me with the twins in a silent standoff.

Eli is the one to break it,

"Why the sudden interest? And why Charlie, you can't go find your own girl?" He sounds tired, and I'm sure he is after the drive back home. But this is more of a resigned tired, like he's tired of the arguing and bickering between all of us since mom and dad died and with Maverick ever since Charlotte came into the picture.

"Because she's fucking special. I didn't expect to have feelings for her, but the more I'm around her the more evident they are. She's a little spitfire, she's kind and brilliant and just so different than anybody I've ever met," I tell them sincerely, "I'd be stupid to let that go just for the sake of not stepping on anyone's toes."

They both contemplate my words, not saying anything but looking to each other to have their weird silent twin communication that they do.

Kai finally sighs and drops his hands to the countertop.

"Fine. If you really care about her and you'll do whatever it takes to make her happy then we're okay with it." he concedes.

"But only if Charlie is okay with it. It is her choice at the end of the day, and everything has to go at her pace." Eli adds, "Which is slow, in case that wasn't obvious before. She's never had a relationship." He stresses, which doesn't surprise me based on the conversations I've had with her.

"Thank you guys, really. I appreciate you not shutting me out and giving me a chance."

We all go back to our breakfast and coffee when Kai speaks up again.

"Wait, are we all really buying that Maverick isn't interested?" He asks.

Snorting a laugh, Eli shakes his head.

"Not for a second."

I laugh too, "No, he's definitely interested. It's just a matter of getting him to admit it."

I will just have to find a way to get him to admit it, first to himself and then to us. There is no denying that Charlotte has all of us wrapped around her little finger. It's going to be quite a show when she and Maverick both come to that realization.

20

~ *Charlotte* ~

Ever since the rage room with Cooper and Maverick, things had shifted. All the guys, with the exception of Maverick have been a lot more forward with me, initiating contact, holding hands and sneaking quick kisses here and there. With Eli and Kai, it wasn't that shocking, it was Cooper that really stunned me. It drove me crazy for days, battling with myself over what it all meant and tearing myself down for my feelings I had towards all of them before the three of them locked themselves in my office with me and demanded to talk about it.

They had all listened and been very reassuring and patient with me as I tried to express everything to them. All three of them had assured me that they shared feelings for me as well and explained that they wanted to try a relationship, and how that would work. Most importantly, they wanted to make sure that I understood that it was one hundred percent my choice, if I had even the smallest shred of doubt about any of it I was supposed to call it off.

I think I surprised myself the most when I told them with almost no hesitation that I wanted to give it a shot. I had been stressing over these feelings for months, so I was just relieved that they weren't angry with me over what I felt. I was still determined to try new things, and I trusted the guys more than anyone I'd ever met, so I took a chance.

So far, it hasn't been any different between us, other than the guys initiating more contact with me, not hesitating as much to put an arm around me or grab my hand. They still respected my boundaries and if I was overstimulated then they still gave me space, but there wasn't any fear of setting me off by touching me now.

The biggest difference had to be Kai trying to use their new status into reasoning for him to drive me to work every day, so we'd repeated that argument. I was afraid that Cooper and Eli would side with him but to my surprise, they actually backed me up and got Kai to drop it and leave me to my long walks to the office after class. I still let them drive me home, so he wasn't too upset.

I was happy for now, though I'd be lying if I said a small part of me wasn't a little disappointed that Maverick had seemingly been ignoring me since the night at the rage room.

I know it's selfish to want more with all the others were offering me, but I can't ignore how I'm drawn to

Maverick just as much as his brothers, or the sting I feel over his subtle rejection.

I push all of that to the back of my mind as I watch the program running on my screen before me. I was so close to finding something, I could feel it. It was why I had kicked all the guys out of my office hours ago, insisting that they don't disturb me so I could finally snag something to help us with this case.

It was late, I wonder if any of them are still here with me or if they had all gone for the night, knowing that I probably wasn't leaving. Knowing them, at least one of them is bound to still be here, hopefully not Maverick. His silent rejection of me embarrassed me enough that I'd been doing my best to avoid him all week, even as he was avoiding me. Double avoidance meant a better chance of not ever having to face each other and address the elephant in the room, despite working in the same office every day. That was a typical twenty-something year old's problem....right?

The small chime from the computer drags me from my thoughts, bringing my attention back to what I was working on. With little luck finding anything on the security feeds I had decided to scour the dark web to see if I could find anything linking to Ivy.

I hoped that I didn't find anything due to the fact that if I did then that would mean something way worse than a simple kidnapping that was suspected now.

Luck isn't on my side though, and I have to fight to hold back the bile I feel in the back of my throat when the results flash on the screen, showing a posting just over a month ago with a picture matching Ivy.

The image is posted on a listing, a listing for Ivy. A listing to *purchase* Ivy.

What the fuck?

Unease makes my stomach roll as I put the pieces together. Ivy was targeted at the bar, led away from her friends and kidnapped, only to be sold into some sort of sex trafficking scheme.

Giving myself a minute to control my rolling stomach I focus on just breathing and not throwing up at this new information. What were we going to do now? This has instantly become a much bigger case, we thought we were just dealing with some sick fucker who kidnapped a girl at a bar, but now? Now we have to figure out how far this stretches and how to get Ivy back from the fuckers who are selling her body to other like-minded, twisted individuals.

Printing the posting from the screen I grab them from my printer and rush down the hall to Maverick's office. Voices filter through the door, stopping me for a moment.

I don't mean to listen to the conversation, but I can't help it when I hear a mention of my name.

"Why don't you just admit that you feel something for Charlotte already?" Cooper's voice questions from inside the office.

"Drop it, we've already had this discussion, and I told you my stance on it." Maverick fires back, sounding annoyed.

"I just don't see why you want to deny yourself an amazing girl when we've all discussed it and told you that we're all on board! Why disregard that and miss out?"

"I don't need to hook up with some kid, especially not with my brothers. I don't know why you insist on arguing with me on it." A thump sounds from the room, sounding like Maverick slamming his fist onto his desk. "I feel nothing for her. This is a bad idea; it's going to blow up in all of your faces. But I'll be here to pick up all the pieces when it does, just like I always do."

The venom in Maverick's voice stuns me for a moment and I have to blink back the tears that form instantly at hearing the disgust in his voice. I was fairly sure that he didn't feel the same for me as I do him but thinking about it and hearing it are two different things.

Collecting myself, I glance at the papers in my hands, reminding myself why I'm here. I take a breath before knocking on the door, loud enough for them to hear and put an end to their conversation.

"Come in." Maverick calls out roughly.

Stepping into the office, their eyes are instantly on me, I only meet them for a moment before opting to look at the floor to ignore my embarrassment over what I overheard.

"Hey babe, you done for the day?" Cooper asks, shooting me a smile, tension lingering in his features just under the surface.

"No. I f-found something." I hold up the papers indicating to both of them the new information.

"Did you finally get a clear shot of the guy from the bar?" Maverick asks, leaning forward on his desk on folded arms.

Shaking my head I step forward, laying the papers on his desk and ignoring their confused looks.

Maverick finally snags the stack and starts flipping through the listing that I printed, his eyes going wide as he scans over them.

"Oh fuck," he growls.

"What is it?" Cooper's brows are pinched, and he tries to peak at the pages across the desk.

With an angry huff Maverick tosses them onto the desk so they slide towards Cooper who picks them up and looks over them, wide eyed.

"Ivy wasn't just kidnapped. She's being trafficked."

"What?!" Cooper scrambles to grab the papers, scanning over them, his eyes frantic as he tries to take in the information.

Both Maverick and I stay silent as he looks it over, seeming to understand the severity of the situation.

"Okay, so what's our next move? How are we going to find her?" Cooper asks, looking between the two of us.

We all think it over for a moment, the silence and tension growing between us.

"I c-can try to d-dig into the posting that I f-found," I suggest, "See if w-we can link it to any o-of the people involved."

It seems like the only option we have, there was no other way to find out where Ivy was than to find the people that posted the listing for her and follow the trail. I could still try to identify the guy who grabbed her from the bar but I'm just not sure if that will give us the answers we need like finding the source.

Cooper looks concerned, Maverick is unreadable with his usual stance, arms folded, and his brow drawn down as he looks at us, calculating.

"Where did you find this? Is it safe to be digging deeper into it?" Cooper finally asks.

"It was on the d-dark web," I admit, pulling at my fingers anxiously as I wait for their reactions. "B-but I have p-precautions in p-place so it's s-safe." That's not technically true, anytime you dig around on the dark web there's always a risk. A lot of shady people use the dark web, hence its name, and those people often are very skilled in covering their tracks or digging into matters by any means necessary. I will take precautions, but I have no way to completely protect myself while looking into all of this.

Cooper looks ready to launch into a full-blown meltdown at my admission, but before he can Maverick beats him to it.

"Absolutely not," He all but growls, causing me to jump back closer to the door. "No, no digging into this posting. I will give it to my contacts at the police department and their team will dig further into it. You will only look into the guy from the bar and get a profile on him which we will also turn over."

My hackles raise at his tone. I get his concern, truly I do, but handing this back over to the police is going to lead to the case going nowhere and there will be no chance of getting Ivy home.

"T-the police a-are just going to s-store it for y-years until they m-maybe find something else to b-build a case and by then it w-will be too late!"

This has to be the first time that I've raised my voice at any of the guys, the shock is evident on both of their faces as well as mine at the outburst. I can't feel sorry about it when Ivy's life is on the line.

"Babe, I know it's not what you want to hear but there's only so much we can do with a case when it takes on this extreme." Cooper stands, stepping towards me to try and pull me in for a hug to offer me comfort but I can't be touched right now. I jump away from him, trying to ignore the look of hurt on his face.

"No! W-we said w-we were going t-to bring Ivy h-home. We can't j-just hand over the c-case without f-finding her!" I'm getting more worked up by the second. I don't understand how they are okay with just giving up knowing that kind of fate that waits for the poor girl that was snatched away from her life. And they want to just hand over what we've found and throw away months of work because it's more in depth than they thought?

"Charlotte, this is how it goes. You don't get to solve every case, some things are beyond our skillset, and this is one of them." Maverick is firm in his words, not showing even the slightest bit of sympathy. "I mean it, do not go digging into this. Find the profile and get it to me when you have it but other than that do no go looking into this."

Having given his orders, he turns back to his computer, done with the conversation and done with paying me any attention.

I'm fuming at their lack of sympathy and at Maverick's blatant dismissal. Too many emotions are raging through me between Ivy and Maverick. I know he's a generally cold-hearted person but outside of our first meeting he had seemed to be warming up to me over the last few weeks, him shutting me out on top of all this crumbling down around me is causing me to feel like I'm being punched in the chest, shattering me from the inside out.

It's too much, I can't deal with this. All the thoughts are bashing against my skull, a migraine blooming as all the feelings and rational thoughts fight one another. Turning on my heel I stalk out of the room, ensuring I slam the door behind me simply because it's the only way that I can make sure Maverick sees how pissed off I am.

Immature? Sure. Do I care? Not in the slightest.

Storming into my office, I slam that door too, just for good measure and pace the length of the room, trying to calm down. I try my hardest to ignore all the noise in my head and the rage that's causing my face to burn.

Fuck Maverick for trying to tell me that I can't pursue this lead. This is the only solid lead that we've had since we found out that we can hack into the security cameras at the bar. This has been months of work that he just wants to throw away.

No, I'm not doing that. I refuse to give up and let Ivy be left to the horrid fate that waits for her. If I were in her shoes and I knew that the only people looking for me were giving up because of how complicated it was to find me I think I would lose any hope that I had, any fight in me would be gone and that thought alone is enough to plant the seed of determination in me that I will find out who took Ivy and I will do everything in my power to bring her home. If I have to do it alone then so be it, I won't sit around on the information that I've found and hope the police pull their heads out of their asses in time to do something for her.

I just need to remain calm and not let any of the guys know that I'm still going to be digging into all of this. With how protective they were, they will definitely lose their minds if they figure out what I'm doing.

A knock sounds on the door, and I take a second to shove everything I'm feeling down and lock it up tight to be unpacked later, leaving a blank mask on my face that would rival Maverick's. Once I have everything tucked away I open the door to find Cooper waiting hesitantly just outside.

"You alright?" he asks eyeing me up.

"I'm fine," I tell him, still pissed off but wanting to keep a lid on my emotions.

He waits for me and doesn't say much as I pack up all of my stuff so he can drive me back to the dorms. It isn't until we're in his Jeep and halfway back before he breaks the silence.

"Look, I know you're upset but just know that we would do everything to follow the lead and find Ivy if we could." His eyes flick between the road and mine as he squeezes my hand, like he's begging me to listen to him. "Some things are just too complicated for us to handle, and unfortunately sex trafficking falls into that category."

Sighing I give his hand a gentle squeeze.

"I g-get it. I'm just a l-little upset right now." It's not a complete lie.

"I know, and I know it's probably disappointing that your first case with us is coming to this but there will be plenty of other cases that you're going to crush and it's going to feel so great when you close that first one. I'm sorry it's not this one but you did a great job, I just hope you know that." He's so sincere that I almost can't be annoyed at his ability to just throw in the towel. I'm still upset at his easy surrender but for his sake I give him a small smile and nod to show that I hear him.

He seems to relax as he thinks that I've accepted defeat and am willing to throw in the towel.

Cooper drops me off and I waste no time firing up my personal computer and get to digging on the post that I found. Using my own computer means that Maverick can't track what I'm doing, it might set me back a bit considering that when I'm at work I can't actively work on this but if it means I can still do what I'm setting out to do then it's no bother to me.

I will take the long days and sleepless nights after work if it means I can find something to help Ivy escape from whatever hell she's found herself trapped in.

21

~ *Charlotte* ~

I should not be here.

I should be in my dorm searching and digging through the endless trail that I started to unravel from the post that I found about Ivy last week.

Instead, I somehow let Cooper, Kai and Eli drag me out of my room to go Christmas shopping, which is how I find myself standing in the middle of a crowded mall with screaming children and horrible holiday music blasting through the speakers.

I don't know why I let them talk me into this, I don't even really celebrate Christmas since I'm usually alone, and it's not like I exchange gifts with my parents. But the relationship with the guys is stressing me out, I think that because we're dating now I'm obligated to buy them gifts. What do you get your three boyfriends for Christmas when you've never really bought presents before?

Gift cards were always a good idea right? Was that too impersonal?

I should have googled this before coming out today.

Kai is bouncing around like an excited chihuahua on crack while Eli and Cooper look at the directory.

"I love Christmas! I know exactly what I want to get you, you're going to love it!" He throws an arm over my shoulder, pulling me off balance with his excitement.

Righting myself I shoot him a look, trying not to kill his mood. It's not his fault that this mall is overstimulating and ticking every last one of my nerves.

"You really don't need to get me anything, just focus on your brothers." I try to tell him for the hundredth time.

"Pft, I'm getting you a gift." He waves me off, "No way am I not going to get my girlfriend a gift! That's criminal."

I feel the blush in my cheeks at hearing the sentiment. Yes, I'm aware that they're my boyfriends, officially, but hearing it still sends a small rush through me, a warm feeling of acceptance that I've never had before.

"What do you even want for Christmas? I have no clue what to get you, and I have to figure out something for three of you! This is hard." I pout jokingly, but really the idea of having to pick something out for all of them that's appropriate to give as a gift is stressing me out. What if I pick something stupid, or what if they just hate whatever I pick out for them?

294

"Lottie, it doesn't matter what you get. I will love anything you get me, just pick anything that makes you think of me." Kai tells me sweetly, always having to be perfectly reassuring. "Or just get me a gag gift that will make me laugh, whatever you want."

Cooper and Eli join us, dodging the crowd of people pushing around each other in the walkway.

"Alright, so you guys want to split up for an hour and meet back at the food court? Or do you want to do pairs and then switch halfway through?" Cooper asks, looking to each of us.

"I'll take Lottie!"

"I'm with Charlie."

Kai and Eli both speak at once, Cooper raises a brow their way before looking to me for what I want to do.

I don't want to dull their excitement, but I have no clue what I'm looking for, so to save them from my indecisiveness I decide to go at it alone and suffer by myself.

"M-maybe we should just split up," I suggest, trying to avoid their matching bummed out expressions. But Cooper swoops in to save me.

"I think that's a great idea, we can all get all of our gifts knocked out at once with no interruption." He smiles at me, I think reassuring me that there was no right or wrong choice here.

Although they don't seem crazy about the idea, they reluctantly agree to split up and we each head in a different direction to find our gifts. I walk through a handful of stores to try and come up with some ideas but come up with nothing as I make my way through each.

Coming out of a clothing store I look up to see a small jewelry stand centered between the walkways, an idea starts to form in my head and I make my over to see if they have what I'm thinking of.

After arguably too much time spent pondering over the options laid out in the case, I manage to walk away with one set of silver and one set of diamond studded snake bite piercings for Eli. He seems to like his piercings, and these could be a change from his plain black rings that he normally has in.

Finding my first gift makes me feel a little less anxious at the idea of picking stuff out for the guys, I just have to think practically about things that they'll actually use and look from there. But just in case, I can include gift receipts with all of the gifts...

A few stores down from the jewelry stand I see one that's filled with electronics and accessories, walking in I look for something that Kai might like. Kai already has a great set up, both at work and at their house, so I skim past the computers quickly. The keyboards catch my eye and I lean down to study the different options, finding a newly released keyboard designed specifically for gaming. I look over the specs, liking it. This seems like a good gift for Kai, when I stayed at their house and played with him

I noticed his keyboard had a few keys that were sticking, and I know how annoying that can be when you're in the middle of a game. I grab one of those and then continue looking.

There's a display with gaming headsets of all different colors, another idea hits me, and I quickly pick out a blue headset, figuring that I can give it to Eli so if he ever wants to learn to play Dragonlight with Kai and I then he'll have his own.

The store also has a selection of LED signs that can be customized within minutes, I ask the guy behind the counter to make one with Kai's gamer tag to put up in his room.

Checking out, I feel like I'm getting the hang of gift buying and set out to find Cooper's gift next. I search through a few stores, not finding anything before I end up in a sporting goods store where I find a cool vintage metal printed Jeep Wrangler poster. I pick that up, figuring he might like it with how much he seems to love his own Jeep, but I keep looking for something else. Searching the whole store, I finally find a pocketknife and decide to have it engraved, that way it will be something practical that Cooper can keep on him but the engraving will make it more personal. I keep the engraving simple, 'Remember the little things - Charlotte' to reference him always telling me that the little things are how we show we care. It feels silly once I see it, but I hope he understands that I'm grateful for him always making a point to show me that they care about me and make me feel seen.

The sporting goods store also had a huge selection of dog collars, so I pick out Zeus a pretty new collar. The giant fur ball that I thought was a bear has really grown on me; Maverick had even brought him into the office a few times since I met him, and he always found his way to my office to lay on my feet while I was at my desk.

I check the time and realize that the one-hour time limit that we agreed on is almost up so I decide to start heading back in the direction of the food court. Walking by all the massive window displays, with their flashing signs and tacky holiday decorations I try to focus on carrying all my bags and avoiding bumping into people.

People are bustling around on every side of me, brushing against me or shouldering past, knocking me off balance once or twice. Coming around the corner there's a store that seems quieter than the rest, only one or two people inside, I duck into the store if anything to catch a break from all the people surrounding me. The quiet atmosphere of the store helps calm me instantly, taking away the assaulting sound of music through the speakers and hundreds of conversations blending together into a buzz.

Right inside the store there's a small display with coffee mugs, I step closer to take a look, so I'm not left standing in the doorway like a weirdo. The cups seem to be fancy mugs that are self-heating, so your coffee doesn't go cold even if you leave it sitting for a long period of time. Instantly, I think of Maverick, he's always reheating his coffee in the microwave at work because he makes a cup and then gets sidetracked before he can drink it, every single time it grosses me out.

Mentally, I want to slap myself for considering grabbing the overpriced mug for him when he's been nothing but an asshole to me. Sure, he took me to the rage room when I was stressed out, and yes, he did give me a job and take care of me when I was sick. But overall, he's been cold towards me, and I overheard him saying I'm just a kid he wants nothing to do with me just last week in his office! So why am I reaching for the damn cup that I know he'll enjoy and use every day?

Because I'm an idiot, obviously.

Frustrated with myself, I pay for the stupid cup. He'll probably let it collect dust in the cabinet just to spite me, but whatever, I can at least say that I was nice and thought of him despite his attitude towards me.

Finally having a gift for everyone and not being able to carry anything else, I set out for the food court once again. Still trying to avoid everyone as I walk through the crowded walkways I start to get an uneasy feeling. The hair on the back of my neck stands up and chills wash over me. I don't know what's bringing this on but I have the distant feeling of eyes on me, like someone is watching me.

I look around at all the people around me, not finding anyone's eyes looking back. Scanning the rest of the walkway around me, my steps slow, causing someone behind me to collide with my back, knocking some of my bags to the floor.

Quickly, I scramble to grab my stuff as the passerby mutters an insult about me not paying attention.

I guess not everyone has the same holiday spirit as Kai.

Standing back up I step to the side, out of the traffic and look around again. Everything looks normal, no one is looking at me yet my skin still crawls with the feeling. Not finding anything out of the ordinary I keep walking, picking up my pace so I can find the guys.

With each step, my heart rate picks up. By the time I reach the food court my breathing has quickened and sweat beads on my forehead. Frantically, I look around again, for the guys or for whoever is watching me.

I can't see anything and my panic builds.

Hands wrap around my middle, trapping my arms by my side and I'm swooped up off my feet as a small shriek is torn from me.

"Lottie girl! How'd it go? You're going to love your gift, I found the perfect one!" Kai's familiar voice settles me some, but the panic is still buzzing under my skin as he spins me around.

"Kai, put her down!" Eli barks from beside us.

Kai quickly puts me back on my feet, my legs slightly shaking under me. A bright smile shines on his face as Eli looks over me with concern.

"What's wrong? You look scared." He asks me, looking over me from head to toe.

"N-n-nothing. Kai j-just took me b-by surprise." I fight to get the words out, not wanting to tell them about the strange feeling I had making my way back here.

Eli slaps Kai across the back of the head, making an audible thumping sound.

"Way to go! Can you calm down for five minutes," He chastises Kai.

"I can't help it, I love Christmas! It's my favorite holiday. And I was excited to see my Lottie, I missed her." He pouts, giving me puppy dog eyes. "Forgive me? I didn't mean to scare you."

Taking a deep breath, I steady myself.

"I-it's fine." I tell him, instantly rewarded with another beaming smile. "Come on, Cooper saved us a table." He grabs some of the bags from my hand and begins dragging me through the crowded food court, navigating effortlessly through the maze of tables.

Eli follows behind, grabbing the remaining bags in my hands, offering a wink when I turn to meet his gaze making butterflies flutter in my stomach.

They both drop my bags into one of the empty chairs as they settle at the table where Cooper sits with a spread of food in front of him. Seeing us approach, he pockets his phone and waits patiently.

"So, how did everyone do?" He asks, looking around the table.

All three of them look to me to answer first, heat floods my cheeks at their attention zeroed in on me.

I dip my head to look at the table, letting my hair fall to cover some of my face so I don't feel as put on the spot.

"G-good." I reply, lamely.

They must look at each other because Kai answers next,

"Not to pat myself on the back, but I did fantastic." Peeking up I watch him do exactly that and reach a hand around to slap his own back, "I definitely win Christmas this year."

Eli rolls his eyes, "It's not a competition."

"Says a true runner up." Kai shrugs, starting to dig into the food containers laid on the table.

I look between Cooper and Eli, waiting for their replies as we ignore Kai and his antics.

"I think I found some really cool stuff for everyone." Eli says.

"Yeah, it took me awhile, but I think I managed alright." Cooper agrees. "Anyway, after all that shopping I figured we'd all be hungry, so I went ahead and grabbed some food for us." gesturing to the containers on the table. I feel some nerves about eating in front of them after the Thanksgiving disaster as I hesitate to grab a container.

Cooper must sense where my mind is taking me because he just chuckles softly as he pushes one of the containers over until it sits before me.

"Chicken tenders and fries okay?" He asks with no judgement in his tone, only curiosity. It's clear that if I say no then he will jump out of his seat and go find something that will be suitable for me, and that thought brings that warm feeling crashing into me that I tend to get around them.

Nodding I open the container, instantly hit with the mouthwatering scent of juicy chicken and crispy fries. The only thing that would make this better would be some ranch to pair it with.

Just as I think it Cooper presents me with a small container of the heavenly pairing condiment, bringing a smile to my face almost as big as Kai's.

We all talk as we eat our food, in our own little bubble in the middle of the chaotic space. After the mall we stop by Target to grab some gift wrap to go with our presents and then the guys drop me off. The heat in my cheeks makes me feel as though I'm about to spontaneously combust as all three of them stand just inside my dorm, kissing me before leaving.

I had kissed Kai and Eli once before, and that had left me breathless, but this was my first time kissing Cooper, and it made my legs go weak. I thought they'd completely give out as he dominated the kiss, taking full control and leaving me to try and keep up with him. Kissing was still so foreign to me, I still didn't fully comprehend how it could make me feel the way that it did, or how kissing the three of them was so vastly different. But I also wasn't complaining, so far, with my very limited experience I was becoming addicted to the way that kissing them was able to silence the raging thoughts in my head and just give me a few moments of peace.

Earlier in the day I had been reluctant to buy gifts for the guys, but now that I had I was excited to give them to the guys and still very nervous that they might hate them. But I don't let it stop me from spreading everything out on the floor in the middle of my room to start wrapping them up. I take extra time and care making sure all of the edges of the wrapping paper are straight and lined up evenly, matching the patterns on the paper so that it's nice and symmetrical all the way around. I even found some really fancy ribbon at the store that I use to make bows to wrap around each package.

I put a tag on each gift, addressing who they're for and as I pick up Maverick's gift I feel the same conflicted feelings that I did when I bought it earlier today. I already decided to buy the gift, so I'm obviously going to give it to him but he brings out a defiance in my that I'm not sure how to tame.

So, for his gift tag, rather than writing 'To: Maverick' I put 'To: Captain Dick, From: Your Favorite Employee'.

That's not mean or petty right? He should know that's a joke...right?

I mull it over for a minute before just deciding to go with it and slap it onto the package.

I move around the workspace I set up on the floor, collecting all the scrap paper and trash to throw away, storing the wrapping supplies in my closet in case I ever need it again. All the presents get stacked on the kitchen counter so I can drop them with the guys at some point this week.

I need to work more on Ivy's case since I spent the day out with the guys but exhaustion weighs heavy on me, too much social interaction and people for one day. I stumble over to my bed and bury myself under my weighted covers, savoring the feeling of being crushed and warm as my mind drifts. I'm not able to hold onto a single thought as sleep pulls me under instantly.

22

~ Charlotte ~

I am officially running on empty.

My brain is fried, and my body feels like it's been run over with a truck labeled 'exhaustion'.

Days and days of sitting hunched over, staring at a computer screen. Between work and my extracurricular self-involvement with Ivy's case, I'm running on fumes. My only saving grace is that classes were on a break right now for the holidays, otherwise I'd probably be failing with how much time I've spent not thinking about anything related to school.

At least it wasn't for nothing, I had compiled a list of ten names. Ten vile people who had some sort of digital footprint on the posting I'd found of Ivy. I had already been creating profiles on each of the names, trying to figure out the best way to figure out how each person was involved, and which one could lead me to the information I was really looking for, where Ivy is now.

All of this work and still finding time to spend with the guys so they wouldn't figure out what I was doing was taking a toll on me though. I needed to find some time to rest, but every time I tried I just felt guilty about it, my thoughts jumping to how much I could be getting done if I wasn't being lazy.

Today, I had to take a break though. As much as the guilt forms a knot in my stomach, today was Christmas Eve and Kai had been bugging me nonstop with his plans for the day, we'd bickered about it briefly. I had insisted that the guys spend time as a family and enjoy most of their day before I came over to join them for dinner and to exchange our presents. It had taken days to get Kai to let it go that I wouldn't spend the night and spend Christmas day with them, but I was used to being alone and they didn't need to break all of their traditions just to include me. I had already spoiled one holiday for them, I didn't want to add another.

Eli had texted me this morning, letting me know that he'd be by at three to pick me up and bring me over to their house, a look at the time tells me I have about three hours left. Three hours isn't enough time to dig further into the profiles, so I save all the progress I've made and shut down the computer finally standing to stretch. My body cracks, enjoying the change in position and finally releasing some of the tension it's been holding.

I definitely need to shower before going to the guy's house, but I have more time than I need to get ready. I change into some leggings and a cropped tank top with a jacket thrown over top of it, deciding to go for a jog to get my blood flowing and wake me up. Running will at least give my mind a chance to clear and keep me from crashing into a much-needed sleep.

Grabbing my earbuds and phone on the way out, I set out for the trail that loops around the campus. Even though running is normally my escape it doesn't keep my mind from wandering today. I think back to the recent events of the last couple of weeks, shopping with the guys, continuing to work at GLS and this damn loose thread that I'm trying to unravel. Just a few days ago, I had finally gotten a clear image of the guy from the bar and turned it over to Maverick, officially ending GLS's participation in Ivy's abduction investigation. After that was done Maverick had me working on a few security systems that they run for various businesses across the city, I was looking for flaws in the codes and any weak spots, making the necessary adjustments. It wasn't very exciting work, but it was something that I didn't mind doing especially with how much I was getting paid.

I had spent a considerable amount of time with Kai, Eli, and Cooper as well. Cooper had taken me to a local hockey game and taught me all about how the game worked. I smile thinking about his excitement when the players started brawling on the ice, I on the other hand was terrified that someone was going to get hurt. Eli had taken me on a couple coffee dates to give me a break from being cooped up in my office. We spent our entire lunch hour just sitting with our flavor of the day holiday themed drinks, talking about everything from coding, our favorite movies, favorite books, and anything else that we could come up with in a game of twenty questions. He had told me a lot about his and Kai's childhood and how they came to be adopted by their parents. His face lit up when he talked about his mom and dad, recalling his favorite memories with them. It was foreign to me to hear such great stories about their close-knit family, but seeing the fondness and warmth shine through him as he talked made me happy.

My time with Kai had been very chaotic and high energy, just like him. He had taken me to a retro style arcade bar, a pool hall where he taught me how to play, a walk through a park right on the river where we got to feed ducks and watched the sunset, and he'd even taken me axe throwing.

I'd gotten to spend time with each of my guys individually, getting to know each of them on a deeper level and understanding them more but we also had gone to dinner together, they had taken me to their favorite diner and raved over their favorite dishes. We had all gone out to get ice cream after work and we had even skipped out on work on a particularly slow day to go bowling. All of it was so much fun and so entertaining, just being around the guys, together or separately.

With everything we'd been doing it was no wonder I was so exhausted.

Maverick had still kept a wide berth from me, giving me the cold shoulder and only talking to me when it was necessary for work. There was no more rage room or shared meals in my office. I continuously pushed down the hurt that it caused me and told myself not to be selfish, to enjoy the three amazing boyfriends that I had and forget about him and his dislike for me. But every time I thought I had it pushed down I would catch his eye in the office, and it all came bubbling back up, full force.

And then today, I was going over to their house, so I know I'm going to have to share space with him and see his cold and detached expressions and continue to act unaffected by it.

I really just wish I knew what it was that I did that made him go cold again. For a while, it seemed like he was warming up to me being around but now he couldn't get far enough away.

A car alarm blaring seeps through my headphones and I come back to my surroundings. Taking a look around I notice that I've run most of the trail and just have one more curve until I'll be back at my dorm.

I slow down to a walk to give myself time to cool down, checking the time to make sure I'm not going to be rushed before Eli gets here to pick me up.

As I walk, I take in the scenery. The weather in Florida doesn't get cold enough to have the leaves change colors with the seasons like in most places. Although today is fairly brisk at 64 outside, most of the trees are still fairly full and lush. The ground is littered with crunchy brown leaves, making it feel like fall, but the sun is shining bright and breaking through the cover of the trees.

Chills work their way through my body and a feeling of panic washes over me. Looking around, I don't see anything that would be putting me on edge. Campus is empty due to the holiday and I haven't seen a single person out here during my run. I pull my earbuds out to listen for any sounds around me but am met with an eerie silence.

This feeling reminds me all too well of the feeling I had at the mall when we went shopping, I had all but forgotten about it with how busy I've been but the same sinking feeling of being watched was ringing alarm bells in my head and making my skin crawl.

I pick up my speed, keeping my head on a swivel, looking in every direction for anyone or anything that could be making me feel this. The only thing in my sight is one of the campus security cameras and alert stations, other than that I'm completely alone out here as far as I can tell.

The feeling doesn't lessen the closer I get to my dorm. My heart is pounding in my chest, and my hands are shaking as I open the door to the lobby. My ragged breathing echoes off the walls as I rush down the hall to my room, looking over my shoulder every few seconds, waiting for something to jump out at me.

I rush into the room and slam the door shut behind me, flipping the lock and as an added measure, I prop up one of the bar stools from the kitchen under the knob.

I watch the door, rooted in place just waiting for something to happen. Nothing does.

Closing my eyes I draw in a deep breath, trying to steady myself.

I feel like an idiot.

The lack of sleep must really be getting to me, that's the only logical explanation for this feeling.

Checking the time again, I see that I have just around an hour before Eli will be here. I make my way around the room, gathering my clothes and putting away my running gear before jumping in the shower.

I let my head drop down as I stand under the full spray of water, blindly reaching out to turn the dial as hot as the water will go. The water burns my skin, feeling like a thousand little pin pricks all over my body, but I welcome it. I let that feeling wash away the tension coiled up in my neck and shoulders, letting that and all of my anxious energy wash down the drain like it never existed in the first place.

A thick wall of steam fills the bathroom by the time I finish showering. I don't even bother trying to clear the mirror of the fog as I throw on the clothes I picked out. I open the door as I set to work blow drying my hair, so I don't feel suffocated in the enclosed space and then I run the straighter over it.

I'm just finishing up when I hear a noise coming from the front door. A rattling sound of the knob hitting the chair I propped up as someone tries to push the handle down.

The panic I felt earlier is back full force, spiking my heart rate in an instant.

I wait and listen, for any sounds to indicate who's trying to get in here. Was someone actually following me? Did I lead them straight here, should I call someone? I should definitely call someone.

"Charlie?" Eli's muffled voice sounds through the door, putting a stop to my panic.

Shit, I must have been in the shower much longer than I thought if he was here already.

I scramble across the room, quickly moving the chair back to its spot, straightening it with the other before flipping the lock and swinging the door open.

"H-hi." I greet him, taking in his green buffalo plaid button up thrown on over a fitted black t-shirt, black ripped jeans and a black beanie to match his glasses. His face shows his concern, but he doesn't voice it as he looks me over in return.

Unlike my usual hoodie and leggings, today I decided to throw on a pair of fitted skinny jeans and paired that with a red tank top, showing just a sliver of my midsection with a black zip up to throw over top of it.

"Hey," he finally greets me in return, offering a small smile and looking over my shoulder at the mountain of presents stacked up on the counter, his eyes going wide. "Wow, those all are coming with us?" he asks.

I nod as I shuffle to the side, letting him into the space.

He looks me over once more, looking like he wants to ask me something but decides to drop it as he gestures to the gifts.

"I can go ahead and run them to the car if you're almost ready to go?"

"Sure, I just n-need to grab my shoes and m-my phone and I'll be good."

I set out to do just that as he carries the gifts out of the room, returning only a minute later for the ones that remain just as I finish lacing up my Vans.

"All set?" He asks, standing by the door, perfectly balancing the gifts in his arms as he waits.

"Yes, but I can h-help carry those." I offer and try reaching for some on the top of the stack, but he spins away from me, effectively blocking me from touching them.

"I got it, you just look cute and lead the way." He winks as he flashes me another sweet smile, waiting patiently as I lock the door behind us.

We ride in a comfortable silence, holding hands over the center console as we make our way to their house.

"So, are you excited to open gifts with all of us?" Eli asks, breaking the silence.

"I g-guess." I shrug, not really sure of how I'm feeling about exchanging gifts with the guys. I'm more nervous than anything that they might not like what I got them but I'm also nervous about being awkward while opening mine, not being used to receiving presents from anyone.

He looks over at me for a moment, assessing before focusing back on the road again.

"Was everything alright when I came over to get you? You seemed off." He trails off at the end of his question, not sure how to address how panicked I was when he showed up today. Rather than entertain his questioning I stick with avoidance once again.

"Y-yeah, I was j-just rushed. I went f-for a run before you c-came over and was finishing getting ready." It's not a lie but it's not the whole truth either. I can see that he wants to ask me more so before he can I change the subject. "S-so what do y-you guys normally do f-for Christmas?"

Taking the bait, he lightens up as he talks about their normal traditions.

"Not a whole lot really. Christmas is Kai's favorite holiday just like Thanksgiving is Mav's. We usually bake some cookies for Christmas eve and then watch some of the typical movies, Christmas morning Mav usually makes a huge spread for breakfast, and we open gifts then

315

hang out and watch football before dinner. It's usually a really laid-back day overall."

It does sound nice, it beats my plans which are to order Chinese takeout and get lost in the computer for another day. But it's what I'm used to.

The neighborhood is busy as we approach the house, cars lining the street on both sides in front of every house down the block.

Kai rushes out the front door as we pull in the driveway and both him and Eli refuse to let me carry any of the gifts into the house as we all shuffle inside. Inside the house looks different than the last time I was here, the living room now accented with stockings hung on the wall, an eight-foot tree nestled in the corner with an array of mismatched ornaments and colorful lights strung over it.

Maverick sits on the couch with Zeus, watching the TV while Cooper stands in the kitchen laying out ingredients on the counter tops. Zeus notices my arrival and quickly sprints across the room to greet me while Kai and Eli set the presents around the tree. Once they're done, Kai races over with a Santa hat bouncing on his head to wrap me up in a hug, making Zeus bark as he picks me up to spin me around.

"Hey, babe!" Cooper calls from the kitchen, "Merry Christmas!"

"Y-you too." I'm a bit breathless as Kai finally puts me down, giving me the chance to squat down and love on Zeus where he waits patiently.

Once I'm done giving all the love to Zeus I stand to meet Cooper, who is also patiently waiting for my attention. He wraps me up in a quick hug, kissing my temple before pulling back to give me my space.

"Are you ready for presents?" Kai bounces excitedly next to me, looking between me and the tree in the corner.

"Presents are after dinner. The same as every year." Maverick barks from the couch, not pulling his attention from the TV. Kai just pouts in response, and I feel ready to join him with how Maverick won't even look in my direction.

Eli silently grabs my hand and pulls me to follow Cooper into the kitchen where an array of baking ingredients and materials are laid out along the counters.

"What are we making?" I ask as a white and blue apron gets thrown over my head and Eli begins tying it around my waist.

Cooper looks me over, eyeing the apron up and down while smirking before shaking himself and looking back to the ingredients.

"Peanut butter balls, sugar cookies, pecan bars and then when we're done with that we'll make a gingerbread house while dinner gets cooked." My eyes widen with each dessert on the list, it seemed we were really going to spend the entire afternoon baking. This should go well, considering my zero experience with baking, or anything remotely close to it.

Cooper chuckles, clearly seeing the panic on my face,

"Don't worry, it's easy and I'll walk you through it."

And so we dive into the world of baking. The peanut butter balls are easy enough, Eli helps me mix all of the ingredients and is patient with me as I roll the balls, taking extra time to make sure they're all evenly sized and spaced on the baking sheet before popping them into the freezer. The same goes for the sugar cookies, with Cooper's help before they go into the oven. The pecan bars are a bit more challenging, but Cooper is there helping me every step of the way as Eli retreats to the living room with the other two to watch some hockey game.

After a couple hours, both the cookies and the bars are out of the oven and cooling and the peanut butter balls are dipped in chocolate and setting in the fridge. I feel accomplished at what we managed to make, and I feel myself beaming with pride as I help clean up the mess we made.

Just as we're finishing up I feel my positive energy plummet, turning around I see Maverick has joined us in the kitchen. He briefly looks over the baked goods we left to cool on the counter before making a beeline for the fridge, pulling out chicken from the fridge and a variety of other items from the pantry. He doesn't acknowledge Cooper or I as he sets out to start making dinner.

I feel frustrated at the fact that he's able to suck the joy out of me by just stepping into the room and I'm determined to ignore him just as he's doing to me. Spinning back around to face Cooper I plaster a huge smile on my face.

"So g-gingerbread house?" I ask, desperately looking for another distraction.

Kai and Eli join us in building and decorating the gingerbread house. We decide to make teams, each team decorating one side of the house. Eli and I work on one side while Kai and Cooper work on the other.

Eli and I are quiet as we work, only sharing an idea here or there but working flawlessly to make a very well-organized design on our side of the house. Kai and Cooper on the other hand, bicker constantly about what should go where and what the overall design should be.

"Why do you insist on making this damn house every year?" Kai grumbles as he tosses down another peppermint stick that he's broken while trying to glue it to the roof.

Cooper is focused on piping icing onto the house as he answers, distracted,

"We always do a gingerbread house. We've done it every year since you guys came to live with us."

"It's a waste, it just rots here on the table." Kai tries putting the peppermint on again and we all watch as it just falls back to the table. "And they're impossible to build and make look at least halfway decent!" he huffs, throwing himself back in his chair to sulk.

"Tell that to Eli and Charlotte," Maverick's voice calls from the kitchen, a small spark shooting through me at hearing him mention my name.

Kai shoots him a confused look before getting up and rounding the table, stopping in his tracks and gaping at our side of the house.

"What the fuck?" He shouts, leaning in to examine our work closer as Eli and I scoot back to avoid getting head butted. "How? That is literally impossible!"

Cooper stands to take a peek at our side, his brows raising as he appreciates our craftsmanship.

"Some people just have raw talent," Cooper says, sitting back down to work some more. "And you are not one of them."

"I have talent! Just not at decorating a house made out of baked goods!" Kai argues back.

I sit back and just watch them bicker, enjoying the banter. From the corner of my eye, I see Maverick leaning up against the counter, watching us all interact.

Eli is focusing on adding the finishing touches to the roof on our side, I can't even tell if he's listening to his brothers when he suddenly speaks up,

320

"Do you remember how frustrated dad used to get with these?" he asks no one in particular.

The room stills for a few moments, each of them lost in their thoughts.

Cooper snorts, "Yes, he used to threaten to smash the whole thing after the walls would fall two or three times."

"Oh yeah, Mom refused to get the pre-assembled ones because she said that was cheating. Dad dreaded it every year until he finally figured out how to put them together." Kai perks up, forgetting about his sulking for the moment.

Maverick snorts from the kitchen, drawing all of our attention.

"If by 'figured it out' you mean he started assembling them with the hot glue gun, then yeah."

Cooper bursts out laughing,

"Oh yeah, he used to make us stand guard while he glued it and warn him if Mom was coming." He smiles fondly at the memory while Kai gapes at both of them.

"Are you shitting me?" He sounds utterly shocked at the new information, and I find myself laughing at his shock.

The atmosphere in the room is lighter after their reminiscing as we put the finishing touches on the house. It looks absolutely horrible by the time we're done, one side completely put together and the other looking like a candy bomb went off. But it's standing and it has personality, so we accomplished something.

By the time we clean up the candy and put the house on display in the center of the table, Maverick announces that dinner is ready and we all help set the table before settling around in our seats. We end up in the same seats as Thanksgiving, putting me directly next to Maverick. I try to ignore his close proximity, but find myself tensing and glancing his way every time he shifts in his seat. Each time though, I'm met with the feeling of disappointment as his attention remains elsewhere.

Again, I force it down and inspect the food that's been set out in front of us. The spread includes a dish filled with homemade corn bread, a pot of chicken and dumplings and a small meat and cheese board complete with crackers and jam.

Looking over all of the food, it looks and smells amazing. Looking up, I'm met with Maverick's gaze firmly locked on me.

"Do you eat chicken and dumplings?" He asks simply.

Dumbfounded that he's speaking to me I just nod like an idiot, he nods once then turns to start plating up the food, dismissing the entire exchange.

I end up with a small bowl of the dumplings and with a side plate of some crackers and cheese and a piece of the cornbread.

We all make small talk throughout dinner; Maverick goes back to ignoring me after his one question. I mostly listen in as I'm too busy shoveling food into my mouth, it's all just so delicious. After we eat, we all help clean up and then sample all of the sweets that Cooper and I worked on.

By the time we've each tried at least one of everything, Kai is vibrating with excitement next to me.

"Please say we can open presents now?" He looks to each of us, hopeful and eager.

Eli rolls his eyes and Cooper just shakes his head at his brother's behavior, but they all look to Maverick for the final verdict. He eyes Kai for a moment, not amused in the slightest but nods towards the living room, giving him the green light.

Kai whoops excitedly, startling me as he scoops me up and runs to the couch,

"Be careful!" Eli calls out as he follows us at a much more reasonable pace. I'm breathless as I right myself on the couch. Kai settles in to my right and Eli takes the empty spot to my left, sandwiching me between them. Zeus jumps up from his bed to come and join us, settling between my feet to face the room. I run my fingers through his fur, letting it calm my nerves about exchanging gifts with the guys. I'm second guessing all of the gifts I got and there's a sinking feeling in my stomach that they're going to hate them.

Cooper takes a seat across from us, leaving Maverick to start handing out the gifts from under the tree. We each form our own little piles, waiting for all of them to be given out. My nerves only double when I see Maverick's own pile is mostly just envelopes and no actual gifts. I may have gone about this all wrong, I knew I should've just gotten them all gift cards.

Maverick picks up the last present, but makes no move to hand it over to anyone, instead he just studies it with a raised brow and a dry expression.

"Am I correct to assume that I'm 'Captain Dick'?" he asks simply.

Oh shit.

I completely forgot I wrote that when I was wrapping the gifts.

I can't think of anything to say, I should probably apologize now that I can see that he wasn't amused by my attempt at a joke but I'm too mortified to speak. The rest of the guys, however, find it hilarious if their roaring laughter is any indication.

"Oh my God! Did she actually write that on there?" Kai asks, almost in tears from how hard he's laughing.

Eli composes himself enough to nod thoughtfully, fighting a smile as he looks over at me before looking back to Maverick still standing with the gift in hand.

"I'd say that checks out."

Maverick's jaw ticks as he stares down his brothers, I focus on Zeus, not able to meet any of their gazes on me.

Did I just screw up another holiday?

23

~ *Charlotte* ~

I try to ignore the awkward tension that seems to settle around me as Maverick takes his seat with his gifts and we wait to see who's going to open theirs first.

Do we all just start ripping open gifts? Or do we take turns? I don't know what the appropriate behavior is here, so I'd rather wait until everyone else starts.

Kai wastes no time, grabbing the first gift off of his pile and ripping into the paper violently, tearing it to shreds. Eli and Cooper also pick a gift to start unwrapping in much more reasonable manners. Maverick on the other hand just stares at Kai with annoyance, eyeing all of the pieces of paper being thrown around.

Part of me wants to watch the guys open their gifts, but a larger part is nervous for their reactions so instead I pick up my smallest gift and start gently tearing the paper off. I hear Kai and Cooper talking as I work on unwrapping the gift to present a velvet jewelry box. Pulling open the lid I see a beautiful silver necklace with a sea turtle pendant nestled in the middle. It's very dainty and stunningly beautiful and I love that it showcases my favorite animal. Not only that, but it also shows how much Eli listens when I talk, remembering one of our games of twenty questions where we discussed our favorite animals. He had thought turtle was a weird choice until I expanded on the fact that I was really interested in sea turtles and how beautiful I thought they were.

Looking over to Eli, I see him watching my reaction to his present eagerly. I thank him and turn so he can help me put the necklace on, admiring how it settles perfectly in between my collar bones.

Kai opens his gamer tag sign that I got for him while Cooper unwraps the Jeep sign and they both seemed pretty pleased with the gifts. Eli opens the new piercings I got him and much like me with my necklace, insists on putting them on right now.

Picking up another gift I see that this one is from Cooper, ripping through the paper I find a small box. The box has a new pair of earbuds, with extra cushioning for the ears and a removable cord so they can be hung around my neck.

"Thought you could use an upgrade, yours looked a little dated last time you had them at the office." Cooper tells me, looking up I give him a smile and let him know that I really like them.

I have two gifts from Kai to open, I opt for the larger of the two first. A laugh bursts out of me when I open the gift to find a giant case of instant noodles. Looking to Kai he just winks back,

"Lifetime supply, baby. You'll never run out with me around."

Thanking him for the silly gift that reminds me of a time months ago before I had met any of them I reach for the second. The second gift is a personalized case for my e-reader, in a pretty teal color and embroidered with sunflowers, daisies and ivy vines. It's so beautiful, and it has a handle so I can hold it easier while reading. I absolutely love it.

Kai, Eli and Cooper all three open their second gift from me at the same time. Kai freaks out over the new keyboard, saying he's excited to test it out and also thrilled when he sees the headset for Eli so he can join in with us. Eli seems really pleased with the idea of all of us gaming together. Cooper looks to be pleased with the pocketknife and smiles wide while he inspects the engraving on the side.

"Oh good, you got Cooper something we can stab Kai with finally." Maverick comments drily from his seat in the middle of us. My jaw drops at the comment, but Kai just laughs it off before gesturing to the gifts sitting before him.

"We're all done now, are you going to open yours?" he asks.

Maverick huffs but reaches for one of the envelopes from his pile, opening it up and reading the card inside.

"Maverick always waits until everyone is done before opening any gifts," Eli explains quietly from my other side, "He hates the chaos of all of us opening them at the same time." I appreciate the explanation, though I can't say that I agree with his logic. It seems like it'd be more nerve wracking to have everyone watching as I tried to open gifts. I for one, would be too worried about what my reaction looks like than what the actual gift is.

He opens three cards, each with a gift card or two for either a coffee shop or some athletic brand for clothing I assume. He pulls the gift that I wrapped for Zeus and eyes the tag for a moment before ripping the paper off. He inspects the collar, turning it around in his hands as Zeus barks as if he knows it's a gift for him.

"Zeus has a collar." Maverick tells me plainly, holding the collar loosely as if it offends him.

"I k-k-know. I found i-it and l-liked it. You don't h-have to use it." Even through my stutter I think my annoyance at his reaction is obvious. I feel much better about keeping his gift labeled to Captain Dick at this point because that's what he's acting like. Despite his constant attitude towards me I still made a point to grab something for him as well as for Zeus. I've really come to love Zeus and his constant comfort he offers anytime he's around, and I thought the collar was really nice and cute for him. I didn't think it would be such a big deal to grab it for him.

"It's nice, I really like it." Cooper tries to reassure me, but the mood is pretty much in the garbage at the moment.

Kai obviously doesn't care about not rocking the boat though as he snatches the collar and works on taking the old one off Zeus to secure the new one on.

"It's bad ass! And it looks amazing, see." Zeus sits proudly in his new collar, and it brings a smile back to my face despite Maverick's shitty reaction.

Maverick seems less thrilled to open up his gift but tears through the paper anyway, looking blankly at the coffee mug.

"Is that like the old one you had that you broke?" Eli asks, trying to look around me to see the mug.

Maverick doesn't respond but Cooper leans over to get a closer look,

"Oh yeah. You used that last one until it was literally cracked and couldn't hold coffee anymore. But you refused to get a new one once it was done with." Maverick remains stoic while Cooper talks about the mug, showing nothing on his face as he continues to stare at the box.

"Yeah." He finally rasps out, "Well Dad got me that mug before he died, so it didn't feel right to replace it."

And there it is. I feel like the asshole, again. Not that I would have any way to know that when I picked out the gift, but I still feel pretty awful now.

Is there going to be anything that I don't screw up in regards to Maverick? I feel like no matter what I do or try to do it just isn't the right thing.

Without another word Maverick gathers his stuff and retreats to his office, closing the door quietly behind him.

"I-I'm sorry, I d-didn't know." I tell no one in particular. Everything else from today is washed away and overshadowed by the sinking feeling of guilt for dredging up painful memories and spoiling yet another holiday.

Eli wraps an arm around me, pulling me in for a hug.

"It's all right, you couldn't have known about that." He tries to reassure me, with little success. I still feel shitty about it.

"He'll be alright." Cooper chimes in, "It was a really great gift, he just doesn't like to show emotions, and I think it sparked some feelings in him."

"It'll be fine." Kai agrees, "I think you're officially the winner of gift giving this year, I need to step up my game." he jokes, always trying to lighten the mood.

I'm lost in overthinking my screw up and how I upset Maverick and gave him more of a reason to hate me while Eli suggests that we clean up and get ready to watch some of their usual Christmas movies.

I end up lying in the middle of the couch with Zeus resting on my lap. Eli lays to one side of me and Cooper beat Kai to his spot so he takes up my other side. After pouting for much longer than necessary Kai sulks to a spot in one of the chairs off the side of the couch.

The guys are into the movies as soon as they start, sharing their commentary throughout. Two movies in they rotate spots so Kai will stop pouting about not sitting next to me and Cooper grabs us all some popcorn and more of the sweets we made. I try to enjoy the movies along with them but my mind is elsewhere, my attention keeps getting drawn to the light coming from under the door to Maverick's office.

I don't know if I should try to apologize to him or if I should just leave it alone. As far as I know, he disliked me before and today probably didn't help that any. I hate the idea of trying to address any of it with him but the thought of not apologizing leaves me unsettled.

I fall asleep while contemplating, startling awake sometime later when Zeus gets down off the couch.

Looking around the room is dark, only a slight glow coming from the lights strung up on the tree, the TV having shut off at some point. Zeus starts whining at the back door, so I move to let him into the yard, waiting for him to do his business.

I need to get back to my dorm so the guys can enjoy their Christmas and so I can get some work done, but I don't want to wake any of them, they all look so peaceful passed out of the couches.

I pull out my phone and order an uber, not giving myself a chance to dwell on it. I don't want to wake them up and I just want to get home and rest some before diving into another day of work.

Sitting with Zeus while I wait, I look over each of the guys. They all look so relaxed and peaceful in their sleep, not a worry line in sight.

The notification pings on my phone that my ride is approaching, so I find a notepad in the kitchen to write a note to leave on the coffee table so none of them freak out any more than they probably already will when they wake up.

I gather up my stuff and tell Zeus to go to his bed before quietly slipping out the front door.

Getting settled in the backseat I glance back at the house as we pull away. For a moment I think I see a shadow of someone in the window of Maverick's office, but in a blink it's gone.

Overall, my time with the guys today was nice, I enjoyed getting to give them their gifts, with the exception of Maverick and getting to spend time with each of them. Even with the fun and enjoyment of the day, I'm relieved to be going back to my dorm to soak in the silence. I'm also determined to make more progress on Ivy's case and figure out where she's at, regardless of if I'm supposed to or not.

24

~ *Charlotte* ~

Campus is just a eerie and deserted as it was earlier in the day, but with it being the middle of the night it's creeping me out how empty and quiet it is. Stepping into my room I'm immediately reminded of the unsettling feeling I had this morning after my run. It feels like much more time has passed than just a few hours but being back in here alone makes the unsettled feeling slam right back into my gut.

I'm not actually worried that anything will happen, I'm clearly overthinking things. But just to be safe I put the barstool back under the door handle as an added precaution once I sit all my stuff down.

Walking over to the windows, I pull all the curtains shut, making sure the view from outside is completely cut off.

I already left a note for the guys at the house, but just as an added reassurance, I send them a group text to let them know that I'm home and that I'm safe. I don't want any of them freaking out thinking anything happened.

Falling asleep at the guys' house meant that I got some much-needed rest, but I could really use a couple more hours to fully refresh myself so that I can get some work done on Ivy's case. The exhaustion I was feeling this morning is still lingering, making me feel weighed down and sluggish.

I go through the motions of taking my pills, setting up everything for bed, grabbing a change of clothes before moving to the bathroom to start up the shower, turning the dial as hot as it will go to try and wash away this sluggish feeling.

I spend longer than usual in the shower, standing under the spray and just letting the warmth from the water sink into all of my muscles and warm me up. Getting out of the shower I take the time to blow dry my hair, working through all the knots and conditioning it to try and give it some type of nourishment after having it thrown in a messy bun for days on end and rushing through washing it earlier in the day.

Shutting off the blow dryer I quickly throw on the clothes I brought in, needing to just brush my teeth and do some basic skin care before finally passing out for the rest of the night. I hear a small thump through the door and freeze in place, holding my breath while I wait to hear something else.

When no other sounds filter through the door I carry on with my routine, shaking it off as something in my imagination with how tired I am.

I quickly finish up and grab my phone off the counter, ready to collapse into bed.

Swinging open the door I'm instantly frozen in place.

My computer chair is across the room, on its side like it's been tossed away from the desk. The computer itself has a cracked screen, the keyboard broken in half and laying in pieces on the desk and the floor.

That's about all I can see from the doorway. I stay frozen, looking around and not finding anyone in the space, not hearing any sounds coming from the room. I step out of the bathroom, intending to see what other damage is done.

Looking to the front door, the barstool is still firmly in place where I left it. The curtains are still drawn as well, so I can't see outside.

The kitchen is in a state much like my computer desk, cabinets open and items from each ripped from the shelves and strewn about between the floors and countertops. Broken glass litters most of the floor and my gifts from the guys have been thrown off the counter and to the floor over by the bed.

My hands start going numb as my breathing picks up the more I look around. Someone was definitely in here, but why?

I don't understand why anyone would come in here to trash all my things or who would do that.

Other than the blankets being tossed around, the bed seems to be untouched. The weighted dinosaur that Cooper got for me remains untouched on the pillows at the head of the bed. With the state of everything else, it seems stupid to feel the relief that I do at a stuffed animal being unbothered, but it means something to me and I feel a rush of relief at knowing it isn't tainted.

I don't know what to do now, I'm on the verge of hyperventilating as I continue to look at all the destruction. It's all just stuff and it can all be replaced, even my computer is backed onto an external hard drive that I keep secured under the desk so everything can be recovered.

I just feel violated that someone was in here while I was feet away and I didn't even know it.

The panic is growing the more I think about someone in my space. My hands shake violently now, sweat coating my palms as the numb and tingling sensation travels further up my arms. My breathing comes faster as the seconds tick by. I'm on the verge of a full-blown panic attack, but I need to think logically.

I can't pass out or freak out. I just need help; I need to call someone. I can't stay here.

Clearly I can't stay here if someone was already in here, having no clue as to who it was or why I just need to get out of here, preferably before I black out.

Looking down, I try to get my hands steady enough to unlock my phone, finally getting it on the third try.

I dial Cooper's number first, trying to count my breaths as I listen to the line ring multiple times before finally going to voicemail. Next I try Kai with the same result. Finally, I dial Eli, my heart sinking further and further into my stomach with each ring and no answer.

Tears finally start to blur my vision as I hear the automated voice telling me that Eli is not available at this time.

It's not their fault that I left in the middle of the night while they were sleeping, but it still sucks that I need them now and I can't get through to them.

Sobs begin to choke me as I think of what to do. Where I can go.

With no other options and very little hope I click on one more name.

The line continues to ring, crushing my hope and building my panic with each pass.

"Hello?" The gruff voice comes through as I almost collapse with relief.

"M-M-M-Mav-v—v-verick" I can't form words through my chattering teeth as the panic and relief both battle to overwhelm me. My knees shake, threatening to give out under me.

"Charlotte? What's wrong?" His usual annoyance rings through his words but it's overshadowed by the amount of worry I can hear as well. It's the most that I've ever heard from him, a stark contrast to his usual tone.

Closing my eyes, I try to force myself to take a breath before speaking. Reminding myself that I'm fine and that as much as I freaked out, I'm alone and safe for now.

I'm past the point of calming down now, as is clear when I try my hardest to speak.

"S-S-Someone w-was h-h-h-here." is the only statement I'm able to get out, choking on my own words each time I try to force them out.

The tears keep streaming down my face despite the relief I felt moments ago when Maverick answered his phone.

The annoyance is wiped away and only concern sounds through his voice as he starts talking rapidly,

"Charlotte, calm down. Just take a breath, what do you mean by someone was there? In your dorm? Why did you even go back there in the middle of the night? Are they still there?" He rapidly fires his questions as the sounds of rustling fill the background, like he's grabbing things and moving through the house while talking.

"I-I-I- d-d-d-d-"

"Okay, just breathe. Breathe, calm down for me." He gently tries to coax me. "I'm on my way, it's okay. Just try to breathe."

I try, I try my hardest to listen to his words and try to slow my breathing but nothing I do will dissipate this overwhelming feeling of fear ripping through me.

Through a haze, I can still hear Maverick speaking to me with urgency but I can't make out any of his words anymore. Half blind I try to stumble over to the bathroom, to throw some water on my face or to cower in fear until Maverick gets here.

Just before I make it to the bathroom I feel a crushing weight slam into me from the side, tearing a piercing scream from me, sending me flying to the floor as my phone flies towards the wall.

"CHARLOTTE!" Even from feet away I can hear Maverick's panicked voice screaming into the phone.

My arm screams in protest as I roll off of it and my head is pounding from it getting acquainted with the hardwood. I try to look behind me, my vision now blurred from the hit and not just my tears.

I only manage to catch a glimpse of some dark clothing as I roll over before a weight is crushing down on my midsection. Looking up, I'm met with a dark shadow looming over me.

My glasses must've fallen off when I fell because no matter how hard I try, I can't make out any details of the masked man that's currently pinning me down.

Maverick's distant voice is still yelling through the phone from somewhere, adding to the ringing in my head.

A sharp blow stings my face, the force sending my head to the side and quickly followed by my burning cheek as a backhand is delivered, quickly followed by another.

I can't make sense of what's happening as I feel hands roughly wrap around my throat. Immediately, I try to gasp for air but get nothing as the hands on my throat only tighten past the point of letting any air into my lungs.

"You stupid bitch! You brought this on yourself!" The voice growls.

Desperately I grab the hands at my throat, using all my strength to try and pry them off of me. I'm not able to make any progress as the hands feel like they tighten even further. Kicking my feet, I try to land a hit on my attacker, but I may as well be a child fighting an adult as much of an impact as it's making.

Dark spots start to fill my hazy vision, making me use all my concentration on just trying to get some air.

Just as I feel myself starting to slip, falling off the ledge, the hands release my neck. I alternate between coughing and choking and sucking down as much air as I can.

Another blow lands on my face, the force of this one feeling like a fist before the hands that were just on my throat grasp handfuls of my hair pulling my head up off the floor before slamming it down against the hardwood one, two, three times.

My head is pounding, and all my thoughts are scrambled together as I fight the urge to vomit.

While I fight to stop my head from spinning, the weight on my midsection finally lifts off of me. Nothing happens for a moment as the dark shadow stands tall, towering over me.

I feel another blow, this time to my stomach. A foot kicks me repeatedly alternating between my stomach and my ribs as more screams are ripped from me. Fire engulfs my entire side as I try to curl into a ball to stop the blows from landing on what I'm sure are now my broken ribs.

A loud banging fills the space around us, thankfully stopping my attacker for the moment as we both listen.

The sound, I think is coming from the front door and only continues to get louder and more aggressive as we both stay frozen.

Within a split second my attacker scrambles, sprinting for the windows as the sound of the door being thrown open reaches me, complimented with the crashing of the barstool that was propped under the handle.

I can't focus on anything. Between the pounding in my head, the fire in my side and the urge to finally slip into the darkness and just be away from this all.

A familiar voice that I wasn't sure would ever bring me comfort roars throughout the small space.

"Charlotte!" I can hear him rushing towards me, "No. No, no, no, no. Charlotte, look at me! You're okay, you're alright, just look at me please." He's closer now, I can feel his hands gently running over me, checking to see where I'm injured.

I wince when his hand runs over my arm that I landed on to begin with. A whimper escapes me at the pain that shoots through from his touch.

"Shit, sorry." I think I've finally lost it if Maverick is apologizing. "Charlotte, open your eyes for me, now." Ah, there he is.

Using every ounce of strength left in me I pry my eyelids apart, wincing again at the light in the room that assaults my vision. Seeing my eyes, Maverick releases a harsh breath.

"Oh thank God." His hands hover over me, not able to decide where he can touch me. "Keep your eyes open. Tell me where all you hurt." He reaches for his phone as he speaks to me, getting it unlocked and raising it to his ear as he looks expectantly at me for an answer.

"I'm f-f-fine." I mutter, my eyelids already fighting to close again.

"Charlotte, I swear to - Hi, yes I need an ambulance sent to Oceancoast University…" I lose track of what he's saying as my eyes finally draw shut, blocking out all the noise and pain, chasing the bliss of nothingness.

"Charlotte! Open your eyes, now damn it! Charlotte!" Maverick is frantic, alternating between yelling at me and whoever he has on the phone, but I don't have the energy to open my eyes.

The darkness is pulling me under and I'm tired enough to accept it. The pain lessens the deeper I slip under and I just want to feel nothing.

Maverick made it here, he came for me. He'll watch out for me, and that gives me enough peace for now to drift away.

25

~ *Maverick* ~

I haven't enjoyed Christmas since my parents died. Once they were gone it was just a day of reminders, reminders of the traditions we used to have and the memories that we shared with Mom and Dad.

Every year, my brothers try to keep up their own traditions and make the holiday enjoyable, but every year I feel the dark cloud looming over me, reminding me of all the memories from years ago.

Mom used to do everything she could to make Christmas magical and memorable and extremely cheesy. She was all about matching ugly sweaters and pajamas, the tacky decorations, the over-the-top wrappings on presents and all of the traditional baked goods. Dad was all about doing whatever my mom suggested, always intent to just bring a smile to her face and make her happy. So, every year dad just about killed himself hanging the lights on the outside of the house and moving lawn ornaments around for hours until mom deemed they were in the perfect spot. Every year he spent hours hot gluing a gingerbread house together because it made mom happy, and he sampled every single dessert for her, even if it made him sick.

These days, all of the traditions feel forced, like we're all trying to relive the past and it just doesn't feel right.

This year was more of the same routine, just with Charlotte thrown into the mix. Having her presence in the kitchen with Cooper all day for our Christmas Eve traditions was different but not unwelcome.

She truly cares about my brothers, that much was obvious with the gifts that she had selected for each of them. She took into account each of their individual interests with each gift. She even went as far as getting me a gift, and my dog. To say that was a surprise is an understatement.

The emotion that hit me when I opened the mug from her, thinking about my dad and how he had bought me the same gift when I started working for another security firm, hoping to move up and working long hours I'd always had a cup of coffee within reach. He always said that there was nothing worse than cold coffee and that I couldn't put out good work while choking down shitty coffee, I should always have a fresh cup to give my best work.

I know my reaction to opening Charlotte's gift wasn't the best, but this time of year is already hard enough for me without extra reminders of the past getting tossed at me. I could tell that she was hurt by my reaction to Zeus's gift as well as my own, but I wasn't in the right headspace to try and smooth that over.

I've been in my office all evening, going through emails and glaring at the gift sitting on my desk, listening to the others watching movies in the living room just outside. The noise had died down a couple hours ago, and I heard Charlotte sneaking out just around two am. I had to bite back my irritation at seeing her climbing into an uber in the driveway, reminding myself that it's not my place to be annoyed at that.

Looking down I notice the time is creeping up on three thirty in the morning and decide to turn in for the night, knowing that Kai will be waking us all up in the morning for more 'family fun traditions'.

Heading quietly past my sleeping brothers in the living room, I make my way upstairs to go through the motions of getting ready for bed.

Just as I lay down in the bed with Zeus curled up at my feet I hear my phone vibrating on the nightstand. Reaching over to grab it, I see Charlotte's contact on the screen. Why would she be calling me?

"Hello?" I try to keep the annoyance from my voice, but I'm tired and ready to crash for the night.

"M-M-M-Mav-v-v-verick" Charlotte's voice instantly puts me on edge, panic clear in her voice. I'm used to her stutter at this point but she can't even get a word out, and her ragged breathing bellows through the line, making it even harder to try and make out what she's trying to say.

"Charlotte? What's wrong?" I try to get something from her as I jump out of bed, pulling on the first shirt I find and gathering my shoes and keys to rush back down the stairs.

Silence meets me through the phone, aside from Charlotte's panicked breaths.

"S-S-someone w-was h-h-h-here." she manages to choke out.

What the fuck does she mean here? Here, as in her dorm?

What the fuck is going on? I wonder as I bolt out the front door and into my car, fumbling with the keys in my rush to get it started.

I can hear Charlotte crying, full on sobbing but still not able to tell me what happened, only ramping my panic up further and further. In the time I've known her she hasn't been one to show a lot of emotion, usually preferring to break down in private and never one to ask for help. This whole situation is freaking me out and making me antsy as I drive through the empty streets, blowing through stoplights and stop signs, just hoping for the best.

"Charlotte, calm down." I'm not the best at trying to comfort anyone but I need to get her to calm down. The rate she's going she'll pass out from hyperventilating before I even get to her. "Just take a breath, what do you mean someone was there? In your dorm? Why did you even go back there in the middle of the night? Are they still there?"

Okay, so my attempt to comfort her didn't last long, my curiosity and need for answers quickly overpowered that.

"I-I-I- d-d-d-d-" Great, I just made this worse. Charlotte can't even form a single word now. I need to calm her down first, answers later.

"Okay, just breathe. Breathe, calm down for me. I'm on my way, it's okay. Just try to breathe." I don't know what to say, I usually ignore emotions and emotional people. I don't think this will actually help her, but she needs to breathe.

I keep mumbling nonsense to her, trying to calm her down. I don't think she'll manage to talk to me before I get to her but for now it's working in the sense that she's still conscious. Small victories.

I'm only five minutes away now, pushing the pedal towards the floor to make it to her when a crash sounds through the speaker, followed by Charlotte's terrified scream.

"CHARLOTTE!" I yell, waiting for a response, any response from her but being met only with some rustling and her pained whimpers. I keep trying to talk to her, to get any response but am met with a muted silence.

As I pull in the parking lot for her dorm I can almost make out a muffled voice, followed again by more of Charlotte's whimpers and cries and a thumping sound.

Abandoning my car I sprint to the front doors, slamming them against the brick wall in my haste to get through them. Rushing up to Charlotte's door I push the handle, surprised to find it locked. I recall Kai complaining when they first started dating that she never locked it, and when I'd come to check on her when she was sick it was unlocked then too.

Charlotte's cries pull me out of my thoughts. Immediately I start shouldering the door, trying to break it in. It only moves slightly each time I hit it, never giving away fully. Stepping back I center myself, pulling in a deep breath before lifting my foot and kicking the door right in the center, watching as it swings inward, giving me entry to the dorm room.

My panic doesn't ease at seeing the state of the room. Utter chaos and destruction covers the room, glass and other items strewn about the floors and every surface. All the cabinets in the kitchen are open, the shelves bare any of their normal items.

Rushing around the island I'm stunned to see Charlotte crumpled on the floor, curled into a ball to protect herself, whimpering and crying and shaking violently.

"Charlotte! No. No, no, no, no." I rush over to her dropping to my knees and trying to gently feel her over, seeing where she's hurt. Ignoring the glass I can feel piercing my legs.

"Charlotte, look at me! You're okay, you're alright, just look at me please." I'm begging her now, just to open her eyes and let me know she's okay.

I frantically try to pull my phone out of my pocket, still feeling her over. I feel her arm, it feels like it's swelling and there's a lump sticking out on the side. She winces hard as I touch the spot on her arm, whimpering as she tries to pull it away. I feel bad for a moment, but it's overshadowed by the relief I feel at seeing some sort of reaction from her.

"Shit, sorry." I apologize while trying to coax her awake. "Charlotte, open your eyes for me. Now." I force the demand at the end, not able to help myself.

Studying her, I don't miss the moment her eyes finally slit open, giving me a glance of that sweet hazel color looking back at me.

"Oh thank God. " I'm relieved to see her awake, now I just need to keep her that way until I can get help. "Keep you eyes open. Tell me where all you hurt." I finally look down and dial 911 on the phone, putting it on my shoulder to keep feeling for injuries on her, making a mental note of every time she winces when I touch her.

Her head rolls to the side as she winces again.

"I'm f-f-fine." her raspy voice mutters, low enough that I almost miss it.

Irritation flares in me at her usual response, clearly she's not fine and I'm not seeing the humor in this if she's aiming to make a joke.

"Charlotte, I swear to-" I'm interrupted by the operator's voice coming through the phone, asking what my emergency is. I start explaining to them that I need an ambulance as soon as possible when I see Charlotte's eye flutter shut again. The phone slips to the floor as I try to rouse her.

"Charlotte! Open your eyes, now damn it!" I try shaking her gently, I know I shouldn't move her but I need her to wake up. I need her to stay awake and stay okay just until help is here. "Charlotte! Wake up!"

"Sir, sir are you there?" The operator's voice sounds again, coming from the phone on the floor. I scramble to pick it up and hurriedly explain where I need help and a basic overview of what I can tell them happened.

Hanging up the phone I keep talking to Charlotte, trying to get her to wake up again. No matter what I say, her eyes stay firmly shut, my only reassurance is that her chest continues to rise and fall.

"I'm sorry, I know I've been an asshole to you." I admit to the quiet room as I wait for help to show up, not able to endure the silence that lingers around me. Knowing that she can't hear me makes the words easier to say. "My brother's care so much about you and it would tear them apart if you're not okay." She still doesn't respond. "It would honestly tear *me* apart if you're not okay." I admit

352

quietly, "You've been a bright light for all of us since you stumbled into our lives and we can't be without you, Charlotte. I don't *want* to be without you."

As much as I've denied feeling anything for her to my brothers, I can't lie now. These feelings that are rushing through me are more than just concern for my brother's girlfriend, or for an employee. This is deep rooted panic of losing someone that I care about, someone that I may possibly love. That sounds ridiculous to say, but she's truly made a mark on my life, from the moment she came to the office and refused to answer my questions. From the start she's challenged me, tested my nerves and done nothing but be a sweet and caring presence for all of us.

"I need you to wake up. I need all of your anxious ticks and your hyper fixation on the smallest things. I need you to challenge me under your breath and to be the warming presence that reminds me and my brothers that life isn't all dark and depressing." I finally hear the sirens approaching outside, but I need her to hear one more thing, even if she can't hear what I'm saying. "You have brought my brothers closer together Charlotte, and I need you to wake up and keep doing that. Keep bringing us all together because they need you. *I* need you."

I press a kiss to her forehead, hoping to see her eyes again, but she remains still as the EMT's finally rush into the room.

In a flurry of motion, they start working on her, securing her neck and loading her up onto the gurney, rolling her out of the room. I don't hesitate to follow behind them, rushing out the front doors and to the ambulance waiting just outside.

The EMT's let me ride with her, not that I would have given them a choice. I sit beside her, holding her hand throughout the entire ride. Once we arrive to the hospital they rush her away from me, leaving me standing in the waiting room staring at the doors they disappeared through.

Worry threatens to crush me as I'm left in the sterile, white-walled room alone.

Dropping into one of the plastic chairs I let my head fall into my hands, trying to filter through everything that's happened tonight.

I need to call my brothers, as much as I dread having to make that call I know I need to do it. They need to know, and they would want to be here.

Taking out my phone I see it's just shy of six in the morning, Cooper is probably going to be my best bet in answering the phone this early.

Sucking in a deep breath to steady myself I click on the number to dial, waiting as the line rings a couple of times.

"Hello?" His groggy voice comes through, telling me I woke him up.

"Cooper," I keep my voice firm, making sure he's paying attention. "Something happened last night."

He's instantly more alert, hearing the seriousness in my voice.

"What is it? What happened?" he asks, concerned now.

"It's Charlotte."

To be continued…

Golden Locke Security Book 2

Coming Soon…

Afterword

What a journey!

I can't believe that I actually finished my first book!

I hate to leave you hanging, but I had to leave you wanting more. I hope I did just that.

This story has been a work in progress for an entire year, and I am just so excited to end the year with closing out this first part of Charlotte's story. This story started out as one single idea and slowly transformed into something that the characters just began writing it themselves, and I was just as anxious to see where it was heading as hopefully you were as well!

I can't wait to see where it leads and to find out who is after Charlotte and how her men react when they get the news! Stick around if you want to find out as well... And if you want a story with a bit more spice then definitely stay tuned to see Charlotte and her men as they only grow closer.

In the meantime, please feel free to leave me a review to tell me what you liked or disliked about the book. Give me all of your feedback so the continuation of Charlotte's story can be nothing short of amazing.

Come find me on social media, and let's talk about it!

About the Author

B. Lynn Hedge is wife and 9-5 worker by day, and a writer by night. She runs on diet coke, energy drinks and power naps.

Born and raised in Florida, she still resides there with her husband and fur babies.

She has been working towards her goal of finishing her first book for years now, starting to write at the age of 19 but finally reaching her goal at 26 with this debut novel.

Her extensive book collection showcases her favorite genre, romance and has everything from YA to the darkest of dark romances.

More about B. Lynn Hedge and her upcoming works can be found on social media!

Instagram

TikTok

Facebook Group

www.ingramcontent.com/pod-product-compliance
Lightning Source LLC
Chambersburg PA
CBHW030553260626
47157CB00006B/2297